I0822300

KILLERS NEVER DIE

KILLERS NEVER DIE

CHELSEA BURTON DUNN

DEAD MAN'S HAND
BOOK 2

4 Horsemen
Publications, Inc.

Published By: 4 Horsemen Publications, Inc.

4 Horsemen Publications, Inc.
PO Box 417
Sylva, NC 28779
4horsemenpublications.com
info@4horsemenpublications.com

Cover & Typesetting by Autumn Skye
Edited by Blair Parke

Library of Congress Control Number: 2024941177

Paperback ISBN-13: 979-8-8232-0603-7
Hardcover ISBN-13: 979-8-8232-0604-4
Audiobook ISBN-13: 979-8-8232-0606-8
Ebook ISBN-13: 979-8-8232-0605-1

Table of Contents

Chapter 1

The sky was dark, the air damp with mist and clinging to everything, making the pavement shine in the dim streetlights. The small trio of college students walked on the pavement, their steps wavering slightly after having had a little bit too much to drink on their last stop, a pub known to house those at the university nearby. Despite it being a celebration, they had decided to end their night a bit earlier than the others they had been out with, moving away from the excitement and activity of the pub toward the darker, shadowed, little alleyway that acted as a shortcut toward one of their flats.

This group had gone through this alley many times in the past and never had a problem passing through the poorly lit passage before. The liquor in their veins only added to their nonchalance, despite the way the shadows of the night seemed to be creatures unto themselves, reaching out toward the three as if they wanted to drag them into their dark depths.

A woman stumbled out from one of the narrow door insets in one of the buildings, a cloak covering her so only her long hair was visible beneath the hood. Her shoulder hit one of the three, a girl who seemed to have the biggest trouble with her steps, causing her to stumble back, trying to grasp at the arms of the man of the group, but failing, instead falling with a burst of giggles against the pavement.

"I'm so sorry," the cloaked woman said meekly, reaching out a gloved hand to help her up, but the girl merely shook her head, grinning up at her friends and not at all paying attention to the woman who just caused her to tumble.

"Not to worry; James will help me up," the girl said, humor still vibrating through her words as her friend, presumably James, pulled her to a stand.

"I should have been more careful," the woman said, though she tilted her head a little further up to make eye contact with James. He was tall but thin. His face held markers, clear signs of his lineage; the blond hair was a bit tussled from the night out, but his dimpled chin, pale skin, and piercing blue eyes were unmistakable to the cloaked woman.

"It was probably our fault. We aren't exactly walking in a straight line," the other girl said with a grunt, as she finally got her friend in an upright position, placing her hand protectively through her arm.

"It's just as well," the cloaked woman said.

"What are you doing out so late?" James asked, steadying his friends and pulling up closer behind them, almost protectively. His eyes held an air of suspicion as he looked at the woman before them. James may have been just as human as the two girls with him, but he *knew* things about the world that most humans didn't. The way his skin prickled in this woman's presence, the air of strangeness about her, told him that he needed to be cautious because something was very wrong about this encounter.

The woman's chin lifted a fraction, a small smirk playing at the corner of her mouth.

"I'm looking for something," she said. James's brow furrowed at her tone. It was odd, not at all frantic or pained like someone would be if they had lost something in the dark, but eager. James searched through the darkness under the cloak for her eyes, like perhaps seeing into them would contradict the strange way she sounded.

"It may be better to do that come morning," one of the girls murmured, still not looking at the woman like he was. But why would she? She had no idea of the things that lurked in the dark, not like James did.

"Morning wouldn't do," she said, shaking her head and lifting her chin just enough that he could see the eerie smile that spread across her lips. He felt an odd hum within him, a vibration as James looked into that darkness of her hood, as if he were trapped there by nothing more than her unseen features. "The night brings more to light than the sun. Purity shines best when in shadows. I had to find someone whose blood is pure enough to use. Someone who is valuable."

The words didn't register with the girls for a moment, still looking at one another with amusement, before they truly sank in. Their eyes glanced back at their lanky friend, whose face showed the horror he felt at the woman before them.

Pure.

James was certainly considered pure. He was still a virgin, which was so unheard of these days, but additionally he was valuable too. His friends didn't know why his family was so rich, but they knew he was set to inherit quite a lot. He had value to his family; they just didn't know why or for what.

Almost as if they were afraid to look upon her again, the girls slowly turned toward the woman, eyes taking her in more fully than the passing glance they had given her before. The woman's face, though still slightly hidden by the hood of the cloak, was perfect, too perfect. Her skin seemed to be luminescent on its own, glowing from beneath the shadow, but it was her eyes that pierced through the darkness: vibrant green, like two emeralds in the sun. Whatever façade she had put on before was gone, as her smile showed the maliciousness now. She intended them harm.

"You two may go; you have nothing I seek," she said, spitting as if they were revolting, eyes locked on their tall friend behind them.

"Run," the girl who had stumbled whispered, but it was enough to break her friends from whatever power the woman had that locked them in place.

Fear?

Magic?

They weren't sure.

The three of them turned abruptly, walking quickly back toward the pubs they had just vacated, hoping to find solace amongst others, but it was far too late. As if they had materialized from the shadows, others in cloaks stepped out into the light, boxing them in the alley. There was nowhere for the three of them to turn. Nowhere to run as the menacing eyes behind the shadows of their hoods stared them down.

James stood still, his breath struggling to pull as his lungs spasmed with fear. These weren't the creatures in the darkness that he knew. They were not the ones who his family had served for centuries. They were something else, something he had not encountered before, and they wanted *him*.

"Yes, he will do perfectly," the cloaked woman said, her voice quiet but holding the promise of pain as the cloaked figures stepped closer to the group, boxing them in even more.

The city was alive. London was lit up, teaming with energy. The skies were clear of rain, the weather warm, and the mortals were taking advantage of the summer night with vigor. This kind of weather brought everyone out of their homes, so the mixture of different people made it easy for anyone to blend in. It was the perfect opportunity for Immortals to walk amongst them; no one would be the wiser as to what they were up to with so many bodies around. Screams could be masked with the sounds of unrestrained laughter and loud voices. People disappearing would go unnoticed.

Werewolves and Vampires alike could snag a meal, Witches could take their next blood sacrifice, and Chenjas could steal the very soul from a human's body, with most of them left completely unaware.

Perfect.

However, the crowded streets were not met by all Immortals, though. Not every Vampire was eager to seduce away an unwitting human from their group. Ace crouched on the balcony overlooking the crowd as two of her Necare moved through the masses. Lotte and Nyprat slithered through the humans, moving with purpose as their noses tracked the scents of their targets. They weren't going to kill anyone tonight; no, this was reconnaissance. They had been watching the Witch coven and the local Werewolf den closely. Something was going on between the two allies, and Ace wanted to know what.

Ten years was a long time. It went by in the blink of an eye, especially for an Immortal, but a lot can change. For Ace, that was certainly the case. Ten years prior, the war between the Immortals had been at a high. The Werewolves preformed a ritual that their previous leader, Lukis, was certain would win it all for them and their allies, the Witches. But it didn't go according to his plan and, along with it, went his head.

The ritual was like a tremor that seemed to grow into a tsunami, hitting every Immortal group at its core. Those not directly affected by what had taken place in New Orleans soon got word of what had occurred in that abandoned hospital. Each group had faced losses, each group unsure of where this new tide would take the war. Alliances were being tested in this span of time. Each moment, each decision made by the leaders of the individual Immortal sects were now so much more important.

And more individually, Ace's life was never the same after the ritual either. Both more and less complex. More so that she went from being a Coven Judge and head of the Necare to now being an Elder. Her role within the Vampires was not only more important but imperative to their success. But personally, as well, much had changed. Not only did her progeny, Six, die as a sacrifice, but shortly after, with barely enough time to grieve that loss, something seemingly impossible happened to her. She shivered at the memory, the horrible pain, the feel of her body being broken from within. From the ashes of one progeny, another was born. Quite literally from within her.

The revelation, that Vampires were capable of procreating alone, would have been enough of a puzzle to last several decades, but that of course was not the only thing that they had to contend with. There was no time or room to rest with their enemies so weakened. The Vampires took every advantage they had, tearing through Werewolf dens and Witch covens alike, dismantling as much of their structures as possible. They needed to cripple and hurt them into submission. It was the only way that Ace and the other Elders thought it possible to end the war with the best possible outcome.

But they didn't submit. The Werewolves may have been scattered, weakened, and divided, but they were not caving. Their stubbornness was exasperating and only spurred Ace to want to push harder to stop them. It didn't help that the new leader of the Werewolves held her mind in a precarious position. On one hand, Ace knew that if they managed to kill the newly installed leader, the remaining weakened Werewolves would most likely fold to their will, but on the other hand, that new leader was none other than Alexander, her brother from her former human life centuries ago.

Ace and Alexander had not spoken in the last decade, though she knew he wanted to. Note after note had been sent to her. She could feel his eyes on her as she moved through London over the years. Each time she considered meeting with the Werewolf that was once her brother, she would look upon her son, the first and only Vampire that she knew of to be born and not made, and she knew whatever feelings she had for her brother could never compare to what she felt for the life she had created with her partner Nero. She could never be torn to choose between her blood and the creature she had become again because now her son was both.

But recently, something had changed over the last year.

Though the war had not slowed, not really, with all the missions the Necare across the globe had been on to keep the Werewolves and Witches on their toes, she sensed a shift. They were no longer defending one another and not fighting their enemies as a team.

The weaker covens of Witches were falling like a house of cards and began pulling further into the darkness to hide themselves away. The Raven, the leader of the Witches for the last three hundred years, had moved her coven's base so many times, the trails had become too convoluted to follow. The Werewolves, on the other hand, tried to regroup on their own. Alexander was attempting to recruit rogue factions of Werewolves who had split from his leadership when their dens fell, focusing all his time and effort on rebuilding their wealth and forces but not aiding their allies.

Ace knew the Witches, being the weaker of the two enemies, needed more help from their partnership. However, she wasn't sure if the cause of their apparent rift was because of the actions of her Vampires, or if it was something else entirely. Ace's new approach, while not wanting them to gain too much strength, was to pull back and watch. They needed to *see* and determine what was actually going on with their enemies. Thus, the Necare went back to watching in the shadows, waiting for the inevitable moment when someone would slip up and give away what was happening.

Either they were putting out strange signals to throw the Vampires off or Ace's suspicions that the alliance between the Werewolves and Witches had ended was correct. Whatever the problem, she knew it originated with Alexander's den; there was no doubt in her mind.

Ace's silver eyes followed Lotte as she neared the techno club that most of these humans were lined up to enter. She saw the Witches standing very close to the door, a door that happened to be manned by a Werewolf.

This club was Werewolf-owned, one of the institutions Alexander had tried to put in place to regain some of the wealth that had been lost along with their numbers. The Werewolves needed money, as money, no matter if it was human or Immortal, brought power with it. Alexander needed power to return to the Werewolves on all fronts, both in his ranks and in the bank. Ace knew, based on the subtle moves she saw him doing, that he was making strides in becoming more organized with Werewolf-owned establishments. Seedy clubs and pubs were good ways to bring income, both legally and illegally, as well as feed the baser appetites of those under his command.

If things didn't improve for them, Ace knew it was only a matter of time before the Werewolves were weakened enough to no longer be considered a threat. With Werewolves practically out of the war, the Chenjas and the Witches would fall in line, succumbing to the inevitable fate of having Vampires rule over them all. It was the best outcome for the Immortals. Vampires were organized, meticulous. They would protect and provide for all, while continuing to maintain the Masquerade that kept the humans of the world unaware.

That was ultimately what the Vampires wanted out of all of this. They simply wanted to keep the secrets that they had been so beholden to for all these years. Secrets that were constantly threatened with exposure with each encounter where humans were left as witnesses.

This was exactly what Ace was trying to avoid on this very occasion, watching as the large bouncer's lip curled, taking in the Witches that were waiting in line.

"I'm getting closer. I can't hear what they're saying over the other voices," came Lotte's voice from the device in Ace's ear.

"Careful," Ace said, watching Lotte's approach.

The Witches stiffened at whatever the bouncer said to them. A shimmer seemed to swirl around them, barely noticeable but still there. The mortals who encircled them didn't seem to see it, but it was clear what was brewing below. Ace shook her head at the blatantness of their actions. That shimmer of magic was the sign they were not above using it openly.

Fools.

"None of your kind here, Witch." The sound of the man's voice came now that Lotte had position herself closer.

"...the disrespect!" The quieter voice of the Witch came through, only at the end of her sentence, but the growl the Werewolf made in response to her could easily be heard.

The magic pulsed over the two Witches there as the Werewolf's arms flexed with a promise of a change. Ace's body stiffened as she watched. Were they all insane? They were going to fight right here in the middle of this crowded street?

"Nyprat," Ace hissed into the microphone, eyes darting to where the small Vampire pushed closer from the other side of the line than Lotte. Ace didn't need to elaborate. They all heard that exchange and could all sense what was coming if they didn't step in; the mess would be obscene. How many hundreds of humans were standing in this bright, crowded street?

Ace prepared herself as she watched, her muscles tensing from where she stood. Nyprat and Lotte were closer, but if they didn't neutralize this situation in time, she was ready to burst into action.

"On it," Nyprat murmured, her voice rough with determination as she moved at a human's pace through the crowd, since the people were too tightly pressed for her to easily maneuver at her true speed without notice.

As Ace watched, her body coiled and ready to step in, her mind was fitting the pieces together. Her suspicions were confirmed. If the Werewolves weren't letting the Witches join them in their spaces, something was seriously wrong with their alliance. Perhaps it wasn't completely torn apart, but the damage was done. Cracks in their relationship had been established, and it only needed a small *push* to send them from friends to enemies. No matter how much Ace wanted that push to happen, she did not want to have to deal with the aftermath of the fight that was threatening to break out on this human-filled street.

"You'll only cause us problems. Go before I must remove you," the Werewolf said. Ace watched from afar as his eyes glinted their warning in the darkness. There was far too much anger there. Something very wrong happened between these two Immortal sects.

"You know our Mistress is devising a plan. She told Alexander, and he does this? Bars us from entering your clubs? Does he even want to win?" one of the Witches asked, her voice getting shrill with the anger radiating off her.

What could the Witches possibly plan that would make Alexander push them away?

"He doesn't want to win that way. Your kind is all the same, finding others to do your dirty work because you're too weak to do it yourself," the Werewolf growled. The energy in the street changed then, as the power within the Witches was surging. A hum came over the bud in Ace's ear, a hum that she knew all too well was the start of a spell.

"Now," Ace hissed.

She watched as Nyprat almost unnoticeably flicked her wrist over her shoulder from several hundred feet away, tiny glints of metal sparkling through the air before the three figures' bodies stiffened with the sudden prick of pain. Darts. Not enough to kill or even hurt either the Werewolf or the two witches, but enough to keep them away from one another. The concoction hidden within the dart was a mixture of silver and a sedative.

For a moment, the three other Immortals stood shocked at the sudden pain, but then the darts began working. The two Witches slumping a little against one another, their magic that had been swirling around them stopping almost immediately, while the Werewolf roughly rubbed his eyes as if the night was finally getting to him. The Witches staggered from the line, clutching one another, and Ace watched as Lotte followed them. Nyprat pushed her way through the line to meet up with her.

Ace stood from where she crouched, high above the crowd below, jumping from the balcony to the next roof over, and slipping down into the alleyway that the two Witches were heading into. Their stumbling footsteps slowed as the sedative continued moving through their systems. Even if they could have reduced the progression of it with their magic, now that they were away from human eyes, it had moved too far through their systems. There was no use in trying to stop it. Ace had to act fast before they finally passed out.

"Just a little further, Poppy," one of the Witches murmured, a slur in her words.

"I think this is far enough," Ace said, stepping from the shadowed part of the alley into the yellowed lamp that hung from one of the walls.

"*You,*" was all the other Witch said, as her eyes rested on Ace's face. Ace knew she was well known, rather infamous within their secret world. Her black hair and porcelain skin may not have been enough, but the silver of her irises and the tattoo over her eye always gave her away to those who knew what to look for.

"Me," Ace confirmed with a smirk, as the Witches tried to maneuver themselves to turn around and go back where they came down the alley, but Lotte and Nyprat were both there, slowly walking toward them and caging them in. "Odd that you weren't allowed in a club owned by your own allies," Ace said, her voice holding the questions there.

"It's none of your business what goes on between us and our allies, Vampire," the Witch who spoke earlier said. She was clearly having an easier time of fighting the drugs than her friend, who now let her head loll to the side, eyes closed completely.

"It's all of my business what goes on with my enemies," Ace said back, her smirk widening to a grin, showing off her fangs. "Tell me, what will happen to the Werewolves if the Vampires were to attack the tunnels under the city as we speak?" The way the Witch's face lost its color at those words made the sinister smile spread even further over Ace's lips, exposing her white teeth.

"Just let us go. We can't harm you now," the Witch whispered, her voice frantic, fear polluting her scent and making Ace's eyes glow brighter. Hunting fearful prey was instinctual.

"No, but you had no qualms about exposing everything back there, did you? How strange to want to fight amongst your own allies right in front of the humans on that street," Ace murmured, bobbing her head toward the entrance to the alley.

One glance at the two Vampires behind them, and the Witches were whisked away, the movements of her Necare practically invisible, as they dragged the Witches off with barely a sound to indicate it had happened at all.

What could the Witches be planning that would be cause for the Werewolves to write them off? Torture was in those Witches' future. So much pain and suffering that in the end, not only would they reveal what had changed between them and the Werewolves, but they would beg for death after doing so. Because between the stunt they tried to pull in front of all those humans and the fact that it was enough to make even the Werewolves want to distance themselves from them, Ace was certain she would not like the answer.

Chapter 2

The sleek, blacked-out sedan moved silently through the streets of London back to the mansion. It was getting late; the busyness of the central part of the city faded, leaving the quiet darkness of the streets in their wake as Ace drove. Nyprat and Lotte were both in the back, Lotte's eyes trained on the two slumped Witches between them. Though they were sedated, the guns in her hands were trained on them as a precaution. The confined space of the car would make fighting off a spell of any kind nearly impossible.

Normally, Ace would have been happy to just kill the Witches and move on, but there was information that was needed from them. The nature of the rift between the enemy allies was imperative for their next moves, especially now that Ace knew there was a disagreement over a plan the Witches were brewing.

The tall exterior walls that bordered Kurome Mansion came into view. As the car rolled through the gate on the east side of the property, a calmness settled over Ace. She loved the hunt, being out with the Necare, fighting for her kind, but the mansion was her home and refuge. Within its walls, it held everything she loved, and coming back to it always gave her a sense of peace.

She pulled into the garage, watching as Lotte and Nyprat dragged the still sleeping Witches out behind them.

"We'll get them in the cell and make the report," Nyprat said as she passed Ace.

"Good. I'll add to it later," Ace said, watching as they left.

She made her way through the garage shortly behind them, heading toward the Medicus. Hunts always made Ace thirsty, and that was where they stored the donated blood. But more than that, she knew her boys would be there shortly.

Octavian, Ace's son, was a born Vampire, something so rare that it was thought to be a myth. As such, there was nothing to guide them with his development. There was no way of knowing how he would grow, what would be similar or different for him as far as abilities. He was a mystery. And because of that, Ace had Minshin, their head of Medicus, examine him carefully once a month.

His growth seemed to be sporadic. There were long stretches where he wouldn't grow at all and then seemingly overnight, he would change. Limbs would lengthen, his face would lose some of its roundness. There was no way to predict the changes before they occurred, even though they were watching very closely.

The mansion was quiet, but a few House Vampires were still milling about, probably having recently returned from their own fun and hunts. Dava, the oldest House Vampire in the coven, followed Ace's movement with narrowed eyes as she passed through the parlor, her blonde hair down and falling around her beautifully as a human girl sat brushing the long locks. Charles and William seemed to be having an animated conversation with the twins, Melony and Melody, so much so they barely noticed Ace's presence, but not Dava. The gossip monger of the mansion always seemed to be waiting for something to talk about, and Ace, being in the high position she was in, was certainly the one she looked to for juicy tidbits of information to spread. Ace could feel the eagerness in Dava's gaze, barely holding back a snort as she passed without comment.

The lives of the House Vampires were mediocre at best. Ace had lived that way only briefly when she had first been changed. Their main purpose, prior to the facilities Nero had set up to provide the Vampires around the world with fresh, donated blood, had been to procure meals for the other ranks, either by the selected families or other humans who would not be missed. Now that they weren't needed for that, House Vampires did little more than take up space within the covens.

If she had her way, Ace would have preferred House Vampires leave covens altogether, forming their own nests or joining a rank. Since some House Vampires, like Dava, would refuse to train or join a rank, especially at the age Dava was, she knew nests would be a popular option. But the idea of letting so many of their own kind leave the confines and safety of the mansion was what held her and the other Elders back from making that decision. Nests were an easier target for their enemies, and though nests were not part of the war, it was still the Elders' duty to protect all their kind.

Ace took her gun to storage, choosing to make her way through the mansion through the halls, instead of risking having to field questions from the House Vampires she passed when she came through. Stepping into the Medicus, she cast her gaze around to see if her son or Nero was there yet, but she was only met with one set of eyes. Minshin. Ace moved through the space, placing her earpiece back in the foam holder at one wall as she made her way to the back of the large room, toward the kitchen space. It mostly held refrigerators to keep the donated blood cold and provided yet more counter space for Minshin and the other Medicus to use for their work, since there was no need for them to cook food. Humans didn't usually stay in the mansion long, and though Vampires technically could eat human food, it was rather more like eating dirt for them.

"Dava said Nyprat and Lotte dragged two Witches through," Minshin said, having followed Ace through the room and was now leaning against the island that separated the refrigerators from the rest of the Medicus room. Her thin frame and short black bob made her look like she would have been better suited in a different era, but she had a grasp on technology that so few Vampires seemed to possess, making her an integral piece of not only the war but also in keeping them up to date with the current technology. This had become especially imperative in this last century, when it seemed like innovations changed so frequently.

"Dava still seems unable to tame that big mouth of hers," Ace shot back, raising an eyebrow at her friend from across the island as she poured the thick cold blood into a glass. She could have warmed it, but she simply needed the sustenance. Too much to do before the sun began to rise. "Witches were going to attack a Werewolf in front of hundreds of humans. I decided there was no better opportunity than to get as much out of them as possible before we decide to kill them," Ace explained, watching as Minshin's eyes widened.

"In front of that many humans?" Minshin muttered in disbelief.

"We narrowly prevented it. Something is off," Ace stated, recalling the clear hatred between the two types of Immortals. "The Witches mentioned some sort of plan that the Werewolves disagreed with. I'm eager to know what that plan is."

Nero sat in the plush wingback chair in his chambers, his blue eyes moving steadily over the book that was resting against his knee. Across from him in a matching chair sat a child. Silver eyes scanned the pages equally as fast, while his long, white hair flowed over his shoulders. This child was such a perfect mix of Nero and Ace, the long nose of Nero and the shape of Ace's face. And those were Nero's fingers, though more youthful and plump, which turned the page of book in the boy's lap.

Octavian, their son, was something neither of them would have ever dreamed to be possible, but there he sat. He didn't age like a human child; everything about him was unprecedented and unexpected, but the challenge was something Ace and Nero utterly relished in. The fact that Octavian existed at all seemed to be nothing short of a miracle, and though they still were in the midst of war with the other Immortals, they tried to make time to focus on him.

Once they got past the shock of Ace's pregnancy, they were torn between two names. Roku would have been a fitting tribute to two of their fallen comrades in the war. Roku was the Japanese word for six, and therefore would have been for both Codi, Ace's closest Chenja friend, and Six, their progeny. Both Six and Codi died in the ritual that preceded Octavian's birth. However, Ace also reminded Nero that due to Six's sacrifice, their son would be the eighth in their particular bloodline, now that Lucef could be counted as one of them. So Nero had immediately known his name was to be Octavian.

The moment Ace entered the mansion, Nero felt it. He felt her presence like an electrical current, a tether between them, and he knew the moment Octavian felt it too, his eyes popping away from the pages to look up at his father.

"I wonder if she found anything," Octavian mused, his eyes dancing with excitement. He was eager to be part of everything, as was to be expected from someone so young. His thirst for the hunt was palpable, but both Nero and Ace didn't want to risk him getting hurt, not when he was still so young. His body was that of a small child, younger than ten, but his mind had far surpassed that of a human ten-year-old. Not knowing what he was fully capable of made both Nero and Ace wary to unleash him on the world.

"She'll wait until you've finished your studies," Nero said, turning his eyes back down to his book, but Octavian snapped his closed, setting the book on the small table beside his chair and turning toward the open door as the sound of footsteps moved down the hall.

It wasn't Ace; that much Nero knew. Intrigued, he too turned his gaze to the open doorway, watching as Lotte and Nyprat walked past, the limp forms of two Witches held in their grasp. Nero raised an eyebrow at them, gaining a brief smirk from Nyprat as they continued by without stopping.

"Oh, she found something," Octavian said gleefully, a wide grin spreading over his face.

If Lotte and Nyprat were dragging two Witches through the mansion, that could only mean Ace intended to get information out of them.

"Write out your notes before you forget them," Nero said, gesturing to the journal on the table beside his son. Teaching Octavian was both thrilling and frustrating. He had flown through all basic knowledge, his reading level far surpassing any human child quickly. He could rival great mathematicians, would probably thrive in a scientific debate if he was given the opportunity, and had already mastered several languages. His thirst for knowledge was voracious, but as with all children, he could grow impatient, especially when something more exciting was awaiting him.

"I won't forget," Octavian said, rolling his eyes but pulling the journal closer anyway. His current topic was history, since they had all but exhausted common languages, and Minshin was on the cusp of forbidding him from entering the Medicus after he melted an entire table of equipment when he got into advanced chemistry.

History was a safe topic, but also a very important one. If Octavian was to walk through the world on his own at any point in his assuredly long life, he would need to understand it; and to do so he needed to know what made it the way it was. Both human and Immortal history was imperative, and Nero was always there to correct any of the lies the human histories liked to tell to make themselves look better.

Octavian finished his notes, closing the journal with a snap and standing up.

"Can we go now?" Octavian asked, eyes following the purposefully slow movements of his father as he closed the book he had been reading and set it beside him.

"To the Medicus," Nero said with a nod.

They left the chambers, heading toward the Medicus. Each step closer to Ace made Nero feel more at peace, the tether between them blossoming with the nearness. Ace had not been gone long on this particular outing. She had spent much of the evening with the other Elders, discussing her suspicions. Her hunts with the Necare had not been missions of death and destruction for a little over a year. Now she was searching for information—and unfortunately struggling—to find out what the Werewolves and Witches were up to. That was part of the reason Nero had suggested he and Octavian go through the histories. He wasn't certain they would give much to their current situation, but there were always patterns of behavior that could be accounted for. Missteps could be taken advantage of if you know where and when to look.

They stepped into the large room, and his eyes immediately landed on Ace sipping blood from a glass as she talked to Minshin. Octavian didn't wait but a beat before he was dashing through the tables, his figure blurring with inhuman speed as he made his way to his mother. She caught him easily when he came around the counter, pressing him to her and smoothing the back of his head.

"We saw Lotte and Nyprat," Octavian said, his body practically vibrating with anticipation once he broke away from the hug.

"There was an interesting situation near the newest club Alexander has opened. The Witches nearly exposed themselves," Ace said, bending over to kiss Octavian's forehead, leaving a tinge of blood from her meal on his white skin, before turning to Nero, who had come up behind him. She pressed her lips softly to Nero's, watching with amusement as his eyes flashed bright blue for a moment when she parted from him. He licked his lips, loving the taste of *her* and blood there.

"Hence why we took them with us. I have some questions," Ace murmured, a faint smirk on her lips as she pulled away from Nero.

"I want to come!" Octavian said excitedly. He didn't often show his childish excitement, more often appearing far more mature than his ten years, but with the promise of bloodshed, he was ecstatic, eyes dancing with the wonder of human children his age.

If Ace was still the woman of a thousand years ago, human mother to a human child, she would have been concerned about his lust for violence, but as it was, they were both Vampires. It was their nature to be drawn to the darkness, relishing in the pain and fear of others.

"First, Minshin will see to you," Ace said, eyes narrowing as she looked down at her son. He pouted lightly, eyes flicking over to Minshin, who grinned at his irritation before gesturing for them to follow her over to one of the beds.

Minshin went through the routine, measuring, weighing, and having Octavian smell and taste blood to see how he reacted. His eyes glowed and fangs lengthened, just like any other Vampire. His reflexes were also quick and sharp. She looked over her notes on the tablet from the last time she had examined him, brow furrowing a bit.

"He hasn't grown, but his blood intake has increased?" Minshin asked.

"Yes. We nearly ran out last month, remember?" Ace said, her silver eyes watching everything intently.

"I would assume, based on the last time his hunger increased like this, he will probably grow soon. So strange he doesn't do it gradually," Minshin said absently. "If he's going to exhibit any additional powers, I would suspect they are coming with this change. It's been nearly five years since he's grown; it hasn't been that long before," she continued.

That had been part of their concern. In the first five years of his life, Octavian grew in immediate bursts, going from infant-sized to toddler-sized when he was six months old, then unchanging for only a year before his body changed again, and he grew to be more like a small child, perhaps a three-year-old. At five years, his body drastically changed, making him appear the same age that he was, but then it stopped. The years passed, and he remained the same, though his mind expanded rapidly.

It was enough to concern them that he had stopped growing at all, that he would be trapped as an immortal child, but Minshin's recollection of his blood intake settled some of the worry that Ace had brewing in her chest.

"We'll measure again in a week," Minshin said, eyes still focused on the screen of her tablet instead of on them.

"A week?" Octavian pouted. His monthly visits to Minshin weren't bad, necessarily, just a frustration. He didn't enjoy being poked and prodded when nothing ever seemed to change. Minshin finally let her eyes snap up to look on Octavian, a playful glint in her eyes there.

"Since you've been drinking most of our supply, a supply that should last the entire coven for weeks not days, you should be happy I'm not demanding daily examinations," she said, grinning as his face became horrified.

"A week should suffice," Ace said, holding back her own smile.

"Nero," came a voice from the door. Makiut stood there, phone in hand. "Richard Martin is on the line."

Nero didn't carry a phone on him, seeing as he rarely left the mansion, so anyone who needed to get ahold of him directly had to go through other means. Richard Martin had a line that he called specifically to talk to Nero; the phone was kept in the security room where there was always a Necare keeping watch on their cameras. If Richard was calling, that meant he needed to speak to someone immediately.

It took less than a moment for Nero to have the phone in his hand, stepping out into the hallway as he pressed it to his ear.

"Richard, good to talk to you," Nero said, keeping his tone cool.

"Nero," Richard murmured in response, a slight tremor there. Nero smiled. This man, and practically all his relatives before him, worked for the Vampires, and yet they still held a healthy dose of fear within them at just the sound of Nero's voice. It was for the best, seeing as they and the two other families who were associated with the Vampires were the only humans allowed to know their secrets. The Masquerade may have been in place for humanity as a whole, but the Families were exempt.

"It's not often you call me directly," Nero continued, hopefully prompting Richard to push through his fear and get to the point.

"I-I'm sorry," Richard murmured, the faint sound of rustling, as if he were writhing wherever he sat uncomfortably. "We've sent reports over. I didn't know if you'd received them, but today something troubling happened. It seems to be accelerating."

"Reports?"

"About the women who keep coming to the facility. None of them have gone in, but we've seen them watching quite often," Richard said. Nero had not, in fact, read any of the reports. He had left that task to Trunist and Makiut, who both seemed less inclined to field work than they once were after the Ritual. Trunist had gone to Redeamond with Nero prior to the Ritual and Makiut never seemed to fully recover his vigor for the hunt after his arm had been taken off by a Werewolf.

Nero was walking now, heading toward the security room not far from where the Necare would train. Makiut had already headed right back there once he passed the phone to Nero, so he was certain that's where he'd find both Vampires.

"Women? Just women?" Nero asked as he entered the room, his eyes glowing slightly with his irritation.

If there were reports coming from the facilities, he expected to be told about them. The facilities were where the Families would go to have their blood drawn for Vampire consumption. In years past, they would come to covens and nests, giving their blood straight from their bodies, but with advancements in technology over the years Nero created these facilities, making donations easier on the humans and more efficient for the Vampires. Any problem or threat to the families could mean their supply would be negatively affected. Any decrease in the amount of blood they had access to meant the Vampires were back to hunting humans like they did in the past. That would be much harder to maintain, especially in this day and age with all the cameras tracking every human's move. Hunting still happened, but it was on a much lesser scale, not drawing attention.

"They seemed strange. At first our staff thought they were yours. Vampires, I mean," Richard said, clearly still shaken.

"Reports from the Martin facility?" Nero hissed at Trunist and Makiut, who seemed bewildered when he came through.

"Reports?" Trunist asked, her black brows furrowing and glancing at Makiut, who seemed to swallow thickly.

"I didn't—"

"You didn't what, Makiut? Think?" Nero hissed again, as he snatched the laptop where Makiut had quickly pulled up the reports. Nero's eyes scanned the words typed there as Richard continued to nervously babble about them from the phone.

They started as nothing, really. Suspicious women seemed to be coming by, looking at the exterior of the building every so often. The occurrences started to increase in frequency, clearly trying to determine something about who and what the facility was, though what they wanted that information for was unclear, since they spoke to no one. But as Nero's eyes finished reading the last of the reports, Richard's voice caught his attention again.

"...And she stopped a few of the girls as they were leaving this morning."

"One of these women stopped someone from your facility?" Nero asked.

"Yes. They called me as soon as they sped away. Apparently one of them felt drawn to going with her, and that's when I knew I needed to call you. Are we safe here?"

There were only two Immortals that possessed the power of enthrallment: Vampires and Witches. Any Vampire, even those not affiliated with covens, were able to receive blood from these facilities. They would only have to appeal to the Elders or the nearest Coven Judge, but it was strictly forbidden for any of them to approach that place on their own. That, along with all the other information gleaned from those reports, told Nero that for some reason, Witches were trying to gain access and knowledge of the facilities, but he had no idea why.

"Richard, lock it down. Anyone in the families who is involved with the facilities at this point is to either stay within or stay away for the time being until we find out why these women are approaching. I'll be keeping this phone on me and expect you to reach out if there are any other incidents immediately," Nero said, carefully setting the laptop down so he wouldn't throw it against the wall with how frustrated he was.

"T-thank you, sir," Richard said, before he abruptly hung up the phone.

"Nero, I didn't—" Makiut started.

"Do you know how disastrous it would be for us if something happened to that facility, Makiut?" Nero's voice was far too calm for the rage that was brewing within him.

"I'm sorry. It won't happen again," Makiut said.

"Trunist, I'll have you take over on that duty. Hire more security to watch the facilities during the day and see if there are available Necare in the Coven nearby to guard at night," Nero snapped, shooting them one last glare before he turned and left.

Chapter 3

The sun was shining brightly, casting the hill in a soft glow of its golden hue. It was warm against Lucef's skin, familiar, as if he had been there a hundred times before. And he had ... hadn't he?

He watched in amazement as small tendrils of magic seemed to float around him, almost like little creatures in and of themselves, dancing around his head as he sat in the grass.

"You keep playing like that, and Mum will find out you're misusing your magic," said a girl from behind him. He turned to look at her. Her hair was long, slightly curly at the bottom, but otherwise straight. Though Lucef knew he hadn't seen this girl before, he did *know her. This was his sister, his best friend. His twin. The twinge of guilt at her words had him cringing. She was right. He shouldn't have been using magic that way, but it was so pretty.*

"I don't want to stop," he said, his voice coming out not his own, as the small, dainty hands that were his continued to make the swirling magic continue. The moment was perfect, exactly as it should have been, as it had been once, but then something changed.

The air seemed to chill, and he turned to look upon his sister once more.

"You're going to turn to ashes if you keep using your powers that way," the girl said to him this time, her face twisting into a horrified mask, eyes darkening to black holes, face going pale and gaunt as the sunny hill around them seemed to suddenly be covered in shadow.

The scene around them shifted. The ground beneath him was no longer the soft grass but that of hard stone. The sun was gone, replaced with the poorly lit ceiling tiles of a cafeteria.

He felt hollow.

Cold.

Terrified.

Just as he started to turn his gaze to look more completely around him, the scene shifted again.

Now he sat at the edge of a little pond. He was careful to keep his feet clear of the water as he looked down, eyes taking in the beautiful koi fish just below the surface. Their orange, white, and black scales were tantalizing from where he sat, but he knew he could not touch. If he reached his hand in the water, it would hurt him.

"You're too close to the edge!" cried a voice from behind him. The language, though he understood it, was not English. He turned around and looked back at who spoke. She was small, her black hair flowing over her shoulders and framing her face, accentuating her almond- shaped eyes.

"I will not fall," he said indignantly, though his words also came out in that other language; his voice was once again not his own. His sister's mouth opened, as if to say something, but instead of any words coming out, a strange rattling sound did instead. Her face went gaunt, mouth continuing to extend open unnaturally like her jaw had unhinged.

"You'll be nothing more than a puddle yourself. You will be nothing anymore. It will all be for nothing," the girl said, her voice sounding almost metallic as she spoke through her strangely warped mouth.

Once again, the soft ground beneath him changed to stone. He was back in that dark room, the soothing sounds of the water and the fish splashing beneath it replaced by whispers and growls. He tried to raise his head, tried to look around and see where the sounds were coming from, to know where he was, but he was too weak to lift himself from the stone.

The scene shifted once more. He sat on the plush rug in his room from childhood. His hands holding firmly to the gameboard, only they weren't his hands. No ... he knew this moment; he had lived it before, but he hadn't been the one to sit on the floor and set up the game.

"Bridgit, I don't want to play that one again," came a small voice from the doorway. He looked up, only to see himself staring back at him. The very little version of himself stood there, perhaps only five years old, a pout on his face as he crossed his arms over his chest. He felt the smile pulling at his lips, looking at himself from years ago. Was he *smiling or was it the person who was looking at his younger self? Bridgit?*

"You'll never get better if you don't practice, Lucef," came the voice of Bridgit from his own mouth. The sour face of his younger self fell, the

expression becoming blank and unreadable, eyes lifeless as they stared into Bridgit, and therefore his, from across the room.

"Your sacrifice meant nothing," the younger him said, causing a chill to run down his spine as the chessboard within his grasp became chains, the murmuring hum of a Witches' spell filling the air as he stared only at the stained ceiling tiles above him.

No, no ... not this. Please, not this.

The scene changed again. He felt satin against his fingers and chest. He basked in the contentment, the happiness, but also the pain he knew was to come.

He looked down at her. She was lying beneath him, her fiery red hair a mess around her as it splayed over the sheets beneath her, framing a heart-shaped face. Red eyes staring up at him almost in awe as her hand came up to touch his chest. His Six was there before him. This moment had already come to pass, he knew, but he couldn't push it away. No matter that he knew what was coming next.

"Just kiss me," Six whispered to him. The hum of her computer was the only thing that could be heard as he leaned down and kissed her gently on her lips. The feel of her against him was like heaven, his heart beating wildly in his chest beneath her fingers. As he pulled away, she had the most beautiful glow and a genuine smile on her lips.

"I would kiss you forever if I could," he whispered to her.

"And why can't you?" she asked, her voice hushed, as if this conversation was a secret only they could share, before reaching her hand up to touch his cheek.

"We'd never do anything else."

"We'd never need to do anything else," she retorted, her thin fingers tracing his face. "But we won't get that chance, will we, Lucef?" she asked, her contented face falling, eyes going flat and lifeless.

No, no, no! NO!

"No! We'll get the chance," he said aloud, but it didn't matter. Before his eyes and under his hands, her skin began to crumble. There was nothing he could do, no way for him to fix it as she slowly turned to ash in his arms.

Lucef sat up in bed, screaming just as he had been in his dream. He let his voice fade to a pant, eyes wide as he took in his surroundings, trying to remember where he was, what he was doing there. He always awakened disoriented.

The dreams of Six never ended, not in a decade. Nearly every time he succumbed to sleep, which wasn't very often, he had the same dream, only more recently they also included the memories of the others who had been his sacrifices: the Witch, Codi, Bridgit, and Six. But it always ended with her. It always ended with Six crumbling to ash in his arms. Her life slipping through his fingers as he sat there, helpless to do anything about it.

He ran his fingers through his sweaty hair, shoving it off his damp forehead. His body was shaking head to toe as he wiped away tears that had fallen from his eyes. Disgusted with himself, he stood from the small twin bed, stained from previous tenants. He was staying in a hostel, in the seediest part of Paris, where his screams every night he slept would only be thought of as ordinary.

The last ten years had been a waking nightmare, only to be fueled by his actual nightmares when he allowed himself to sleep. He had spent time at Kurome with Ace and Nero off and on, but the way they were fighting the war now was too uncomfortable for him. He hadn't liked being potentially caught up in it and never wanted to be involved. The war between the Immortals had never been his fight. Though his father had tried everything to force him into it.

Ten years of avoidance when you've been made into the most powerful Immortal being was quite a feat. He was sought out by all the other Immortals, either to kill him or to convince him to join. Ace never asked anything from him. She never demanded he fight with them, didn't mind when he decided to take his extended stints away from London. All she ever seemed to want was to know that he was alright.

He liked Ace and Nero. He loved Octavian. But he didn't want to be part of the war. He never had. Paris's Werewolf den had never recovered from the Vampire raids. The Werewolves scattered, mostly out into the countryside or joined other dens in other countries rather than try to rebuild. That's why he had chosen to come here. It was a small pocket of peace in the Immortal world. No other Immortals who remained in the city had anything to do with war, except for the local Vampire coven, but even they often sent their Necare out to neighboring countries to help take down Witch and Werewolf operations.

He knew he couldn't stay out of it forever though, not with what he was. He was in that book for a reason. Ancient books, full of history and prophecies, had revealed that he was essential, inevitable. The prophecy that had changed his life and altered everything within the Immortal world had clearly and distinctly shown his face and described only him. His turning into what he had become after that ritual was exactly what was supposed to pass, according to the prophecy, but until something obvious changed, needing his attention, he would try to forget what happened.

Try to forget the sacrifices that were made to make him what he was.

Try to forget Six.

But there was no forgetting about her. His dreams saw to that.

Lucef paced around the tiny room, continuing to rake his fingers through his now red locks. She was part of him, and he would never be able to put her in the past.

And what ignorant bliss that would be, to forget his love, his only true love, who had died to make *him* stronger.

It would only be a matter of time before Lucef would go back to Kurome. Something about Ace grounded him. His nightmares still came, but the internal torment was not nearly as bad. He wasn't sure if it was because she too was tormented by the death of Six, or if it was just the proximity of being around Six's sire that gave him more strength. As if he was now tethered to Ace as Six had been. The only thing he seemed to understand after all these years was the longer he stayed away, the crazier he seemed to become.

Ace had been his only comfort, suffering almost as much as he did, and he admittedly didn't make it any better for her. He didn't assist her in the war and did not do much of anything when he did decide to come around, other than simply ... be there. He paused, looking down at the stained sheet he had just emerged from.

Was living in these places worth it when he could try to find a purpose?

Was hiding going to do anything other than make his torment worse?

His computer dinged from his bag where he had thrown it coming in. He didn't keep a phone on him, but he did like having a laptop. He pulled it out, setting it on the end of the bed and opening it. The email was from Ace.

Of course it was.

She had a sort of sixth sense when it came to him.

He hadn't checked his email in a few weeks, guiltily looking at the red notification saying he had ten unread messages. Ace sent him updates. Most of the time, it was related to what was happening with the war, and occasionally Octavian and his progress. Sparingly, Octavian, himself, would send an email. He pulled one up on the screen, skimming it.

Ace was having suspicions about the alliance between the Werewolves and the Witches. Well ... it was bound to be a bit rocky, especially with a leadership changeover once Lukis had died. His father had been in power for so long, the Witches were simply used to his leadership and domination. Now that Alexander was in power, it looked like they had their own ideas.

...planning something Alexander doesn't approve of...

...Octavian misses you...

...it's almost been a year...

...haven't been able to contact the Chenjas...

...I will have to go to them and try to reconnect. Not knowing the state of them, I think it will be too volatile to take Octavian with me, even if Nero is with us. We would like to see you before I leave. Perhaps have you with them at the mansion until I return. Please just check in. It's been longer than normal, Lucef.

The idea of Ace leaving Kurome stirred something strangely protective in him. He couldn't imagine how Nero must have been feeling about it. Since Octavian's birth, Ace hadn't strayed far from the mansion. In fact, several times Octavian accompanied them out of the country. But never, never had they been apart. And beyond that, in Ace's own way, she was asking that Lucef come back to help watch over her son. Well, Lucef had already thought he'd stayed away for too long. The longer away, the worse his dreams were.

It was almost as if he was supposed to stay at Kurome, but each trip there, despite the reduction in his dreams, he felt guilty for feeling at ease, even happy at times, when the lives of four others were stolen.

When Six's life was stolen.

He was changed so fundamentally after the Ritual. He was still himself ... but he was also *them.*

His heart no longer needed to beat in his chest, he no longer had the need to breathe, and he could change his appearance at will. He didn't have to consume anything. Not blood, not human food. He needed no sustenance to live, but he still craved the taste of blood on his tongue. He still got a thrill from feeling the adrenaline flowing through his victims into him, giving him the most euphoric high.

Lucef shivered in disgust at himself, recalling the last time he lost control. His need to hunt had overwhelmed him just days prior. He had watched a woman for nearly an hour as she ran errands, stopping in little shops as the evening turned dark and the streets started to empty. It was when she was finally walking home that the monster within him couldn't take it anymore.

He closed the distance between them, wrapping his big hand around her wrist and pulling her into a narrow alley that was barely wide enough for one person to walk through. Her surprised scream was immediately muffled by his hand pressed to her lips, large blue eyes staring up at him with fear. The scent of her was intoxicating, her terror oozing out of her pores with her human musk.

He didn't hesitate, as he had already come this far, too far. His need took over, teeth plunging into her shoulder as a growl ripped from his throat. The tang of her blood on his tongue exploded within him like the most delicious bite of food. He couldn't help it as he tore at her flesh, letting pieces of her slide down his throat with her blood.

There had been nothing left of her but tattered pieces of her clothes, bloody from the violent way he had torn her apart. And he left the little alley, feeling both fulfilled and horrified with what he had become.

Lucef tore himself out of the haunting thoughts of his last victim. When he was in London, he never seemed to lose control that way.

One more day in France, then he'd make his way back to Kurome.

Typing one quick reply to Ace's many messages, he told her he would head home. Because what else was the Vampire Coven at this point? He had spent more time there in the last decade than he had anywhere else; it was the place he always continued to end up. He chuckled darkly at this thought. The son of a Werewolf found a home in the coven of their enemies, and not just any coven, but the headquarters for all Vampires. If his father hadn't turned to dust after his mother killed him, he knew Lukis would be turning in his grave.

It was still dark. He had no idea how long he slept, not having been keeping up with the days. He would know that he had given Ace a time to expect him, but the city beyond his window wasn't teaming with life, telling him it was the wee hours of the morning. The near silence and the darkness of the city around him didn't threaten to swallow him in misery like it had the last time he looked out the window, hours, perhaps days ago, just before he fell asleep. Now he felt the strange sense of peace coming over him at the idea of going back to where he belonged.

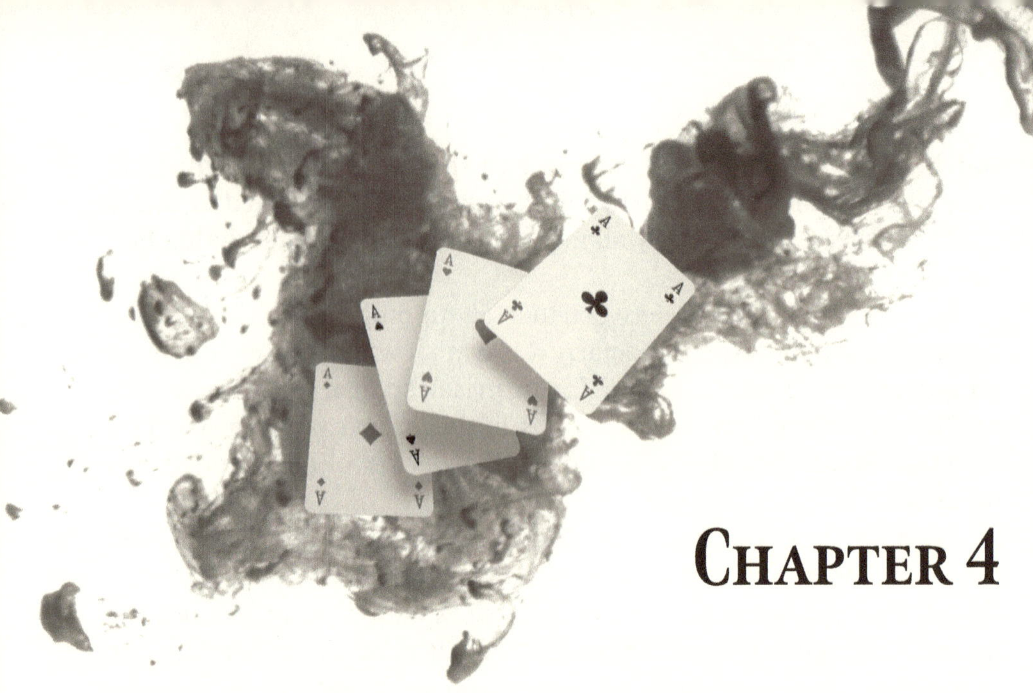

Chapter 4

Nero was heading back toward Medicus, the phone tucked into his pocket felt heavy. And the knowledge that the blood supply was going to be far lessened in the days and weeks to come was harrowing, considering his son had increased his appetite recently. He needed to talk to Minshin and get a ration system going, as well as talk to the House Vampires and make sure they knew that hunting outside of the house would need to be the preferred method for them to sustain themselves until he knew what the Witches were doing stalking their facilities.

It was an open secret. He was certain the other Immortals knew about the facilities but didn't dare interfere. It was in their best interest to keep their enemies fed in such a way that maintained the Masquerade. If Vampires were to exclusively feed off humans as they had in the past, especially with the increase in Vampire numbers since the time before, they would most certainly have human authorities catching on that there were other things to concern themselves with in the dark.

"Nero," Srinta said, stepping in front of him as he stepped back into the hall.

"Srinta," Nero said dismissively, trying to move past her when she put out a hand and placed it on his chest, halting him.

"I have to talk to you about something," she murmured, glancing briefly toward the door of the Medicus, where the sound of Octavian talking animatedly about the experiment he taunted Minshin about doing drifted toward them.

"I have a few things I need to take care of," Nero grumbled, pushing her hand gently away.

"This can't wait any longer," Srinta hissed quietly. He finally looked into her eyes more fully. There was a slight glow, shimmering with fear and anger, in a way he hadn't seen in some time. Although admittedly he hadn't been paying close attention to his sire, having quite a few more important things taking up his thoughts. Their only interactions in recent years had been discussing the war at council meetings, otherwise his main focus had been on Octavian and Ace. "Come with me now," she said, her voice vibrating with her command.

Technically, he didn't have to follow her instruction. He was released from the sire-progeny hold long ago, and they were equals now, both being Elders, but there was a level of respect that he had for her that would never waver. She chose him for this life. At one point, she had been his everything. She would still have been that if he hadn't laid eyes on Ace.

Nero glanced through the door at Ace, who had noticed the two of them speaking just outside. Her lips turned up into the faintest smile, an encouraging one as she nodded.

"Octavian and I have some questions to ask our guests," Ace said, telling him subtly that they would be occupied, and he could go talk to Srinta.

It had been centuries since Nero had seen anything similar to this on Srinta's face, and the bond between them throbbed slowly as she held back from letting him in to see behind the tightness in her eyes to her true thoughts and feelings.

"Where?" Nero asked, narrowing his eyes with suspicion. She said nothing, merely leading him toward the stairwell, moving silently down to the lower levels.

Nero knew this mansion by heart. He knew every room, every crevice, everything about the space around them. There were only a few places Srinta could be taking him to talk. Either she was leading him toward the Council room, which was certainly empty and fairly private when meetings weren't happening, or possibly the library or an antiquities room, where they kept the most valuable and precious possessions. But she surprised him when she stopped in front of the doors that led to Ramses' chamber.

Ramses, the first Vampire, lived, though not in the same way the other Vampires did. He had chosen to take another form, his abilities far *more* than any other Vampire since him. Srinta took in an unnecessary breath, pushing one of the doors open and stepping through the shadowed room beyond. Nero followed her, though cautiously, closing the door and encasing them in darkness for a moment.

"Srinta, what—" Nero started, but was cut off as his eyes fell on the living wall before him.

Ramses had, many years before, transformed himself. Instead of a body, his essence lived within the wall there, able to impart his thoughts to anyone worthy of asking for them. Nero didn't often seek out Ramses' counsel, but he had in the past. Normally, the surface of the wall would move slightly, perhaps ripple when his voice spoke to them, but it was far different now. The surface was more like the rough tides of the sea. The shape of hands came out, like they were pressing to escape from within but were trapped under a thin covering that they could not break.

"It's been like this for some time. It started almost six months ago," Srinta whispered, eyes wide and full of fear as she gazed at it.

Nero knew Srinta visited Ramses often, not that he would always speak back to her or anyone who approached him, but being that Ramses was her sire, her attachment to him was just as great, if not more than other sire-progeny bonds.

"What could have caused this?" Nero asked, his voice hushed, as if speaking louder would somehow offend the wall and cause it to lash out at them.

"I've never seen it this way, Nero. And he has not spoken to me in years. Not since..." She let her voice trail off, her hands clenching into fists at her side.

"Since what?"

Srinta's gaze turned to him, her eyes fiery and glowing with rage. "Since Ace approached the wall last," Srinta said, her voice cold and bitter, echoing around the room.

Ace had felt when Nero and Srinta came down to the lower level shortly before them, but she wasn't surprised. There were fewer ears to overhear down in these rooms than the main floors above, but something about Srinta had seemed odd for some time. Ace had always trusted Srinta implicitly. Her being Nero's sire meant that she was somewhat of a mentor to Ace, but these last ten years since Ace had become an Elder, and then a mother, the way Srinta treated Ace had changed. Not that there wasn't still respect; Srinta certainly still held Ace in high regard and defaulted to many of Ace's ideas as far as how to deal with the war, but something ... something had come to pass between them. Ace wasn't sure what it was or how to fix it.

Octavian looked up toward his mother, eyes moving over her face, which only held the barest hint of concern that only he and his father would be able to see. His small fingers wrapped tighter around hers, squeezing and bringing her attention down to him as they turned the final corner and found themselves near the cells.

"Mum..." Octavian said, wanting to ask what she was worried about, wishing he could press into her mind. Ace wasn't one to speak of her concerns readily. She could even be evasive sometimes when things were going wrong, not even telling his father what was plaguing her, but Octavian wished to know.

Both of his parents were very open with him about what they were, what being a Vampire meant, but also about the other beings in the world. Empathy was something usually left for mortals to feel, but Ace assured him that just because Vampires were blood-thirsty creatures, like the other Immortals, it didn't mean they didn't hold those same feelings within them. And though he wanted nothing more than to know what was in her mind, what caused the slight wrinkle between her brows, he didn't ask, didn't relinquish his thoughts to her. Instead, he turned his head toward the door they stopped in front of, his eyes glowing as he took in the scent that seemed to pour from it.

Ace took in a deep breath herself, catching the scent of fear radiating from the room as the two Witches whispered in haunted tones behind the door.

"You'll watch this one. Perhaps next time you'll get to join in," she said, looking back down at her son.

It was odd to think that not long before he came to be, Ace was worried about attachments getting in the way of her duty and drive for her kind. She had pushed Nero away for so long, only to have doubled her potential distractions. Now, she couldn't think of anything else that would make her simultaneously want to drop everything, as well as fight even harder to ensure the Vampires' success, than her son.

She unlocked the door, letting it fall open to reveal the two Witches, their bodies huddled together against the floor as they looked up at Ace's small yet intimidating silhouette in the doorway. The room was stark, void of any comforts. The cuffs at the Witches' wrists did more than keep them trapped within the room physically, also inhibiting them from using their magic. They both seemed to freeze, breath and all, when Ace and Octavian stepped into the room.

The Witch who had spoken to Ace in the alley let out a gasp when her eyes fell on Octavian. His white hair, blending into his pale skin against glowing silver eyes, was certainly a shocking sight, especially in the child-shaped body he was in.

"What—what is that?" she whispered hoarsely, her face contorting horribly as it dawned on her that he was a child.

"How could you do such a thing? I thought that was against your rules!" the other Witch, Poppy, Ace seemed to recall, nearly screamed, her voice rough with panic as she tried to scramble further back into the cell. However, the chain prevented that, clanging loudly when she had gone as far as she could.

"Octavian?" Ace asked, glancing down at her son with a smirk, wickedness shining in her eyes at the Witches' immediate assumption.

Turning children was a forbidden practice. Too many times in the past, children had been turned and set loose, wreaking havoc. They were wild, untamable hungry beasts. Their thirst for blood seemed unquenchable, and it didn't matter how old they had become; they would completely disregard the rules and the Masquerade in the pursuit of their own pleasure. The practice of changing children was strictly prohibited for these reasons, but Ace knew this was exactly what these Witches imagined had happened as they looked upon her son.

"Oh God, they're turning children again. The world might as well burn," Poppy whimpered, as the chains dug into the flesh of her wrists in an effort to escape. Octavian's eyes zeroed in on the flesh just as it began to break, the scent of her magic-laced blood hitting the air. Unlike Werewolf blood, which to a Vampire tasted musky and earthy in a way that was not favorable, Vampires *liked* the taste of Witch blood. It was close to human with a bit of a bite, which some Vampires in the past liked so much they specifically took to hunting Witches for their meals.

Vampires were the only Immortal that could not be fed from. Their blood was lethal to every other Immortal, since it immediately tried to change any creature from within.

"I'm not turned," Octavian said, licking his lips as he fidgeted beside his mother, wanting to get closer to the delicious elixir that was oozing from Poppy's wrists.

"That's the only way a Vampire is made," the other Witch snapped at Ace, as if she were an idiot and unaware of how her own kind was created.

"Apparently not," Ace said, stepping forward one pace and moving to crouch so she was eye level with the two prisoners. "But this isn't about my son or me. This is about you and what you have behind those pretty blue eyes that I want to know," Ace continued, reaching out to touch the Witch's cheek with her silver nails. The sharp points pressed into her flesh, leaving thin lines of red in their wake.

"I won't tell you anything," she whispered, tears welling in her eyes as she looked at the frightening Vampire before her. Ace was notorious. Cruel, vicious, a machine. There was not an Immortal in this world who hadn't heard her name. To be held captive there, with Ace before them, ready to inflict pain and punishment, was what they considered equal to coming face to face with Ramses himself.

"You will," Ace said with assurance, standing once again and towering over the shaking Witches. "Because if you don't, I'll make sure you live so long and in so much pain, you'll be begging me for death, and still it won't come."

Lucef's eyes flashed opened at the sound of a heavy door slamming closed somewhere in the distance. He was vaguely aware of the sounds of screams in the distance, the scent of burning, blood, and filth. His eyes moved around the room, taking in the scene that seemed oddly familiar, even though he was certain he had never been in a place like this. The rough stone was encasing them, like he was in a cave of some sort. Clearly underground. There were metal objects hanging above him, most of them crusted with blood. But within them, he caught his reflection. Well, not his *reflection.*

Six.

It wasn't Six as he had known her. She looked different, changed. Her eyes looked like that of a serpent; blood red every which way as they shifted with vertical pupils, like a cat. Her eyebrows were non-existent, simply smooth white flesh where the delicate red arches used to reside. The lack of hair there made her heart-shaped face more alien. Her red, spiked hair now had the consistency of metal, protruding from her scalp like a gruesome crimson crown. Her red diamond tattoos seemed to have spread, the sharp, pointed red designs littering more of her skin, which had an unnatural glow even for a Vampire.

She was naked, chained to a flat stone table, which was eerily reminiscent of the ones they had been chained to for the ritual, but this place was not the ritual. This was nothing like the dreams Lucef had been tormented with before.

He felt her hunger, her anger, her pain. He was within her somehow, but not the same distant way he felt in his other dreams; no, this dream felt so different. It was new. This wasn't the Six he had known, nor was this a place he had ever seen her before.

Six flexed her fingers a bit as her thoughts of hunger made that insatiable feeling take over her thoughts. She could use a drink from a warm body right about that moment. The movement of her hands rattle the chains that held her to the flat stone table, making her hiss at the sensation on her torn skin. Her lips pulled over her teeth, baring them to the empty room, as if it could help her escape her confinement. Her teeth were yet another change. They were no longer the four pearly white canines that she had developed after being made Vampire. She now had six, long pointed fangs.

A low growl could be heard outside the door. Somehow Lucef knew that sound—no, Six knew that sound.

Chomic.

It was a thought, but not Lucef's.

Six instantly became still, retracting her fangs and letting her eyes glaze over, head lolling toward the wall as the door creaked open. Chomic, a torture demon, looked as if he had been tortured a bit himself. His arms were like a body-builder's—huge and bulging—however there were a few chunks of muscle and flesh that seemed to have been ripped away from the bone. His hands and feet were more like claws, with missing bits here or there, while his skin, a charred blue gray, was heavily scarred and stitched.

As the demon brushed past, his arm touching against Six's flesh, Lucef felt an immediate piercing fire running through him from the faint, inadvertent touch. If this had been his own body, his own mind, he would have cried out, but within Six, he remained silent and still, just as she was. She had gotten used to this feeling, Lucef realized. There was no other way she'd be able to completely not react to it, as it scorched its way through her.

Lucef pushed through her thoughts, her new memories, seeing that this Chomic touched her quite a lot when he was inflicting all sorts of other painful forms of torture on her. Quickly, horrific scenes flashed through his mind from her memories. So much blood and pain, fire and torment. If he was in his own body, he would weep for the torture she had already endured. But instead of letting her body react to the slight brush against her skin, she kept it motionless, eyes deadened.

Initially, Chomic didn't seem to notice her lack of reaction, too busy letting his fingers brush over all the instruments of torture, stopping at one serrated knife, caked with her blood from some previous bout of torture.

Perhaps we can start with this one today, *he spoke into her mind and, therefore, Lucef's.*

Chomic didn't speak aloud often. Lucef realized Six wasn't sure if it was something normal for all demons, but much like Vehekan, the demon who had inhabited her blades previously, he predominately spoke directly within her head, reading her thoughts easily.

Chomic's head turned slightly, eyes looking over at her when he heard nothing within her thoughts in return. When there was still nothing from her, not even a movement after a beat, he stood over her lifeless body, scanning it and finally resting on her detached gaze. He stared into her eyes for a long minute, waiting for a thought or a shift in her pupils, but there was nothing reflected to Lucef from the demon's black eyes that looked down at her.

Chomic let out a disappointed huff, his nostrils flaring. He tossed the knife back on the instrument table with frustration, moving to begin unlocking each of the clasps around her wrists and ankles. The chains clanked against the stone as his massive claws cupped the tiny figure of Six into his arms. He cradled her as if she were a small child. As if he cared.

The door was opened once more, and Chomic walked with her in his arms, his clawed fingers lightly brushing over her skin, caressing her. Honestly, it seemed a bit bizarre that a demon demonstrated such an odd act of kindness, even if he didn't think she could feel it. From the brief set of memories that Lucef had witnessed, he relished in her pain and anguish. The softness of his touch was, while painful to her and to Lucef, comforting and confusing. Lucef didn't understand, but quite frankly, neither did Six, and she was doing her very best to remain unthinking, unfeeling. If she didn't maintain this, she, and therefore Lucef, knew she would go right back into that torture chamber, all to begin again. The fire from his skin on hers covered a good majority of her body, but she remained limp, showing no signs of discomfort.

It took only seconds once Chomic left the chamber to arrive at another level of the Underworld. The River. For a moment, Chomic was standing there on the stone ledge that protruded from a door, looking down at Six with what seemed like sadness in his deep black eyes.

"I had hoped you would be stronger. You were far too interesting to let waste away in torment, but perhaps now your torture is over, and you can finally sleep," Chomic whispered, before slowly placing her on the dusty ledge before standing once again with hunched shoulders and disappearing with a crack.

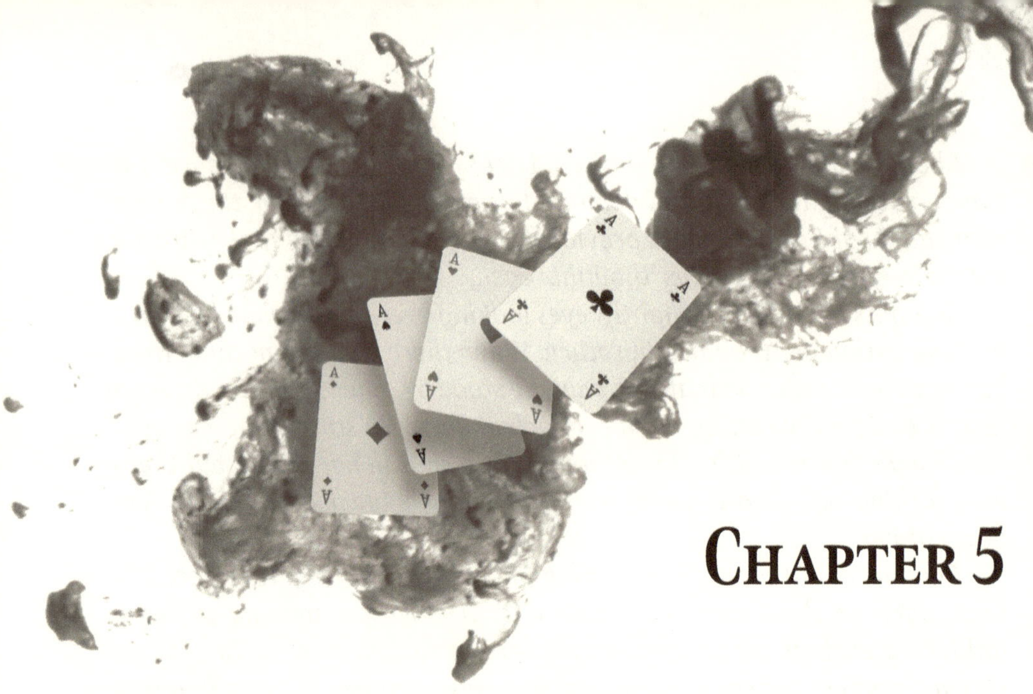

Chapter 5

The bright lights of the city illuminated the darkened room of the penthouse in the heart of Yokohama, Japan. The floors below held the offices and legitimate businesses owned by the figure standing and watching the busy streets below. Cars and people looked so small from the top of the building. Its height wasn't the most impressive, nor was its architecture, but that was by design. The bright rainbow of florescent lights seemed to reflect off the figure's skin, which appeared to be more like liquid mercury than soft flesh. Black almond-shaped eyes looked on emotionlessly, not giving away anything happening in the mind behind them, but as always, there was quite a bit stirring there.

The door across the room opened, the creak of the old hinges breaking the still silence that had permeated the space. Though this building was newer, a steel-and-glass monstrosity like the rest of the buildings in this city, however some ancient fixtures had been salvaged and brought to the penthouse. The combination of old and new in the space showed how vast the passage of time was for the Chenjas. Things may change, but they also stay very much the same.

Soft footfalls followed the sound of the door, approaching the mercurial figure at the window.

"Kagami-sama," the soft voice of the woman who entered the room said.

Kagami turned her black eyes from the window, letting them fall on the meek-looking woman who stood timidly in the center of the mostly empty room. Her black hair fell like a sheet over her shoulders, partially obscuring her face as she bowed her head respectfully toward the figure before her.

"Chiyo-san," Kagami said in return, her voice sounding as liquid and inhuman as the appearance of her skin.

Chiyo kept her head bowed, but her eyes drifted from the floor landing on the being before her. There was no fear, only honor and admiration. As the queen of the Chenjas, Kagami held power beyond what the rest of them possessed, and she also was the only one who could create more.

"<You have visitors,>" Chiyo said quietly in Japanese.

"<Visitors?>" Kagami murmured, her voice hardening a bit more to a normal tone.

"*Hai*," Chiyo said with a nod. "<The Raven.>"

That certainly gave Kagami pause. For The Raven, the leader of the Witches, to have made her way all the way to Japan was quite a statement on its own. The Raven was well known for keeping to herself, never going to anyone but instead setting up a meeting place and making certain that she was protected. For her to have come on her own without setting up an elaborate gathering beforehand meant not only was The Raven asking for the Chenjas' help, but that she was vulnerable and at Kagami's will.

"<Send them in,>" Kagami said, turning back to the window as she let her form change around her.

It was like a ripple of liquid, starting at her feet and traveling slowly up her body. The silver of her skin transformed to smooth, pale human skin, body adorned in traditional Japanese clothes of elaborately embroidered silk.

Chiyo had already slipped back out of the room, but only a moment later, the door opened once again, and Kagami turned to watch the figures who stepped through the door. They all paused, taking her in. Not many had looked upon the Queen of the Chenjas in recent years, and she was certainly a sight to behold.

Her face was perfectly shaped with a pointed chin. Her eyes didn't reduce from their large size in her true form, only took a more human appearance. The blackness of her irises almost seemed unfathomable. Her body was slight, thin, and dainty, but she held herself with such an air of superiority, it was unquestioned how powerful she was. Her lips were unexpected. Instead of pink or red, they were silvery lavender, a color that seemed to be woven through her intricate silk robes. Her black hair was pulled back into an elaborate style away from her face, but fanning around her head like a crown, with jade blossoms placed perfectly in the mound. She was unnaturally beautiful and perfect.

Kagami let her eyes drift over the three women who stood beside Chiyo. They all looked similar in age, but it was well known Witches kept themselves unnaturally youthful through sacrifice. The only thing giving away that there was anything different in the three of them was the way the one in the center's eyes seemed to glow as she took in Kagami. A queen in the presence of another.

"Raven," Kagami said, nodding her head toward only her, eyes locking.

"Kagami," The Raven said in return.

"You come without your protection," Kagami noted, eyes glancing on either side of the group of women, as if to indicate the lack of Werewolves present with them, before returning to meet The Raven's eyes.

"That which tethered us together seems to be failing," The Raven said, her smoky voice sounding almost gravely with barely suppressed anger.

"And you come to your enemy instead?" Kagami asked, raising a delicate black eyebrow. The Raven smirked at that, raising her own.

"Are we enemies?"

"We have been on opposite sides of this war for so long, I would have assumed that to be so," Kagami said, watching when one of the other Witches beside The Raven tensed with Chiyo's movement to be closer to her mother.

"Was that our choice, or did the Vampires and Werewolves choose that for us?" The Raven asked. Kagami cocked her head to the side, her eyes narrowing slightly as she looked across the room and considered what The Raven said.

"It has been so long..."

"How does your alliance with the Vampires fare these days?" The Raven asked, her eyes seeming to glitter with amusement as she watched Kagami's face go from thinking of the past to a simmering fury. Kagami said nothing, her fingers curling into claws before folding into tight fists. "They didn't do a very good job of protecting Codi, did they?"

Kagami's lip pulled back, and a snarl nearly ripped from her throat at the mention of Codi's name. Chiyo whimpered quietly beside her.

"When he died—"

"When *you killed him*," Kagami hissed, eyes blackening further.

"I may have instructed my Witches to perform the ritual, but it was under Lukis's command," The Raven murmured, her face showing only a bit of remorse.

"The Vampires failed to protect him, but it was *your* magic that tore his soul from his body. *Your* magic that made it so we could not even reabsorb him," Kagami spat.

"But that never would have happened if the Vampires and the Werewolves weren't the ones who held all the power," The Raven said, her voice a bit more forceful to be certain that Kagami heard her words. When the Chenja went quiet, eyes still burning with fury, The Raven continued. "Weaker than them. That's what they always told us, isn't it?" The Raven murmured, her voice lilting with curiousness, while still edged with bitterness. "Why are we considered weaker? Because my kind doesn't have the physical strength that a Vampire or a Werewolf does? Or your kind doesn't have the same numbers?"

"That seems to be how they have pegged us," Kagami said cautiously, following The Raven's movements as she slowly began to pace at her end of the room.

"The Vampires and the Werewolves will never reconcile. They will never be able to put aside their differences. There would have to be a near annihilation of one of them before any of us could find any peace."

"Neither of us are capable of what you are saying. Neither of our groups have the means to kill off either of the other sects," Kagami argued. It hurt her pride to admit it, but it was true. The Chenjas didn't have the numbers to inflict any real damage on either of the other Immortal sects. They could cause some hurt, perhaps weaken them, but they would very likely be wiped out in the process.

"Ah," The Raven exclaimed suddenly, turning to face Kagami once again, her own eyes showing a vibrant lavender, glittering with an eager hunger. "But what if we, the two *weaker* Immortals, joined together? Would we still be as weak as either of them?"

Kagami let her eyebrow rise on her forehead at the suggestion. For centuries, the Chenjas had been allied with the Vampires. They understood each other to a degree, and Kagami had, at least up until the death of Codi, thought there was a mutual respect between them. The knowledge of the Vampires' operation, of their power structure, and their secrets was powerful in and of itself. If she were to use that knowledge against them...

"How do you so easily turn your back on a centuries-long alliance with the Werewolves? Where is your loyalty? Your honor?" Kagami asked.

"Loyalty and honor?" The Raven asked back, laughing darkly. "Lukis burned any loyalty and honor when his greed outweighed our goals."

"Why did you help him, then?" It was Chiyo who asked, drawing everyone's attention to her now. She had stood silently, watching the entire conversation so far, letting herself blend into the background and become unnoticeable, nearly invisible. The Raven smirked at the younger Chenja, glancing back at Kagami for a moment before returning her green eyes to Chiyo.

"That same loyalty and honor. We trusted him. We had trusted him for far too many years, and what did it get us? Many of ours dead. The ritual completed, but nothing but horror and destruction came after. *The* Immortal was created, but he hides away, helping no sect. None of the triumph Lukis had proclaimed. Had I been given a chance to look at the prophecy itself, and not rely on what he gave me, I would have known. Lukis was no ally to us. He was our slaver, and now he's dead."

Though Kagami never considered the Vampires their masters, they did look up to them for help and guidance all these years. Many of Kagami's ideas were turned down by the Council of Elders in favor of their own plans. And with the death of Codi ... Kagami had lacked something in this last decade. Her soul sat heavy with his loss. The war between Immortals had been fought almost completely without Chenja involvement. But the way The Raven spoke made something strange stir in Kagami's chest. Perhaps it was her need for some sort of revenge for Codi's death, or perhaps it was hope.

"What is it that you plan to do if we were to join together?" Kagami asked, after several long, silent moments. A grin broke out over The Raven's face, and she seemed to take in a breath, her whole body lifting higher and prouder as she did so.

"Oh, I have the start of a plan."

The halls of the Werewolf den were still. Not nearly as many moving through the space as there once were. The darkness of the underground tunnels seemed far more imposing than they once had, no longer cozy and safe; it now felt more like a tomb, complete with the lost souls who inhabited the space. The spirit of the Werewolves had been tested, broken, and was struggling to put the pieces back together in some way that might bring with it even a hint of the power they once were.

Alexander stared out the door from the sitting room he was in, looking out at the quiet, sullen corridor. Though he had gotten many Werewolves back into the fold with promises, favors, and jobs, there were still far more who were reluctant to rejoin him. Preservation of self was proving to be an instinct too strong to fight against when Alexander still had so little to offer them.

They were losing the war.

The frustration was mounting, his rage simmering under the surface. Had his predecessor not been such a fool, none of this would have come to pass. Lukis trading in the strength of their kind in the hopes that he'd be able to pull off some sort of magic to make himself above all others was simply egotistical. If Lukis had truly read the prophecy, he would have seen that his son Lucef, and Lucef alone, was to take up that mantle. Now Alexander was left with no great Immortal, no plan to take his enemies down a peg, and a crumbling army.

To make matters worse, the audacity of Lukis seemed to have spread to their allies, who continuously tried to offer suggestions of how to rid them of prominent Vampires, in the hopes of weakening them as their ranks had been weakened. If there was one thing Werewolves did not do well with, it was letting someone else do their work for them. Alexander was not about to let the Witches summon some other entity to tear down their enemies. If he was to take out the Elder Vampires, it would be him and his wolves doing the killing. No one else.

The footfalls of someone down the hall heading his way grabbed his attention. He was not in the mood for company. He never was.

Prior to taking up the role of leader, Alexander had been a shadow. Second-in-command to Lukis but working mostly alone. It wasn't in his nature anymore to rely on others, and his position now made it nearly impossible to work, hunt, and kill as he had been accustomed to. His fingers tightened on the arm of his chair as steps slowed, indicating whoever was planning on interrupting him was drawing nearer.

The doorway darkened with the figure of Kyle, who had been Alexander's only true confidante in the past decade. There were snakes hidden all around him, everyone having their own agenda, especially with the weakness he inherited, but Kyle never strayed in loyalty, at least not until recently.

More and more, Alexander had noticed odd looks from Kyle and the occasional comment that made Alexander think perhaps his second was not feeling nearly as resolved to the way the leadership of their kind had panned out. It hadn't been what Kyle or many of the other Werewolves in their ranks had wanted, but what Deca had wanted. Deca, in her last moments, made certain Alexander took over. Perhaps whatever initial feelings of loyalty Kyle had felt had been to their late mistress, but now ... a decade with her and Lukis gone, and whatever Kyle's true feelings were had finally started showing.

"The Raven sent word and wants to meet again," Kyle said, stepping through the door as he pulled a letter from his pocket.

The envelope was black, sealed with blood wax. The Raven was the single most powerful Witch. A queen that ruled them. Much like a mafia boss, they pledged their fealty in power and blood, enriching and keeping her in the position, and though the Witches were a weaker Immortal sect, she ruled them viciously.

Alexander glared at the spelled seal for a moment, his grey eyes burning in irritation before taking the offensive thing from Kyle's hand. He knew it was sealed so only he would be capable of opening it, and only he would be able to read its contents. If she were sending him this letter, it was most likely with a location to meet; that was how she had done it each time before.

"Thank you, Kyle," Alexander said, glaring down at the crisp, folded page in his fingers, as he took a sip of the bourbon he had set on the table beside him. It took a lot of alcohol to intoxicate an Immortal, less if a human they ate was drunk, but he hadn't hunted in many moons. Too risky to do so in the city with Kurome's Necare ready to pounce at any opportunity the Werewolves gave them. And leaving the city during this crucial rebuilding time was not an option for him. The beast that he was itched eagerly to tear into flesh and savor the tang of blood on his tongue, but it would be closer to suicide to do so. The twitch of Kyle's fingers as they curled into fists showed his own beast fighting within him for a kill.

"There was one more thing I wanted to tell you," Kyle murmured, as he finally let those twitching fingers clench into fists nervously. Alexander glanced up to see the agitation there in Kyle's face.

"What now?" Alexander asked wearily. He couldn't afford yet more mistakes, either from the Witches or his own Werewolves. The mishaps from both Witches and Werewolves had dwindled some in recent months, but it grew taxing to have to put out fires while simultaneously trying to rebuild what Lukis's actions had torn apart.

"There was an incident that very well could have been catastrophic. One of our bouncers almost tore down two Witches in view of mortals," Kyle said, his voice tight, eyes alight with anger.

If it had not occurred, Alexander was quite sure there was more to the story, especially since Kyle was not at all pleased with what actually came to pass. He could see the tension, the frustration in the set of his second's shoulders, the way Kyle's jaw ticked and eyes glowed.

"Almost?"

"We found him with a tranquilizer in his system. Silver, but not enough to kill."

"Was it the Witches?" Alexander asked, feeling a prickle moving over his skin. He knew the answer before Kyle spoke it.

"It is not their way, nor was it their technology."

Vampires, then.

Alexander furrowed his brow as he thought on the matter. Why would Ace's Necare choose to subdue, but not kill? And he knew it was her. Only Ace would have gone against the instinct to decimate her enemies, especially on the cusp of winning. Perhaps it had been the crowd of humans that kept her from reducing his bouncer to ashes, but he sensed it was something else, something more.

His hand unconsciously moved to his chest. His heart seemed to beat wildly there every time he thought of his sister. The promises he made were not undone just because centuries had passed, and they were no longer the same species. Hidden in the pocket of his inner liner was a lock of black hair, a lock that had stayed with him and close to his heart since that fateful night when everything changed for them.

"Where are the Witches from the incident now?" Alexander asked, removing the hand from his chest to reach for his bourbon once more.

"Gone. When I caught wind of this, I sent two of ours to trace them, but along with them, we scented Vampires."

"Taken, then," Alexander said grimly, glancing back to the red wax seal.

"I would assume so. What should we do? The Raven will not be pleased."

"I will deal with The Raven," Alexander said, holding up the black page as an indicator. "Make sure our people know the Masquerade still holds, and anyone who breaks it will not simply die. They risk us all with that sort of blatant display; they'll pay a price fitting to the risk." The coldness of Alexander's grey eyes chilled even Kyle.

They may be trying to rebuild their ranks, but he would not hesitate to slaughter anyone who threatened the careful balance of secrecy all the Immortals maintained. It was a matter of survival for them all that they remained in the shadows. Humans may be far weaker, good for not much more than the meal that they provided, but they far outnumbered all the Immortals, and their technology continued to grow.

"Of course," Kyle said, nodding his head as he turned to go, but he paused just outside the threshold. "Melissa wishes to—" Alexander's eyes snapped up to look upon Kyle's uneasy face. Melissa, Kyle's sister, had been relentless in the years following his ascension to power. Kyle had been in line to potentially take the role, but Alexander had been Lukis's second, and therefore, when he took it on, there was no questioning him.

But Melissa was hungry for power, power she was denied as soon as her brother was no longer eligible to be leader.

"Melissa is not my concern. She is not my mate nor ranked. She can say anything she *wishes,* but she'll not hold my ear," Alexander growled. Her eagerness had been useful in years past, when he needed to sate other urges than his hunger for flesh, but those trysts were little more than just a means to satisfy himself, not an invitation for a lifelong commitment. She had apparently thought otherwise.

"She's only—"

"Your sister would do well to keep her mouth shut around me, and if you wish to not anger me, you'll do the same."

Kyle stood still as stone for a moment, his eyes on the floor. It was moments like these that Alexander knew Kyle hid his frustration at not being named the leader deep within him. His muscles flexed and bunched as he held down the beast that wanted to lash out.

"Yes, sir," he murmured before quickly leaving the doorway, his footfalls echoing down the hall and away.

Alexander closed his eyes for a moment, waiting until the heavy footfalls faded. He raked his fingers through his long black hair, not wanting to deal with the drama that seemed to continuously unfold around him, as well as not wanting to see the contents of The Raven's letter. He knew already what might be held behind this seal. The Raven was pushing back on his dominance, trying to take control of their alliance by being the one to summon a creature who would rid them of obstacles, and weaken the Vampires as the rest of them had been weakened. He had pushed and argued against her plan, but it didn't matter. She was doing it anyway.

He slipped his finger along the paper, letting the wax pop and feeling the magic float over him. It simmered like a fire was ready to burst over his skin, testing out to make sure he was truly himself, the only one who was worthy of breaking the seal. Once the magic found he was, it seemed to melt off him, the feeling subsiding, allowing him to shake it off before unfolding the page to read what The Raven had written.

Alexander,

> *I thought your problems with us would subside if you and your kind were not involved in my plans; now it seems that all my Witches are no longer welcomed. News of your Werewolves' blatant objection to my Witches joining in your spaces spreads fast through our world. Now I have lost two of mine because of your stubbornness.*

Have you decided the alliance with us is no longer of value? Only a decade into your reign and so different the world has become, how strange the tide shifted after Lukis died. And for what?

If you wish to at least make no further enemies, if not repair our alliance, I suggest you follow the instructions below to meet. Choose not to heed my call, I'll consider you an enemy, along with the Vampires who stole those that are mine.

The letter was signed with a raven's print in blood.

Chapter 6

Ace stood in the spray of the shower, rinsing the blood from her skin. The sun had already risen in the sky, and she had, for once, been grateful for it, since that was one pull that Octavian could not fight. As soon as dawn approached, he would become overwhelmed with exhaustion, the need to sleep taking over.

He had been so eager, watching Ace as she inflicted pain, pausing only often enough to inquire if they were ready to talk and end it all. Poppy, the weaker of the two Witches, finally caved a few hours into the torture, choking out in agony exactly what Ace had suspected and then some.

"The Raven wants to-to—" Poppy choked, blood running from her nose and into her mouth. "There will be a summoning. It's not what... Alexander won't..."

"Tell me or I'll inject you with adrenaline and keep this going for hours to come," Ace hissed, her face coated in the Witches' blood, eyes so fierce and glowing she looked more like a demon than a Vampire. Poppy choked again, her broken limbs moving awkwardly as she struggled for breath.

"Alexander doesn't want to summon..." Her voice trailed away, as she took in a sharp inhale just before a sob ripped through her throat. "The alliance is failing."

"What is The Raven planning on summoning?" Ace asked, watching the tears run down the Witch's cheeks, turning red as it touched the blood there.

"Only Darkness can hunt Darkness," she whispered, her voice haunting. "Only another monster can kill the one who stands in the way."

Her eyes turned from where they had been staring toward the ceiling to look directly into Ace's.

The words felt like a punch. Heavy and meaningful. There was significance to the way the Witch locked eyes with Ace. Something beyond just the outward meaning behind those words. Almost prophetic. But before Ace could even open her mouth to demand further answers, the last bit of air rattled through Poppy's teeth, her eyes dulling with finality as the remnants of her magic and life left the shell of her body.

Poppy must not have been terribly old, because her body didn't crumble and turn to dust but seemed to only deflate slightly once there was no longer anything animating it. Ace let out a sound of frustration as she watched, unable to halt the life from leaving the Witch. Those eerie words would be all that Poppy would offer Ace as explanation for the future.

Octavian had latched onto the other Witch while Ace had been locked onto Poppy, and her breath seemed to stutter in her chest as he drew the blood from her body.

"That's enough, Octavian," Ace murmured, standing from where she crouched and watched as her son detached his mouth from the dying Witch's throat, his eyes still glowing with hunger but drooping with the coming sunrise. "We've gotten all we can from them," Ace said, glancing once more at the Witches before ushering Octavian from the cell and out into the dimly lit corridor.

His hand firmly in hers, she steered him to his room, just next to hers and Nero's, releasing him to crawl into his four-poster bed. He was not as covered in blood as she was, just a bit spilled over his chin and down his neck, but he didn't seem to care. Nor would he have had the energy to wash, as the pull from the sun made it nearly impossible for him to resist closing his eyes. Ace moved past the bed as he settled, making sure the curtains were secure to block out any sun from coming in to touch him.

One thing they hadn't tested yet was his ability to deal with the sunlight. For Ace and Nero, and most other Vampires, the sun was painful, but unless they had a wound that opened their blood directly to the sun's rays, it wouldn't harm them much. Octavian, being born a Vampire, made her nervous when it came to sunlight. Would he react like she did, or would it truly burn him?

When she turned back toward the bed, Octavian had fallen into a coma-like slumber nearly immediately. Ace took a moment to gaze down at his sleeping form. The innocence of his young face, so peaceful as he lay curled over the top of his sheets, made her still heart ache just slightly.

Never would she have thought she would feel so protective over another, the feeling far more all-encompassing and overwhelming than any other. She felt protective of her Necare, and the other Vampires under her. She had also felt protective of the human siblings she once had; and to Six, her progeny, she felt utterly protective and possessive of Nero, but all that, even for Nero, paled in comparison to the fierceness of what she experienced toward Octavian. Despite how utterly impossible his existence had been, he was there, and she was his mother.

Ace had slipped from the room to the chambers she and Nero shared next door, noting Nero's continued absence from the room before taking to washing the blood from her body. He being gone at this hour wasn't terribly unusual. Nero didn't sleep much, being so old, and he often used the time to peruse the findings of the Necare or study an obscure history that he found interesting or useful. But an odd feeling held in the pit of her stomach, recalling that Srinta had called him away.

What could Srinta possibly need to say to Nero that she wouldn't share with Ace? At this point, they were all Elders, and beyond that, Ace and Nero committed to one another in a way that no other set of Vampires had ever been before. There was nothing that Nero didn't share with Ace, and vice versa.

The sound of the door opening from the hall shifted Ace's thoughts immediately. She was scrubbing at a particularly stubborn patch of blood that had spread down her chest, having soaked her shirt and dried there oddly, when Nero's figure stepped into the bathroom. His lean, muscled frame filled the doorway, worry clear on his face as he looked through the glass that separated them.

He didn't say anything, quickly shedding his clothes and moving to join her. Immediately, he stepped close, his hands snaking around her waist to pull her against him. Her body had heated from the water, and she felt the sharp contrast between their skin, his cold and hers almost human warm, sending echoes of their first touches through them both.

"You are worried," Ace said quietly, letting him take the washcloth from her fingers as she studied his face. His blue eyes met hers for a moment before turning her so he could better reach a long trail of blood that had run from her shoulder down her back.

"I have cause to be," Nero confirmed, gently sweeping at the blood, revealing her pale skin beneath.

"What did Srinta tell you?" Ace asked, fighting the urge to turn and look into his eyes. His hand stilled with the washcloth for only a moment. Hesitating to tell her was something she thought they had overcome.

"Ramses seemed to be…" Nero's voice trailed off, his words getting lost, not because he wanted to keep it from Ace but because he wasn't sure what to say. The way the living wall had writhed, its usually calm surface having given way for chaos alongside Ramses' silence and answering none of the questions he or Srinta asked of him, made Nero feel lost.

When Nero didn't continue, letting his words fall away to silence, his hands stilling on her back, Ace turned to see his face. The confusion and anxiety there was plain, making Ace suck in a sharp breath. Nero was strong. Resilient. He was a fighter and a leader. Only a very few times in the centuries she had known him had he ever worn an expression on his face as he did now.

Ace leaned forward, letting her lips touch Nero's softly. If his words struggled, she knew something different could pull him from whatever he had seen, whatever thoughts now plagued his mind. There would be time for words and explanations, but he needed something real to grasp onto.

And grasp, he did. As soon as her lips touched his, it was as if he was jolted with electricity. The force of their connection tearing him from wherever his thoughts were dragging him. The washcloth dropped from his fingers, grasping at her skin, and dragging her so their torsos were pressed together. Blue eyes glowed brightly, looking into hers for only a moment, before he crushed his mouth against hers once again. Lips, teeth, and tongue seeking. He kissed her as if this was their last, as if he would devour her if he could.

Ace let him. The only time she relinquished her power, her dominance and strength, was to him. But the desperation in the way he kissed her, the way his hands gripped tightly to her thighs, lifting her from the tiled floor of the shower to press her against the cold wall, showed her exactly how terrified he felt. He needed to take control of something, because whatever it was that he had seen, whatever Srinta had said to him, had put him on the edge of spiraling.

Ace hissed as they joined, the immediate connection between them giving her that feeling of wholeness, rightness, that it always did. Her nails pierced into the flesh of his shoulders, making a low growl sound from his chest, before he picked up his pace, making the tile behind her back crack with the force.

Her eyes glowed with a hunger only he could sate as she stared into his eyes, which were practically white. Those eyes that had once promised her forever were fierce, hungry … angry. The worry having washed away with his actions to show the true emotion underneath. Whatever he had seen, it didn't just make him anxious; it made him enraged.

Ace looked at the short email that Lucef had sent back to her, stating he was coming back to Kurome. The odd aching in her chest seemed to lessen slightly, as if just the knowledge that he was returning to them was enough to ease some deep-seated pain within her. She knew it was partially because he contained within him what small amount of Six was left, but another part was her own affection for him.

When she had first met Lucef, he intrigued her, chose to trust her, against his upbringing and probably his better judgment. A bond, not as strong as he had with Six, was formed between them, and Ace knew she could never abandon him. It was like he was a part of her now. The seventh in their line from Srinta, not made the way progenies usually were, but then again none since Ace had been made exactly as a Vampire should have been.

The door to the chambers was open, and a shadow obstructed the faint light coming in from the hall outside. Ace followed the movement until a girl stood hesitantly in the doorway. She was thin, her skin was dark and rich, hair curling around her head like a black flame. She was an Obi, one of the three chosen families who donated their blood to the Vampires and had for centuries.

"Madam," the girl said, bobbing her head respectfully, though it was clear she was nervous.

"What can I do for you, Miss Obi?" Ace asked, turning her chair more fully to face her but not moving to stand. There was trust amongst them, trust that unless given permission, a donor would not be harmed, but some Vampires took their very presence in the mansion to be a blanket invitation. Ace didn't want to frighten the girl more than she could already smell coming off her skin.

"A letter came for you. I was going to leave it at the door…" She trailed off, clearly having hoped that since the sun was still high in the sky, she would not have encountered Ace at all.

"You may leave it exactly where you planned to," Ace assured her, nodding toward the floor before her feet. The girl bent over, her back hunched, as she carefully placed the note on the ground at the threshold of the chambers, before turning to walk away.

There seemed to be more of the donors at the mansion as of late, which Ace found odd. More often they had bags of blood sent from the facilities, but someone was having them come to stay here more frequently, and only an Elder could approve such a thing. Perhaps Nero had agreed to bring some of them to the mansion, given the potential threat to the main facility. More often, the House Vampires would bring forgettable humans from the city when they thirsted for blood fresh from the source. Humans they could kill and would not be missed, or if they were particularly skilled at enthralling, make them forget it happened at all and release them.

The ability to enthrall was not a universal gift. It was more common than others, but even if a Vampire was weak in the skill, if they chose a human with a weak mind, they would be able to make the experience not more than a dream. Hence why the bagged blood and occasional unwitting human were far more commonplace than the donor members being in residence.

Ace decided she would inquire with Nero about the presence of the donors in the mansion, but there were several far more pressing things for her to concern herself with first. Pushing the thought away for another time, she stood and moved to retrieve the letter. As soon as she got nearer, the scent coming from the page caused her to halt halfway to the threshold. Werewolf and the distinct scent that she only associated with one other person breached her nose.

She knew who had written that letter before she even touched it.

Alexander.

Her fingers fluttered over the envelope for a moment before she finally let herself grasp it.

Her brother from the life she lived before. Her human life. After centuries of believing him to be dead, he had finally revealed himself to her, just before the ritual tore everything apart. What she said to him then was just as true now. She told him there was no way for them to be anything to each other again. Too much time had passed, and they were far too different now. Her brother had died that night when Werewolves brutalized and murdered their whole family. What remained of him was no longer her brother; he was a Werewolf and her enemy.

Whatever words were written on this page were bound to affect her far more than she liked to admit. The ache for someone lost to her, much like the ache that came with Six's death, tightened against her heart at the thought of him. Stiffening her spine, she stepped out of the chambers and made her way down below.

Some things were meant for her and her alone, and though she loved Nero, he was keeping something from her too. Days had passed, and he had not said a word of what happened between him and Srinta. For that, she felt she could keep this, whatever it happened to be, to herself too.

The corridors were empty. The Obi girl had made herself scarce, and Ace silently moved through the mansion, descending the steps to the lowest level. She paused at the antiquities room. The room was large, but quiet, as every wall was covered either by books or artifacts. The center of the room held the pedestal where the Sister Books rested, and there were several tables and chairs around the room for studying. Nothing was allowed to leave this room.

Ace always felt oddly comfortable in the space, having spent much of her time there the first few years after she was changed. Now, the quiet of the mansion while most of its inhabitants slept, and the security of this room, helped steady her enough to pull open the envelope and let her eyes fall on the script written there.

The gentle swoop of the delicate lettering immediately brought hazy human memories to the forefront of her mind. Sitting in dim candlelight beside the embers of the dying fire of their hearth room while Alexander dutifully taught his sister everything he had learned during his time being taught with the other boys by the village scholar.

Not many families could afford the fee to send their sons, but their father felt it was important his son, his heir, have the advantage. Being able to read and write would keep the farm from being taken advantage of by nobles, help him to deal with the lord more eloquently, and protect them all.

Alexander, knowing his sister would have even less sway in the time they grew up in, due to having been born female, set to give her any advantage he could.

The joy that filled her was quickly chased by sorrow as she watched the memory fade from her vision, the reality of the now swimming back into her view with the letter clasped in her pale fingers.

I know you are not my Grace anymore, and we are very different than we were once upon a time, but I have something I can only tell you in person. If you would trust me only for one hour, I promise there will be nothing to fear. At least not from me.

Your Dearest Brother Always,
Alexander

The bottom of the letter held an address and a time for the following night. The address was for a church in southern London. It would take her away from Nero and Octavian for a large part of the evening, but she knew they had Octavian's studies to occupy them, and Nero seemed busy ensuring the donor facilities were being guarded properly since the Witch sightings.

She was torn, her fingers curling over the page as she warred within herself. Alexander was a Werewolf. He was no longer the brother she had loved dearly when she was human, just like she was no longer his sister. But there was something happening in the shadows with her enemies. Some plot that even Alexander didn't agree with.

Could she allow the opportunity to learn something of this plan slip through her fingers simply because she wasn't sure if she could trust her former brother's intentions?

Ace glanced toward the armchair opposite the pedestal where the books sat. She could picture Octavian sitting there, book in hand, as he read through histories, his father beside him. Octavian's life would never contain the confusion of having lived two lives. He would never have a *before* to grapple with, like she did. Nor would he have ghosts of his past to haunt him, like Alexander was to her, because he was and always would be a Vampire.

Her loyalty, her duty, her greatest loves, her everything was in her vampirism.

Her eyes glanced around the room, shelves lined with artifacts and treasures. The sword of a great Necare who sacrificed themselves to save an army of Necare and Chenja behind him, a singular mummified claw of the first Werewolf to organize them into a united force, and other significant artifacts that only held meaning to the Immortals all rested on the shelves, carefully and prominently displayed.

Her eyes finally landed on a staff mounted on the wall behind the armchair. Its gold gleamed, the large, rare stones shined, and the intricate set of hieroglyphs trailed all along it.

The staff was Ramses', the first Vampire. The one who they all branched from.

She hadn't spoken to Ramses since she became pregnant. The shock of a myth coming to life within her made her desperate for guidance she hadn't sought for hundreds of years.

For so long, she had known her purpose. Her change had been born of a desire for vengeance for the family she had lost, and for the love of the Vampire who had saved her. She had become a weapon. A deadly thing used for the destruction of their enemies. The war had been her single focus.

And then it all changed.

She no longer could hold back her feelings for those around her.

For Nero.

For Six.

And just as suddenly as she gave into that, the ritual transformed them all. Changed the course of everything. Alliances were altered, relationships damaged, and people were lost.

And such a loss it was.

If only Ace had realized what Six meant to her—truly meant to her—before the ritual.

Ace felt shaken, overwhelmed by a searing grief, before the burn of Nero's presence nearing broke through it. Her eyes seemed to focus once again, no longer swimming with the memories as they had been, and she suddenly realized she stood before the door that held Ramses within.

The letter was still clutched in Ace's fingers as she turned away from the door to watch Nero take the final steps down from the main floor.

They still hadn't discussed what Srinta had said to him, what had made him so upset, and the way his eyes looked worried as they flicked between her and the door she stood before told her it had something to do with Ramses.

"I heard you leave the chambers," he murmured, stepping closer to her. She slid the page carefully into her pants pocket as he got closer, making sure her movements were unnoticeable. She wasn't going to let him dissuade her from going to meet with Alexander, as she had to know what he was willing to tell her.

"I came down to look at the Books," she said, gesturing toward the antiquities room.

"Perhaps it's time I have Octavian study those," Nero mused a little playfully, though he could tell she wasn't telling him the complete truth, especially considering where they stood.

"I have some leads I need to follow tonight. I won't make the Council meeting," she told him, moving to pass him in the hall.

"You'll take Makiut or Lotte with you?" he asked, stopping her with a hand gently wrapped around her wrist, but she didn't turn to face him.

"I don't need a partner. Only seeing if it's worth a more detailed mission," she said, trying to pull her arm from his grasp, but his fingers only tightened. He could feel the chasm forming between them. The unsaid words, the growing omissions, and a similar feeling to when they had been apart for years began forming there between them.

"Ace ... don't do this," Nero whispered, eyes focused on her profile.

"I didn't start," she said simply, pulling her wrist from his fingers roughly before moving swiftly down the hall and out of sight up the stairwell.

Nero's fist clenched, nails biting into his cold skin as he stared after where she disappeared. Ace was right, of course. He was the first of them to have kept something secret. But he had a *reason* to keep it from her. If he told her what Srinta had said to him ... he could only imagine Ace's reaction. There was a thin thread holding him back from what his instincts told him regarding his sire, and it was wearing more and more as the time passed without telling Ace, without having an answer.

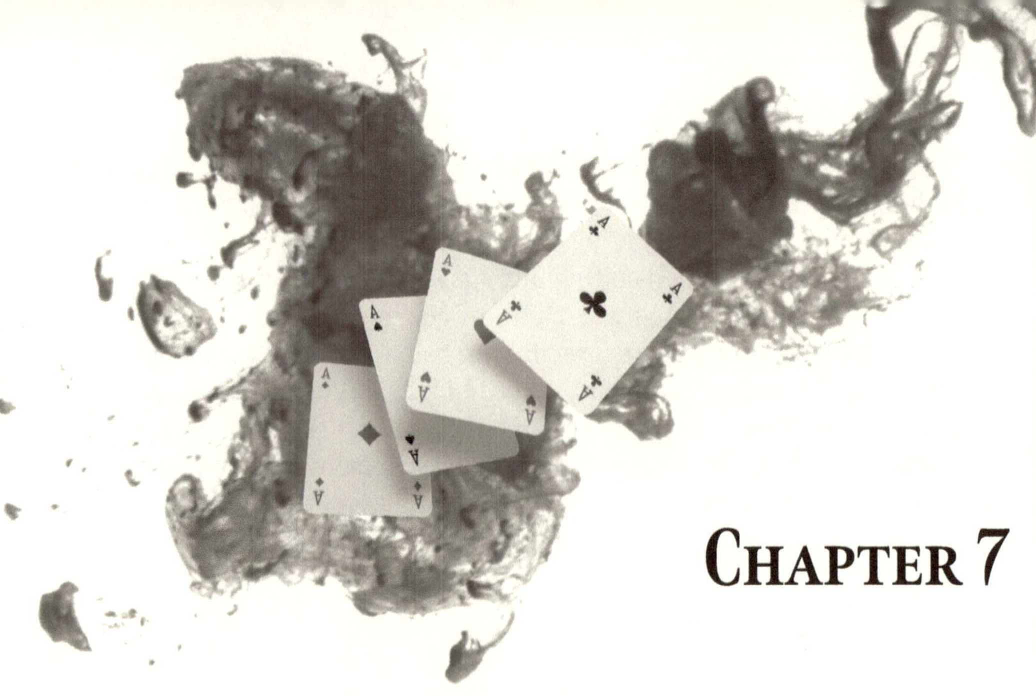

Chapter 7

James Martin opened his eyes, his vision bleary and not aided by the dim light. Before him was a dark wall, the surface irregular as if it had a rough texture, but for some reason, he couldn't quite remember what it reminded him of. His head was thumping rhythmically, and his recollection of what had transpired before he came to be here was like a void he couldn't quite breach. If he was honest, James wasn't quite sure if he was fully awake or still in some sort of dream. He tried to turn his head, planning on taking in more of his surroundings to determine exactly what was going on, but a shooting pain seared through him as he did so. The feeling lanced through him as if he were impaled as his mouth stretched, his throat too hoarse for the scream that wanted to burst forth.

"I wouldn't move just yet," came a voice from somewhere in the room. He didn't dare try to turn his head to find out where, but it sent a chill down his spine at the sound of it. The speaker was feminine, her voice a bit coarse as if she had been screaming a lot recently.

"Where am I?" he asked, his voice like gravel and nearly unrecognizable to his own ears.

"I can't tell you that."

His eyes adjusted a bit more, while the surface he was looking upon became clearer. He was in some sort of stone room; the irregular pattern was the jagged surface of each of the unfinished blocks. It was a dark gray stone, and this place was unfamiliar. He wasn't sure if it was that way naturally, or if time and filth coated it, but what was unusual was that it was clearly the ceiling. The wall he was against was also made of the same stone, indicating that he was in some sort of fully stone structure.

Was he in a cellar? An old church, perhaps? A tomb?

The thought chilled him further, his chest beginning to rise and fall rapidly with his panicked breathing.

"You'll find out soon enough, Martin-boy. Now that you've woken, we can soon begin," the voice said, before the sound of a door creaking open took over the space, and the definitive clunk of it shutting behind them.

His breathing didn't slow, with her absence; if anything, the darkness he was plunged into with the door closing made each intake shorter, his heart pounding in his chest. He tested his limbs, which he just started to feel once again. For some reason, his brain had begun imagining them gone, and that somehow he was blocked from the pain, but no, they were still there. When he tried to move his finger, the same pain he experienced when trying to move his head previously ripped through him, leaving him panting, barely containing the scream that threatened to tear from his throat.

That voice, that woman who had been there before knew his family name. His family, though rich, was not considered important or well-known. They did not donate their riches. They were not entrepreneurs. They did not come from royalty or noble houses. The Martins were only important in one sense, and it was not in the human world where he resided.

His mind desperately tried to come up with reasons why he could have been taken. What had occurred before he found himself trapped here?

He had been out with his mates, celebrating the completion of an exam. Moira may have drunk a bit more at the pub than the rest of them, or perhaps not eaten enough, so they were trying to get her home to the flat she and Kate shared. But they didn't make it there. In fact, they didn't make it fully down the road, merely a few doors down from the pub they had left before they were stopped.

Then the eyes ... the cloaked woman's glowing eyes.

At first, he had thought she was a Vampire, which had put him somewhat at ease. If that had been the case, he would have willingly gone with them, knowing that was his duty. That was his family's responsibility, the reason for their wealth. But she was not a Vampire he had soon realized, but something else.

Martins, Obis, and Stumpfs were supposed to be protected. They were supposed to be untouchable because of what they knew and what they provided. But apparently, whatever this woman was, she didn't consider him untouchable.

He knew how his family got its wealth, its untouchable status. All the children who grew up as one of them were told the only way to maintain their lifestyles and their lives was to continue what was agreed upon centuries, if not millennia, before. His family, along with the two others, were the sole reason that the Vampires didn't ravage the streets, killing humans each night to sate their thirst.

The story that he was told from the time he was a child, the same one he had helped tell his younger brothers and heard murmured to other children for as long as he could remember, flashed through his mind, as it continued to reel in this odd situation he had found himself in.

Cordin Martin was a young farmer. He and his brothers had inherited the land when their father died, but they also inherited his debt. The brothers were so desperate to keep the farm that had been in their family for as long as they could remember, and farming was all they knew. None of them could read or write. None of them could do anything but this.

One night, the desperate brothers stayed up by a fire, contemplating what they could do to salvage their lives, when a man appeared out of the darkness. He was like no one they had ever seen up close. His hair was long, longer than any man's hair they had come across, its ends brushing at the end of his waist. His skin was fair, and his blue eyes almost seemed to shine in the darkness. He was dressed in clothes far finer than any they had ever worn, any they had seen up close.

Clearly, he was a gentleman, a man of wealth and privilege, and yet he was there, walking across their fields, getting dirt on his shiny leather boots, no horse or footman in sight to care for him.

He said nothing, sitting at the fire across from them and waiting.

When Cordin asked who he was, the man simply said, "Nero."

And when Seamus, Cordin's older brother, asked why he was there, the man simply said, "It was to eat you, but I've decided I have a much better idea."

The Martin brothers shook at that revelation. He spoke with no hesitation, his face too serious to indicate he was lying.

Levitt, the youngest of the brothers, asked, "What are you?"

Nero looked at him, a bright, amused gleam in his eyes as he looked him over. Those blue eyes seemed to start to shine brighter, casting their own light as they glowed.

"That was the right question," Nero told him. "Have you ever heard of a Vampire?"

The brothers all shook their heads, never having heard the word before, but they certainly knew stories the people in the villages told of monsters who looked like men that whisked people away, or the perfectly heathy people who would turn up dead on the streets.

Nero told them what a Vampire was, told them the true nature of his kind, and though the brothers all shook with fear, they couldn't bring themselves to run from the man sitting with them by the fire.

When all was said and done, the whole of the night spent talking to this mysterious man, the sky began to lighten with the impending dawn, and Nero stood.

"Tomorrow, I will return. I will give you a choice," he told them before he turned and, almost as if he was never there, seemed to disappear before their very eyes. The only indication that he had been there was the indentation of his boots in the dirt before the place he had been sitting, and the rustle of their grain in the fields from when he passed them faster than any man could move.

The next night, the brothers eagerly waited by the fire. They weren't sure what was the choice Nero would be giving them, but they felt like it was life-changing. Just as the night before, Nero appeared, walking through the fields toward their fire, a new and even fancier set of clothes over his body. His smile, though somewhat chilling with those unnatural blue eyes, was warm.

He settled in across from them as he had been, clasping his hands together and looking at each brother for a long moment.

"The choice, sir?" Levitt asked.

"Yes, the choice," Nero said with another smile.

"For a long time, my kind have had to sustain themselves by killing their prey. We eat humans, but we can take what we need without death. The problem is we must remain secret, and in order to keep that secret, those humans we take from must never wake."

"But you've told us your secret," Seamus whispered, fear taking him over as he shook, watching the Vampire across from them.

"I have told you my secret. I've told you far more than I've told many humans, but they usually don't stay human for long once I've said these words," Nero admitted. "I propose that you and your family keep my secret forever and offer us your blood to sustain us, so we don't always have to resort to murder."

"And why would we do that? Just so you won't kill us?" Cordin asked, glaring across the fire at the glowing eyes of the Vampire. They already had enough problems in their lives, and now this?

"In exchange, I'll be certain your family never wants for anything. Me and mine have many riches. We offer to share them with you, and our secrets, if you only let us drink from you. You sustain us, we sustain you."

And from then on, the Martins and two other families Nero selected had done just that, sustaining the Vampires while they sustained them. But so quickly the tide could change if any one of the Martins chose to reveal these secrets, to betray the Vampires, and most of all Nero. For every piece of riches that they would have gained over all these years, they would take back in the form of every last soul connected to the one who betrayed them.

James's breathing became harsher as he realized he was taken for a reason, a reason that could not only mean his death but the death of his whole family. Memories flashed before his mind as he recalled the look on his friends' faces as they were being torn from him, their screams, before it all went black. What happened to them? Where were they now?

Where was he?

The door opened with a screech, light flooding the room and blinding him slightly.

"She'll see you now," the same voice from before said, just before several faces swam into view. There was a slight hum in the air, a sort of strange electricity that made the hair on his body stand on end.

Suddenly, whatever was holding his body back and causing him pain each time he moved was lifted. He fell forward away from the wall, gasping at the relief of movement, but that relief only lasted a moment, as he felt himself being dragged through the doorway.

The room he was taken to darkened, all the light coming from candles and small orbs of light that floated here and there. There was a round table at the center of the room, which was covered in a variety of things: food, feathers, blood, wine, pages with drawings and symbols on them, sand, stones. It was hard to focus on one strange thing that sat upon the surface, let alone take everything in as any sort of complete picture.

But his focus was stolen away entirely when across the table, he noticed a veiled figure. At first, he hadn't even seen her there; it was like she blended in with all the oddities, but she raised a hand, drawing his gaze to the movement.

Once he saw her, it was a wonder she could ever blend in anywhere. Glowing lavender eyes peered out from behind the veil. Her hand was so pure white, it was shocking against the black lace. The eyes were sinister, more frightening than anything he had seen before, which felt strange considering he had met Vampires at least half a dozen times in his life.

"Why am I here?" he whispered, unable to look away from her piercing gaze.

"We need you to be available to pick up a package. We have someone who will assist you going into Kurome soon. You will make yourself available to them."

"You'd have me betray—"

"I will have you *obey me*, boy, or be forced to obey. There is no other path for you," the woman said, her voice little more than a growl as she cut him off. He swallowed dryly.

"I will not. Centuries my family has served the Vampires. I don't care who you have at Kurome, or what it is you need—"

Her fingers curled, his voice getting chocked as his windpipe was restricted. A murmuring seemed to surround him, voices that didn't seem to be coming from any one direction.

"Oh, my dear. If you think this is something you can fight, you are mistaken. You have no say in this matter. You have no power here. We only need your body, that privileged little body that comes with being a Martin, to walk into Kurome Mansion unquestioned. What you think or feel about it has nothing to do with it at all," she said, and once again James's world went black.

Lucef found himself once again on that small outcropping of stone. The moment he saw the slow flow of the green-tinted river below and the stone that pale feminine feet rested upon, he knew he was dreaming once again.

Dreaming of Six.

The small ledge of stone she stood on was the only safe place within this massive cavern. The river stretched too far to see in all directions; the only indication that there was an end was the domed cave-like ceiling overhead.

Six, and therefore Lucef, scanned the murky water for signs of an exit, but there were only catatonic faces bobbing within the water, looking as if their flesh was being slowly eaten away, and the occasional slithering spine of the river snakes. She shuddered, looking down with a disgusted grimace. Lucef realized that Six's goal was to escape, to get out of this place as fast as she could, and this river was not meant for the likes of her. Only the souls that had been wrung through their torture so long and so hard that there was nothing left of the soul to take were meant to reside there.

Six turned away from the bodies floating through the water to the cave wall. Sitting within the rough stone wall was a door. It was the same thick, heavy metal that the torture cell door had been made of, but it had no handle or knob. Nor was it a swinging door. She soon found out as she rammed her shoulder into it hearing something snap. Lucef felt the sharp pain of shattered bone, as if it had been his own shoulder that was broken, while Six merely sighed, looking at her limp arm. Her humerus was bulging slightly under her skin where the break was made.

"Three ... two ... one..." she muttered to herself as the bone, muscles, and ligaments shifted and healed themselves with a few sickening sounds. It was painful, but nothing that she couldn't handle. Chomic had done far more than break her bones.

The sound of her voice, even the hushed whisper as she counted, was enough to make Lucef want to shiver in pleasure. He hadn't heard her voice in years, only in those haunting dreams of her death. But he realized this, too, was a dream. This wasn't truly her voice. And a pang of longing surged through him as he continued to watch from behind her eyes.

Six began to pace back and forth on the small ledge, tapping her finger impatiently to her chin and glancing at the door every few moments as she tried to determine how she was going to get through. The river wasn't an option. Her eyes glanced back at the sickly-looking liquid the bodies were floating in; there was no way she would risk that.

"On Earth I could set things on fire," she said aloud. She raised her hand in front of her face, looking at her fingers. Previously, rage was what had brought out her fire. She had learned quite a bit about controlling her rage in her time there, because Chomic was only spurred on more when she was angry. In the beginning, she tried to use her fire on him repeatedly, and he would just laugh at her attempts.

Now, she gazed at her fingers as if they were foreign objects. She wasn't sure if she could bring it forth anymore. And then she remembered her blades. The blades Vehekan had possessed, granting her control over them. They weren't imbedded in her clothes anymore ... in fact, she wasn't wearing clothes at all, and she took that moment to look over herself just a bit. The body she had known was ... well, not gone, but different, certainly. The diamond tattoos that had littered her previously were all over her now, almost scaly looking in some places where they clustered. She raised her hand to summon one of her blades, hoping, despite the evidence to the contrary, that they would somehow appear for her, and she would have Vehekan's help.

One of the blades did come forth, seemingly melting out of one of her diamond tattoos at her hips before it fell to the ground. Vehekan was not within them anymore, and the demon metal was essentially useless now, lying at her feet on the stone outcropping. Lucef felt her body go rigid, frustration in her circumstance taking a greater hold over her. She let out a snarl as she bent to pick up the lifeless diamond-shaped metal.

"You better be able to blow this door out of my way," she hissed at the blade in her hand, trying to will it to do as it was told, but knowing it was useless like this. Without a demon to inhabit it, there was nothing there to perform the way she wanted it to.

Six flicked it toward the door and listened to the loud thunk of metal on metal before it fell on the ground once again with a clatter that echoed around the cavernous space.

"Well fuck you, then!" she screamed at it, turning to pace as she tried to keep herself calm. Lucef had seen her enraged before. He had heard every one of these words from her lips in some form or another, but this situation was far different than any memories he had of her. How his mind could come up with the depths of hell, he wasn't sure, but he didn't want it to end. These dreams were far better than watching her die repeatedly.

Six's whole body felt tight as she tried to think of a way out of this. She could not be trapped here. The whole reason she had left Chomic and the torture chamber was to escape, and she certainly intended to complete this mission.

After a long while of cursing and pacing, she let her eyes fall on the thin diamond-shaped metal on the ground by the door. She went back to it, pulling it from the ground and examining it. She didn't feel any presence within it as she had before. Previously, there had been a distinct hum, a vibration that let her know Vehekan had inhabited them. But clearly, he had abandoned them. She vaguely remembered the ritual, when Vehekan had decided to leave just as she was about to kill ... someone. The name of who she had been trying to murder was lost to her.

Lukis. My father, *Lucef thought, feeling her struggle with memories. His heart felt heavy as it dawned on him that this dream Six may not remember him at all.*

Frustrated, she closed her eyes and wrapped her fingers around its sharp edges, creating a fist. She could feel the fire burning within her; her rage was rising. The rage she had controlled so well with Chomic finally coming out, tongues of flame lashing around her.

How was she going to escape this?

At least with Chomic it was halfway interesting; now she was just trapped with a river full of lifeless bodies.

She opened her eyes and looked down at her blazing fist, feeling something buzzing within the metal in her hand. She let her fingers fall away from her palm, releasing the blade and letting it float above her hand. An even smirk found its way to her lips. Well, Vehekan may have left the blades, but she had somehow managed to fill the blade herself.

She tested it, moving it back and forth, watching as flames licked up the sides of the black metal while it flew to and fro. Her eyes shifted back to the door. Quickly, the thud of metal on metal rang once again, but the sudden burst of flames on the door had Six clapping. She called the blade back to her, and she examined the damage it left in its wake. The door was now charred, and there was a deep indentation made by the blade. With a grin, Six summoned her other four blades from within her. Like the first one, they melted from her skin, falling lifelessly to the floor, but she wasted no time, picking each one up and holding them in her fists. Her rage burned through her and into the blades.

Her brows only furrowed slightly when she realized there was not another piece to draw from within her, knowing that she certainly had six of them at some point. But she was on a mission, one that she refused to deviate from. That door needed to open or be blown away so she could move on. She opened her hands again and let her eyes snap back to the door.

Instantly, there was a blinding burst of flames and then a black soot mist, still smoldering as it showered her. Once it cleared, a broken doorway was revealed, like a gaping wound in the rough black rock. She began walking forward, her blades finding their places and melting into her tattoos, as if they had always belonged there.

Lucef felt her determination as she stepped closer to the black hole that was created in the stone, the darkness seeming to swallow Six up before it all simply went black.

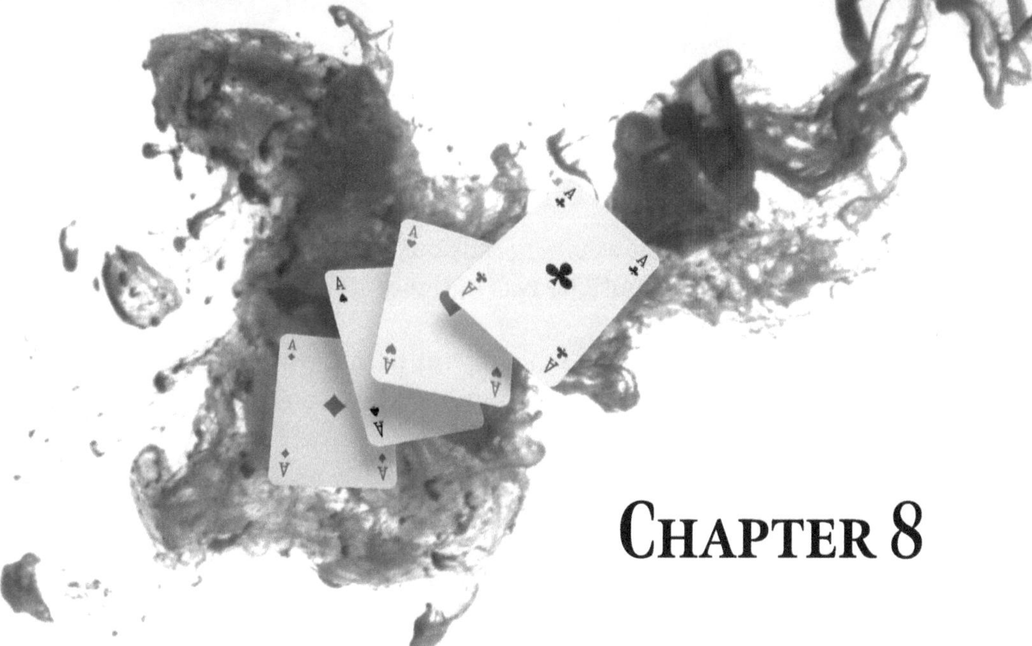

Chapter 8

Ace stepped into the sanctuary of the abandoned church from one of the side doors. Her steps were silent as she stayed to the shadows on the edges of the room, eyes scanning for movement within the tomb-like space. The only sound that could be heard were the rodents that had made homes from the walls and the wind rushing through the hole at the highest peak of the roof.

This had been one of the oldest churches in London, or at least its bones were. The structure was far on the outskirts in what used to be, when Ace was still human, a town and farmland, but had since been absorbed into the capitol it now was. Her eyes fell on the stone altar, which was built into the floor. Ace remembered it when it was a sanctuary much smaller than this, the original outline of the space clear with the different stone floor that bordered the original space. Ace had seen this church before with human eyes, though at the time, women weren't often included in masses. She had been able to come in to be blessed by a priest, a fact which was now laughable, since she would have been considered cursed and damned if they knew what she had become.

A figure appeared in the broken stained-glass window opposite her in the sanctuary. The physique was not new to her; she had now been hunted and watched by this figure for years. She had known the silhouette before she came to be a Vampire, and there was no mistaking it now.

Alexander jumped down into the space, the echo of his heavy boots on the stone floors harsh against the otherwise quiet room.

"You came," he said, his voice rough with some sort of emotion that Ace couldn't determine, as if he doubted it all the way up until the moment he saw her there.

"I did," she said stiffly, watching cautiously as he moved closer, walking between broken pews until he was in the center aisle.

"Grace, I—"

"Ace," she snapped back. "I'm not your pathetic human sister. I'm not that weak thing that could do nothing when monsters attacked our home and killed our family."

Her eyes blazed white with her clipped words. She had shed the name, as well as the life of the human she once was hundreds of years before, and it felt like an insult whenever he called her the name that she had buried, along with that version of herself. Alexander nodded his head, moving to lean forward, hands braced on the back of a pew as he let out a strangled breath.

"I should have done a better job of protecting you," he said quietly, his voice laced with centuries of regret. Regret that had formed into a bitter poison within him, making everything tainted. "If I had known..."

"Known what, Alexander?" Ace asked, pushing from the wall she had been leaning against, fists clenching at her sides.

He sighed, his shoulders tensing for a moment as his fingers clenched against the weak wood.

"That's not why I brought you here. I didn't want to fight," he said, turning to look at her once again.

Their similarities were not lost on her. They still looked as they had centuries ago, and the strong genes of their father showed in their dark hair and the shape of their nose. Only the two of them came through with their mother's eyes out of all their siblings, the other three having had the dark brown orbs of their father. However, while Alexander looked saddened and tortured, she was filled with purpose. She wasn't there to see him socially, to reconcile with him after all these years. She had her own family to protect, her own kind to defend, and that was why she was there.

"You brought me here to tell me something," she prompted, though the previous question still lingered there between them, hovering in the air that was thick with a strange tension.

"The Raven is summoning something," he said, standing tall once again. "They aren't strong enough to attack the Vampires outright, so they're planning on using something else to take you and the other Elders out of the game."

Ace's eyes glowed more vibrantly at his admission. It made sense. The Werewolves were too weak in their current disorganized state to launch any sort of attack, and after what Poppy had said just before she died, Ace had already surmised that the Witches were planning something sinister of this nature. But what she didn't understand was why Alexander was telling her this.

Why would he betray his own kind?

"What are they summoning?" she decided to ask, instead of the other questions burning within her.

"A shadow demon. It's the only thing that can be pulled from the Underworld without possessing something or being released willingly. I don't know more than that. I couldn't help myself. I got..."

He trailed off, letting his head bow slightly.

"You got angry," Ace offered, her eyes dimming back to their normal silver as she watched his shoulder hunch. He often snapped and reacted harshly when they were kids. Even into adulthood, before their changes, he tended to have a hot temper. It didn't surprise her that it followed him and intensified after he became a Werewolf.

"I rejected them before I could learn more."

"Why are you telling me this?" Ace asked, her voice barely above a whisper as she stepped closer unintentionally, placing herself between the two pews with him.

He sighed, pushing his long hair out of his face before glancing up at the strange way the moon shone through the stained glass behind her.

"I don't want you to die," he said it simply, plainly. He had spent the better part of his very long life trying to reconcile that his family was gone. That his family had been the unfortunate consequence of the war he was dragged into. Then when he knew Ace was alive, though unfortunately on the other side of that war, he vowed to himself he would see to her continued existence.

"I've spent years tracking you. Watching you. Making sure you were okay, even if you were my enemy. You, above all others, are my sister, my twin first. We shared a womb. We were once just as well as one. And now?" He chuckled darkly. "How ironic that now we are foes. Enemies, not because of what we did to one another, but because of what we became."

Ace took in an involuntary breath, her eyes rimmed with red, but she blinked back her tears. Her mind flashed with the images of her family that she had envisioned when she made the decision to become a Vampire like Nero. Her parents, her brothers, all of them dead, mangled and ruined from Werewolves who massacred them. Though she loved Nero, she hadn't made the decision to become a Vampire only to be with him forever; it was to have the power and ability to avenge the deaths of her family.

To avenge Alexander's death.

Her twin had been her other half. He knew her better than anyone else for the short years they had together as humans. But that version of her before, who she had been, was just as important as what she had been through since. For Alexander to admit he was betraying everything to protect her, she couldn't help the squeeze of her silent and still heart within her chest.

"I can't do anything for you in return, Alexander. You're the leader. I—"

"I have lived a long time with regrets. I should have found you sooner—done this sooner—before Lukis went mad. I have done nothing more than tell you what I know of The Raven's plan, which is not nearly enough. Just know, that even if you are Ace, the Elder and the most renowned Necare, you are still my Grace. My sister, my twin. And if I had a choice to lose this war, or see you sent to the Underworld, I would choose to lose."

He reached forward, cupping her face gently, his skin so warm it felt like it might burn her cheeks before he pressed his lips firmly to her forehead and turned, launching himself back through the broken window and out of sight.

Octavian sat curled up in one of the armchairs in the antiquities room, his pale brows drawn together as he read through the words on the page once more. He and his father had come down early in the evening to start their studies of the Books. He had been eager to dive into them, having been told over and over again that he was far too young, but as he read through, it wasn't so much his age but the fact that they were so very dry. Whoever had written these had not even attempted to make them interesting. The content was just plainly stated, though in a dead language. Perhaps the language had not much in the way of descriptors?

This passage didn't seem to make total sense to him. It spoke of a creature made of smoke and shadow that was born of Lucifer's darkest wills, but something about how and why it was locked away didn't seem to translate well to him. He glanced up at his father, who was reading the other book that Lucef had obtained from the Werewolves years ago. His brow similarly furrowed as he jotted notes down on the tablet beside him.

"Can you look at this one for me, Papa?" Octavian asked, making Nero's eyes shoot up from the text.

"Let me see," Nero said with a nod, prompting Octavian to move from his chair and over to where his father sat.

Though Octavian was in the body of a human five-year-old, he was ten, and therefore it had become rarer that he would climb into his father's lap as he had years before. But it took no prompting on Nero's part for his son to settle in his lap, the two of them looking over the page together.

"Narthadis," Nero said, having read the name of the demon.

"What does the book mean about it being locked away?" Octavian asked, pointing to the line that had been confusing him.

"It seems this particular demon isn't like most others. It's saying that Narthadis needn't possess anything other than shadow to manifest within this realm."

"Other demons can't do that?"

"Demons aren't truly of this plane. Birthed in the Underworld, most of them can't step foot here without having something to hold onto. An object, or a person," Nero explained.

"So, they have to go back to the Underworld once they no longer have a hold on something here?" Octavian asked, watching as Nero turned the page to continue reading the passage there.

"Exactly, but not this one, it seems," Nero murmured, furrowing his brow as he took in the passage. This creature had been able to move freely between the Underworld and their realm, but only in the shadows. He was powerful, dangerous, and completely unhinged when it came to the destruction he wreaked on the world at that time. How Lucifer could have even created such a creature was beyond Nero, since it was his understanding that Lucifer and Viginti created balance.

As Nero continued to scrutinize the words about Narthadis, Octavian's eyes traveled the room. He had been in here many times, but some strange tingling feeling seemed to pass over him once his father had uttered the name of the demon listed on the page. It had started slowly at first, just a little chill that seemed to travel up his spine at the mention of the creature, but now it was increasing, as if something in this very room had heard Nero speak the name.

"There's something wrong," Octavian said, his voice a hushed whisper. Nero felt it too, a strange and sinister feeling coming over him as well. The two of them looked at one another, then their eyes immediately seemed to drift to the black obsidian box that was sitting on one of the shelves.

Whispers seemed to be growing around them. Like the room had thoughts of its own and was telling them something had heard them and was calling back. Nero turned the page, hoping to see what had occurred with this demon, as everything listed on the previous pages spoke of the threat Narthadis's presence in their realm had wrought on everyone, human and Immortal alike. But the pages beyond it were not there, simply going on to the next topic with no resolution.

"The pages are gone," Octavian said quietly, as if letting his voice increase in volume would somehow bring the eerie feeling within them to a head. Nero looked down, seeing the thin, barely perceptible piece of the missing pages there. Someone, or something, had carefully removed some histories within this book. Who or why they would have done such a thing was just as much a mystery as what happened to the demon itself.

Lucef was falling. He wasn't sure how he knew he was plummeting, considering he couldn't see anything at all. It was pitch-black. There was no indicator of what was up or down. Nothing to feel or sense other than that strange sensation in his stomach that only occurred when he was dropping through the air. The only other sensation he could feel was not something he could fully describe, but somehow, he knew it nonetheless. He was back in another dream of Six.

So, it wasn't he *who was falling, but* her. *She couldn't even see her hand in front of her face, though he felt it when she tried to do such a motion. It was as if she was falling through nothingness and had become nothing along with it. She tried to shout, to call out, but no noise came, as if she had no lips, no lungs, and no throat to produce the noise. But as the immeasurable time passed, the air that she seemed to be falling through became damper. She could once again feel herself breathe as she filled her lungs, enough to make a noise since she couldn't previously, and sense the almost misty quality to the air around her against her skin. Once she was aware of the sensations on her skin and in her lungs, she became aware of her body, touching her flesh with her hands, feeling her lips under her tongue.*

Her body slowed its descent, floating gently to a stop as she landed on the spongy ground. A dim blue light from unknown origin lit the dark space, allowing her to make out what everything was: trees, thousands—no, millions of them, filled with bodies. Some were slumped over branches, wrists slit and bleeding onto the forest floor; others were missing portions of their heads, and then there were those hanging from the branches by—usually makeshift—nooses.

"The Wood of Suicides," Six said aloud. Her voice seemed to cause a breeze to move through the trees, stirring the hanging bodies to sway.

If Lucef could have recoiled at the sight before him, he might have. Seeing all these deaths, displayed horrendously throughout these barren trees, was horrifying. The nearest body snickered liquidly.

"You don't belong here," said the blood-soaked girl, as more blood spewed from her lips. She looked like she could have been twelve, and her slit wrists were a gruesome addition to her child-like demeanor as her body slumped over a low hanging branch, golden hair falling over her face so only one blue eye peeked out from behind its curtain.

"I'm aware," Six grumbled at the girl. "I'm trying to get out."

Another liquid howl came from the corpse.

"There is no getting out."

Six seemed to ignore the girl, turning her focus to a narrow path between the trees. The path was dark, but clear, the bodies unable to move from their entrapments. She walked past, going deeper into the forest.

"I was dead long before I was put here," she said under her breath, almost as an answer to the girl she was already far away from.

Lucef knew that's how Six felt. They had discussed it before, that she was no longer living. She had told him the human version of her had died to make her a Vampire. It had been many years prior to her being sacrificed in the ritual since her heart had beat or she needed air in her lungs. Strange that now he no longer needed air, nor did his heart beat, but he didn't consider himself dead, just different.

The path was long, each step deeper into the forest seemed to make it appear bigger and vaster. As if it were trying to trap her in a maze of death. Lucef wasn't sure how he would help her, but he ached to be beside her, to make sure she wasn't so very alone.

"How the hell do I get out of here?" she called, sending a violent surge of wind through the trees as her frustration over the never-ending path finally came to a head.

"There's no such thing," came a chocked voice from slightly behind her. She turned, letting her snake-like eyes fall on the man hanging from a real noose. His clothes were some kind of uniform, perhaps a policeman or some other type of emergency personnel who had unfortunately seen far too much. The rope's knot was elaborate, and his head sat strangely, clearly having been broken from the impact. "But some have found their way out

of this level that way," he continued, raising his hand slowly and pointing for her to continue forward where she had been headed.

"Thank you, I suppose," Six grumbled in response, as whispers started to fill in the silence around her. The suicides were intrigued, their hushed voices filled with a strange excitement as they watched her pass them.

As she walked, the smell became more pronounced. She hadn't quite noticed anything before, but now the festering stench of decay had grown to a horrendous extreme. She wrinkled her nose, letting her eyes shift around to find the source of the smell but really didn't find one. It was all of them. The reek of death was everywhere.

Deeper and deeper into the trees she went. Neither Lucef nor Six had any measure of time, and of course she never got tired, so she continued at a steady pace through the trees, silently. Through the branches, she saw a glimpse of red a bit in the distance, cutting through the blue light that surrounded her. Lucef simply seemed to know she was meant to follow the light, and she appeared to have the same idea, as she pressed forward with a bit more speed. The whispering of the corpses surrounding Six intensified as she took each step, bathing herself in more and more of the crimson-tinted rays breaking through the trees. When they suddenly thinned, a great open area was revealed at the center of the forest.

The circular clearing was huge, but a giant metallic fountain took up most of the space. Its three tiers were spewing thick crimson liquid over their edges, staining the sides of the silver metal. There was a tall ladder, tilted to reach the top tier. It was made of human bones and seemed to be strapped together with skin. She walked forward, touching the bone ladder for a moment to test its strength before she began to climb. Time seemed to slow further still, making the climb feel as though it was taking forever to reach the top, and Six was moving at her maximum speed.

Once she found herself at the top of the ladder, she looked down at the thick, red fluid that was flowing around her knees, staining her white skin with the viscous crimson liquid. She saw nothing in it at first, but then flashes of faces began to appear. None were faces Lucef or she knew, but he could tell from the way these images appeared in the blood, they were someone else's remembrances.

"Memories..." Six muttered, watching the faces swim against the surface of the blood. Billions of stories trapped within this fountain, the lives of those in the Underworld trapped here for the living to forget.

Chapter 9

The train's horn blared, startling Lucef awake. His eye darted around the small dining car, casting his gaze around to be sure no one was looking at him strangely. He wasn't in control of his appearance when he was sleeping, hence why he tried, very diligently, to not do so in public. But the few people in the car seemed none the wiser. Their eyes turned to their food or the paper in their hands, not to him. He glanced at himself in the reflection of the window he had been leaning on, making sure his appearance was presentable.

His hair had taken on more of a vibrant red once again, that same red he saw in the dream he had been having about Six. He pushed hands through his hair, letting the strands turn to a more mundane brown to go with the backpacker appearance he had put on for his journey back to London. Lucef didn't want to stand out any more than he already did. There was an air about him now that even humans seemed to notice, if given enough time in his presence. Something that told others that he was powerful ... dangerous.

He thought back to the dream he had been pulled from. This had been yet another of the strange dreams of Six he had been having over the past few days. Each time he seemed to sleep, he was transported back into this strange scenario, watching through Six's eyes as she maneuvered her way through the Underworld in her pursuit of freedom. If only it was real and not a fantasy his cracking mind was cooking up for him.

He was glad to have some relief from the constant dreams of her death, but these were nearly just as frustrating. Seeing her, even changed and different, he wanted her. He would have much rather taken her hand and traveled with her through all the things she had to face than to simply be a spectator through her vision.

Just as he was about to contemplate what having these dreams could mean, the door to the dining car opened, and a young woman stepped through. Immediately, his body went on alert. This woman was not human. Most Immortals knew him on sight. Hopefully this one was not stupid enough to try anything in front of all these mortals sitting in the dining car. As if she was sensing the same thing about him, her eyes instantly found his.

She was short, her head only barely clearing the halfway mark on the door she just entered, but she was dressed in business attire. The almond shape of her eyes and the pin-straight black hair, pulled tightly into a long ponytail at the back of her head, were oddly familiar to Lucef, though the strangeness of their circumstances within this train car was enough to make him unsure of why. The clothes and her harsh hairstyle helped her to appear older than her size and youthful face would have one presume, but as her eyes widened at him, she seemed very young indeed.

The seconds passed by slowly as they both took each other in, and then, not even certain why he was doing it, Lucef nodded to her, as if to tell her it was fine for her to join him at his table. She moved quietly, passing by a server with a slight bow of her head, before finally reaching where he sat and sliding into the seat opposite him.

"*Je ne parle pas bien Français*," the woman said, her French accent as poor as her pronunciation. Lucef smiled a little.

"I speak several languages. Which do you prefer?" he asked in English, watching as her eyes brightened slightly.

"I know English," she said with a nod, her Japanese accent coming through a bit.

Lucef hadn't practiced much with all his new abilities since the ritual, preferring that they weren't there to begin with, but he could tell by the way she felt to him and the slightly metallic tang to her scent, that she was a Chenja. And now that he thought it, he had to school his features when he realized the face looking back at him, he *had* seen before. It was the girl from his dreams. The girl telling Codi to stay away from the water.

"Is there anything good to be had in this dining car?" she asked, eyes cast down toward the menu in front of him.

He had only ordered a tea prior to falling asleep in the car, so there the menu sat before him, his tea long since having gone cold in its cup. But he wasn't concerned about the coldness of his tea or anything, really, other than the fact that he could not, for the life of him, remember the name of the girl across from him.

"I hear their salads are quite good," Lucef said, handing the menu over to her, while trying to subtly rifle through the memories of those he had taken within him. It wasn't something he liked doing. In fact, he actively tried to avoid those others inside, not wanting to admit to himself that they weren't separate anymore ... it was all *him* now.

The Codi within him wasn't fighting against the intrusion; rather it seemed more like he was offering it up willingly. The feelings came before her name. At first with just the warm feeling of closeness. This person across from him was someone who Codi cared for very deeply. Then the memories started to flicker through. Images passing so quickly through his mind, he had no way to sort them or really make sense of them, other than the simple knowledge that this was Chiyo. Codi's sister. The last two Chenjas born by Kagami.

With that, Lucef pushed the other memories away to consider later. He had what he needed. He knew she was a Chenja, that she was Codi's sister, but he didn't know why a Chenja was here, on a train bound for London, when Ace's emails indicated that the Chenjas had not been in contact with them, and they were very close to sending Ace to Japan to find out why.

He watched her for a moment as she was puzzling over who and what he was within her own mind. Her eyes moving across the menu but not really reading the words written there.

Lucef wasn't sure what he should do in this situation. His first instinct was to find out as much as he could about Chiyo's motives for coming to London so he could give that information to Ace. But there was a tug within his chest, knowing that if he did that, he would have to deceive Chiyo, because the only person she would willingly give that information to was her late brother.

Chiyo looked up from the menu to see Lucef staring at her, her eyes widening as she looked at him, and some of the features on his face softened into ones that were a bit more familiar to her. She gasped at the recognition there. Lucef either had to explain to her how her brother had truly died, or he had to use this advantage to get her to believe he was, in fact, Codi.

"How did you find me, Chiyo?" Lucef asked, letting his voice move to Codi's intonation slightly. Her lips parted with a quiet gasp, fingers tightening against the menu in her grasp.

"Codi?" she asked, her voice small and strained.

"I didn't think anyone knew where I was, but here you are on the same train to London," Lucef said, letting his eyes dart around the car, as if he expected to be ambushed by others. The small bit of fear in his tone and the anxiety in his face seemed to have the effect on Chiyo he was hoping for. She let the menu fall to the table before her, her hand moving to grasp his but he quickly moved it away, leaning back in his seat away from her.

"We heard you died. The Vampires told us, and we believed it," she said, looking into his eyes and letting her brows furrow in confusion and frustration.

"I may as well have," Lucef said bitterly, giving her a small scowl. She recoiled a little in her seat.

"But if you didn't..." She glanced at her hands that now sat in her lap. "Why didn't you go back to Kagami? To us?" she asked in a whisper.

Lucef allowed himself to cringe. He knew what he was doing was wrong. He was leading this poor girl on in thinking her brother was not only still alive after a decade of silence, but also that he had hidden away from them. Why would Codi have done that? What rationale would the Chenja within him have had to ever abandon his own that way?

Codi would have only had a few reasons to ever do so. If he felt personally betrayed by his own, or if it was to protect them.

If he was going to find out the real reason Chiyo was coming to London, he had to make sure it was for the latter reason.

"Chiyo-kun, I am sorry, but the Vampires had to think I was dead. As did the Werewolves." She looked back up at him then, her eyes scrutinizing as they looked over his face, which held genuine sadness.

"But why?" she asked, her voice breaking a little, and the liquid-like sound that was more natural to Chenjas broke through her fabricated voice for a moment. Lucef glanced toward the man who turned lightly at the strange sound she made a few tables over. "I will tell you that, but not here," he murmured, making her glance over her shoulder at the man who looked at her curiously, before turning back to his paper. They had been noticed now, and it meant whatever veil of privacy they previously had was gone. There was no way for them to talk about anything important until they were alone.

"I have a small compartment to myself," Chiyo offered, having come to the same conclusion. Lucef nodded, the two of them moving quickly from their seats and heading back through the door where she came. They silently moved through the narrow halls, passing through from one car to the other before finally reaching the very small compartment she mentioned. It had only enough room for two people to face each other, and it was quite tight, despite her small size.

Chiyo looked at him expectantly as soon as they were sitting, and Lucef realized he had to come up with a reason for Codi's supposed deception immediately, or there was no going back. He could easily kill her if the ruse wasn't believed, but he didn't want to. Partially because he wanted to make sure he knew everything she had to offer before they returned to Kurome and Ace, but the other part was Codi himself. Though he wasn't whole within Lucef, Codi's affection for his sister made Lucef's chest squeeze uncomfortably with the idea of hurting her.

"I was supposed to die. They all thought I did in the ritual the Werewolves and Witches had plotted, but I simply made myself seem that way. Once the Vampires vacated the building, I moved as far as I could from any Immortals, I recovered and have lived amongst humans since then," Lucef said, hoping his words would answer her questions enough that she wouldn't ask more. Was that what Codi would have done? Lucef wasn't sure, but he was hoping that was a good enough explanation that Chiyo wouldn't fight him for more right now. "Tell me, how things have been going with the war?" he asked, after the silence stretched between them for a long moment. He knew she was gearing up to ask him more, but it was his turn to ask her something.

"It's been frustrating. When we heard about your death, the betrayal was too much. We couldn't keep ourselves aligned with creatures who would so callously let one of ours die. We weren't even informed that the ritual was taking place. We weren't included in anything that occurred in that time. Kagami has been trying to decide how best to proceed with our place in the war, but we got an offer that came at just the right time," Chiyo said, though as the last words slipped from her lips, she realized what she had said, closing her mouth abruptly. She was not supposed to be sharing this information; whatever she was about to divulge to him was a secret.

"An offer from who?" Lucef asked, pressing a bit and letting yet more of his features move to be like Codi's favored appearance.

"Kagami wouldn't like if I was speaking about it. I must complete this, and then I will go home to her before any of it comes to light," Chiyo murmured, looking down at her fingers as they twisted against her lap.

"What do you have to complete, Chiyo? You never left Kagami's side, why is she sending you now?" Lucef asked, having pulled that bit of knowledge from Codi's memories. Chiyo didn't leave their home. She wasn't allowed because she was the next in line to take over Kagami's throne. The only one born from Kagami with the traits necessary to become the next queen. Sending her away from the safety that their fortress provided was extremely risky on Kagami's part.

"My presence will be a sign of good faith. It will help me in the door," Chiyo said, lifting her chin with pride.

Or put the Vampires on higher alert. Ace and Nero were not stupid. They would see the flaws in this immediately, with or without him. However, it would be so much easier if Lucef knew exactly what the Vampires' former allies had planned for them. Was Chiyo going to try to kill a powerful Vampire? Was she going to try and feed information to Kagami about what the Vampires were planning?

"To what? Spy on the Vampires?"

Chiyo's face narrowed slightly, her eyes flashing red as she looked at him.

"Perhaps some of that, Codi, but I am to retrieve something and make sure it gets where it needs to go," Chiyo admitted.

"Maybe I can help?" Lucef asked, and Chiyo scoffed.

"They think you are dead, yes?" she asked, narrowing her eyes at him.

"They think Codi is dead, but I can play someone else. I can be whoever you need me to be to get in there," he said, watching as her face transformed with his offer. Relief was clear there, some of her previous worry melting away at his words. She hadn't wanted to do this alone.

"Do you think it will work?" she asked, her voice hesitant.

"I do, but I'll need to know more about your mission to make sure the plan works flawlessly," he said, pleased when she nodded slowly, taking in a breath to start telling him the details of the plan.

Alexander slipped through the maintenance door that led down to the tunnels below the city. He had snuck away from the den, told not a soul he was leaving or for what, and he intended it to remain that way. No one could ever know he went to meet Ace, nor what he told her of the Witches' plans. But as he slowly eased the door that led into the normally quiet and secluded halls of the den, he came face to face with Melissa.

A scowl seemed to be etched in her features, blonde hair, just like her brother's, curling around her head like a wild mane as she stood there with arms crossed over her chest.

"What do you want, Melissa?" Alexander asked, annoyance clearly laced in his tone as he let the door slam behind him, no longer needing to remain quiet since he was clearly found out.

"Where were you?" Melissa demanded as he walked past her, heading toward the room that held the bourbon he so desperately preferred over her company.

"Out."

He had wanted to be alone. He had wanted to sit with his thoughts and decide what he would do next now that he had finally told Ace exactly what he had wanted to for so many years. No matter the cost, he was always going to choose her.

"You are our leader, and you just abandon us on a whim? What if something had happened? How were we going to find you?"

Alexander stopped and turned abruptly, causing Melissa to crash into him. He gripped the tops of her arms roughly, pushing her away from him, his grey eyes seething as he towered over her. She flinched a bit, making the beast within satisfied that though she may have been acting as though she had some power in their dynamic, she internally knew he was not to be challenged, even if she stubbornly pushed that instinct away.

"I *am* your leader, and therefore what I do and where I go is none of your concern. You are not the keeper of my schedule, and you'd do well to remember your place," he snapped back, a warning growl in his voice.

"You're leading us to death, Alexander! This is not what Lukis would have wanted!" she yelled, eyes blazing with fury.

The clap of Alexander's hand hitting her face resounded off the walls as she flew with its force, crashing against the stone wall a moment later. There was stillness for several beats. The reality of what had just transpired sinking into both. Alexander wasn't one to hit a woman, even if she was a Werewolf like him. He had killed many female Vampires and Chenjas. Eaten quite a few women in his wolfen form, but he was not a woman-beater. He looked away from where she was still sitting on the floor, back to the stone wall staring at him, and down at his hand that still stung a bit from where it hit her soundly.

"What is this?" Kyle's voice hissed out, as he rounded the corner and took in the scene.

"I was merely—"

"You were merely trying to undermine me once again, Melissa. Don't try to say that's not what was happening," Alexander rasped out, his body tensing as he watched Kyle kneel to his sister, taking her chin in his hand to inspect her face, which was now showing a red mark.

"A real man, a real leader would listen to me!" she screeched as she stood up, shoving her brother away from her. "Look at what we've been reduced to, Alexander! We're sniveling when we were once the strongest of them all! You couldn't let the Witches *do something* for once, could you? Needed the glory and the victory for yourself. Well, good luck proving anything to those of us left! Pathetic! Kyle would have been much better suited to this than you. I don't know how you convinced Deca of your worthiness," Melissa spat, turning on her heel and storming through the halls.

Alexander and Kyle stood quietly until the sound of her angry footfalls became distant and then blissfully silent. Kyle didn't speak of the fact that he could have been the leader. It wasn't a topic either of them liked to discuss. Whatever negative way Kyle felt about Alexander's leadership had been left unsaid for all these years, but it was plain in his eyes at the moment as he stared across the hall from Alexander.

"Your sister—"

"My sister is right," Kyle said, his voice quiet but firm. "I know Lukis set us up for failure, but you have barely tried to keep us afloat since. I don't know what your endgame is, or if you even have a plan, but just know, I won't hesitate the next time a choice is laid before me, Alexander. I will choose the good of our kind, whether that be at your instruction or against it," Kyle said, before he too left the hall the same way his sister did.

Alexander could have been angry, but instead he felt ... relieved. What they didn't know, what he couldn't realistically tell anyone, was that if he had a choice to make, he would always choose Ace. Not the Werewolves or their empowerment. Not even the Masquerade. Whatever he would do next, each step he would take, would be to ensure his sister would remain alive and hopefully far away from this war. Now he only had to convince her.

Chapter 10

Ace stepped back into Kurome Mansion, feeling slightly off kilter. Her heart felt heavy in her chest as she moved through the corridors. She just needed to touch her boys. Ace needed to press her nose to the top of Octavian's head and breathe in his scent. She needed to feel Nero's skin against hers. She needed them to ground her because the pain from seeing Alexander unlocked something in her that she wasn't prepared to deal with.

She let the pull of their connection take her to them, down low in the depths of the mansion. She knew what they were doing, trying to search through the Books for anything that might help them, might prepare them for what was to come. Guilt over slipping away and not telling Nero where she was going gnawed at her, making her unstable feeling even worse. She drew closer, and she knew they could feel her. And the way she could nearly smell the old pages and the tanned skin of the covers let her know that Nero knew she was feeling off, that something wasn't right. She felt the nudge of a question there in his mind. The connection they rarely used was fully open, giving her insight into his concern, and him insight into her pain.

But instead of continuing her slow steps to the antiquities room, where she knew he was with their son, she was stopped right as she made it to Ramses' door. Srinta's presence halted Ace in her tracks, pulling her from the strange fog her head was in.

"This is wrong," Srinta said, eyes piercing through Ace's with an intensity Ace had only seen when the Elder was in battle.

"What are you talking about?" Ace asked, brows pinching together as she tried to reorient herself to the now, tried to rationalize why Srinta was looking at her that way. Nothing came to her mind, but the hostility that radiated from Srinta made Ace want to recoil.

"That monstrosity shouldn't even be in that room. He shouldn't be allowed in Kurome. He's an abomination! Why can't you see that?" Srinta hissed, eyes going pale and bright, her arm flailing backward toward the end of the hall where the antiquities room was. Where Nero and Octavian were.

Ace tensed, her body going rigid as the words Srinta said sank in. Srinta was talking about Octavian. She called Ace's son an abomination. And suddenly the pieces fell together. What she had said to Nero that had caused him so much pain ... it was this. Or at least this was part of it.

"He's as much a Vampire as you or I. If anything, he's *more* than either of us, Srinta," Ace said back, trying very hard not to snap at the head of their bloodline. "Eighth in *your* line. Born and not made. A miracle in the flesh. *You* were there at his birth."

"And it is all wrong now, because of him!" Srinta shrieked, her eyes wide and wild, glowing white as her fangs extended.

"I should have known when you went to him." Srinta slapped her hand to the door to Ramses' chamber they stood in front of. "When you went before him while your body was filling with that *thing,* your stomach distending unnaturally. You went to Ramses..." Her voice trailed and she shook her head, as if she couldn't even bring herself to say the words.

"What, then, Srinta? What should you have known?" Ace asked, not trying to hide the venom in her voice. Srinta opened her eyes again, red tears glistening as her irises glowed, casting an odd red sheen to her cheeks.

"He hasn't spoken. Not to me, not to anyone since you."

Ace chanced a glance at the elaborately carved doors of Ramses' chamber. She hadn't gone in since she was pregnant, ten long years ago, and not once in that time had he spoken to anyone else. That was a very long time, especially for him not to give guidance to his own progeny, his favorite progeny.

"He didn't speak to me either, he just..."

When Ace had gone to him, he had just given her a feeling, made her feel that it was the right path that she was following down, nothing more.

"It's because of *him,*" Srinta continued, her tone returning to seething from the vulnerability it held just a moment before. "At first, I was blinded by the rarity of it. Only a myth. Even in my long life, I had never seen such a thing. Vampires procreating? It just simply is impossible. But then I came to understand the gravity of it. This is beyond anything. He has no anchor to the world. No humanity to pull from. He is all monster."

Ace tried to fully absorb Srinta's appearance. Her normally elegant figure was narrowed, fingers twisted in claws like she might attack Ace or pull her own hair out at any moment. Her cheeks were gaunt, eyes sunken, as if she hadn't taken in any blood in quite a long time. Srinta was very old and very powerful. She was the head of their bloodline, the originator of everyone Ace held dear, but Ace would never, nor could she allow anyone to threaten her son.

"You see yourself as a monster, Srinta?" Ace asked after several long moments.

"What are we all, if not monsters?" Srinta asked, a strangely mournful laugh coming from her lips.

Ace stared at her with a look of disbelief. Srinta had been one of Ace's greatest teachers in her early days as a Vampire. And now, after so many lessons about superiority and power, about the beauty of their existence, despite its darkness, *she* was calling them monsters?

Ace felt Nero and Octavian grow closer than they had been when she first entered the mansion. She didn't want Octavian anywhere near this conversation, but she couldn't very well leave Srinta to ensure he stayed put where he was. Srinta was far too volatile for that.

"What is it that you think would solve this problem? You think I would ever allow you to lay a hand on him? You are sorely mistaken," Ace said, not taking her eyes off Srinta, but knowing the moment Nero and Octavian had finally made it close enough to see the interaction.

"I know you won't, which is why I told Nero he had to be the one," Srinta nearly spat. "So the only way to make this happen, to see Ramses back to normal—to prevent *it* from happening—is to wipe out all of you," Srinta said, beginning to straighten. Her body seemed to grow taller and spindly like a spider, cheeks hollowed in the low lighting of the hallway. Her lips pulled back from her extended teeth, a hiss bursting forth as she began her leap across the small bit of space to Ace.

But she didn't make it there. Nero, without a moment's hesitation, caught Srinta at the throat, her body sprawling as it tried to compensate for the change of momentum.

"I thought you understood, Srinta. I thought you knew when I found her that there would never be anyone or anything else for me," Nero said, his voice dark and cold. Ace shivered, both in the feeling of overwhelming hatred she had for Srinta in this moment and for how delicious Nero was in his dark glory. He radiated shadowy power, his muscles bunching in his arm as he clutched her throat, blue eyes glowing icily as he bared his fangs to his sire.

"If that is truly how you feel, Nero, you'll understand that is how it is for me with Ramses! Ace cursed us. I didn't see it when you turned her, or when she turned that red-headed devil. I didn't realize it when Lucef was brought into our midst. I didn't see it until *him!*" Srinta screamed, her white eyes wild as they rimmed with red tears. Nero growled, slamming her against the door to Ramses' room with such force the whole wall shook.

"It's not Ace or Octavian's fault Ramses went to dust, nor is it their fault that he stopped speaking to you. I know nothing of the curse you speak of. To me, it sounds like the mad ramblings of a starving Old One. If you don't want to be held accountable by the Council, you need to calm down!" Nero yelled right back in her face.

The doors behind Srinta's back sprang open, causing both Nero and Srinta to stumble into the dark, shadowed room. She was sprawled across the floor as Nero straightened himself, Ace and Octavian coming to his side in the doorway.

Whispers started filling the room. The same voice whispered a hundred or thousand times over, so it was hard to pinpoint exactly what any of them were saying. There were a multitude of languages being spoken as well, adding to the confusion, but Ace realized when she heard the relieved and exhausted groan coming from Srinta that she actually understood what was being said.

"You speak," Srinta whispered, sitting up and crawling closer to the living wall that was Ramses, its surface rippling and cascading chaotically and angrily.

"What have you done, my black dove?" came one deep voice, the living wall rippled like sound waves with the words, anger clearly apparent as it seemed to cascade around the room.

"You've been—something was wrong, Ramses! Wrong!" Srinta cried, feeling the weight of his rage bearing down upon her and making her crumble further to the floor.

"Change is coming. I feel it all. Many threats, many things that will shift the world as you or I have known it."

"And they are to blame," Srinta hissed, turning her head to glare at Octavian, who stood between Ace and Nero, his small hands held tightly in each of theirs.

"No," Ramses said, his voice shaking the whole room with its power.

"What?" Srinta turned her face back toward the living wall, her shock apparent.

"The Vampire born is not to blame. It is just the way of things. The last time such a change was set in motion, do you know what happened?" he asked, his voice a bit softer now. Srinta only shook her head, bloody tears spilling down her cheeks. "I was made Vampire."

As if a bolt of lightning was struck through Ace at his words. A transformation so great that the last time the tide changed in this way, it was Ramses himself being made Vampire? What were they about to come up against that would be so world-altering as that? The ritual had already taken place, those changes having set so many things in motion. Now the weight of whatever plan the Witches had in store for them felt even heavier as she took in Ramses' words.

She squeezed Octavian's hand in hers, the protectiveness she felt over him beginning to multiply within her. How would she protect her son against something they weren't even certain of, let alone know how to defeat?

"Go now. Leave me with Srinta," Ramses' voice said, the authority in his tone leaving no room for comment. He had to speak to Srinta about her actions, and none of them cared to be there to witness whatever punishment he chose to dole out to her.

"Memories..." came the echo of Six's words, as the image returned to Lucef of the memories and faces floating through the blood of the fountain Six had been standing in. He was dreaming again; it was starting to become expected, but he knew not to count on it being anything more than a dream. It was just another form of torture. His mind had a lovely way of tricking him, letting him feel happiness about Six, only to rip it away again as he watched her crumble to ash. It had happened for the last decade, and simply because his dreams hadn't been ending that way recently didn't mean he could grow complacent.

"Indeed," came an unknown voice. It was far too close to be any of the suicides below. "Blood holds memories and magic."

"Who said that?" Six demanded, tearing her eyes from the swirling images in the fountain and frantically looking about.

"You have to jump in," came the voice again, ignoring her question.

Six's eyes finally travelled to the highest point of the fountain, her gaze landing on the skeleton that was perched there. Her eyes began to trail away, almost dismissively after studying it for a brief moment and realizing the skeleton seemed to be propped there for decoration. She continued looking for the source of the voice, but then the skeleton moved. Bones creaked as it crossed its arms at her, its hollow, eyeless sockets boring into her face. She stared at the face of the skeleton with slight disbelief. Never would she have thought she'd see a skeleton moving on its own. Lucef was equally shocked.

"I am the first suicide. By the rules of this place, I shouldn't even be a full skeleton, my bones having been scattered by animals and used as tools by villagers—" It paused with an angry click, as his teeth snapped together. "But Lucifer is a great man, if a man is what you would call him."

"I see," she said, turning back to the liquid. "And what am I supposed to do?"

"You must jump. It leads you to the Abyss," the suicide told her. As he spoke, the bones seemed to grind and squeak as they pressed together.

Lucef felt Six questioning the suggestion. She was already standing within it, her feet clearly touching the bottom of the fountain's basin. But what was the Underworld other than unpredictable? Things happened here that could never and would never happen in the plane they were accustomed to.

"The Abyss, eh? Will this ruin my clothes?" she asked, as she moved her legs through the liquid. A cackle came from the skeleton, his rib cage moved with the jolts of his laugh, and Lucef felt him smile at her question. So very Six-like to be concerned with her clothing.

"I don't think you need to worry about that, Six," the skeleton said, gesturing for her to go on. But his words confused her. She looked down at herself curiously and immediately recalled she was completely naked. For some reason, that fact had not been retained from before. While she had logically known she was completely nude, the small part of her brain that hadn't been changed by this experience had expected her clothes to still be intact and on her body.

Lucef felt the way the blood slipped over her skin, thickly sticking to her as she waded further toward the center of the basin before she let her body slip under. For a moment, it was like slowly sinking into mud.

Once she was submerged, it was like she was floating through thick air, almost like she was falling, but not quite. Six felt a thumping, a pounding surrounding her body, seeping into her and vibrating her own chest. It reminded her of a human heartbeat, the sound both reassuring and mouth-watering to her and Lucef. She filled her lungs with untainted air, the sickening scent of decay that seemed to hover in the Wood of Suicides having left as soon as she slipped beneath the blood, and the sensation made her feel like she was alive again. But as she drew the second breath, hoping to feel the rush of that bliss once more, her lungs filled with dust and ash, just before her feet hit something solid roughly.

Six blinked a little, letting her eyes adjust to the difference from the red to the dim, harsh light that was now surrounding her, finding herself in a narrow hallway. Smoke filled the air, and screaming bodies littered the floor. Six had made it to the Abyss.

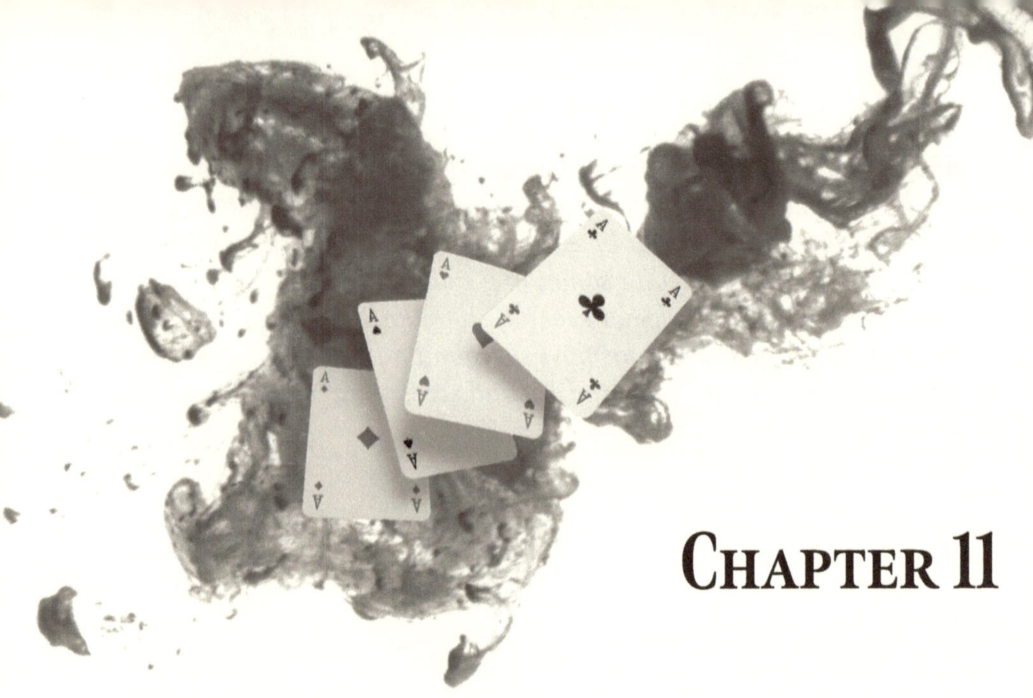

Chapter 11

The whirl of machines filled the silence of the room while Octavian sat staring at the little air bubbles slowly making their way from the bottom of the recently shaken blood bag to the top. He had been sequestered in the Medicus with Minshin while Ace and Nero went to a Council meeting. It wasn't unreasonable that his parents wanted him accompanied by someone they trusted, especially after the display Srinta had put on just days prior, but he was far more interested in continuing to look through the Books rather than sit idly in this room while Minshin and Dietris worked, especially now that he wasn't allowed to touch anything anymore.

"Not drinking all our supply are you, Octavian?" came Makiut's voice, as he strolled through the doors and headed to the counter where Octavian sat. Makiut was one of the handful of Vampires in the coven that didn't seem to avoid him.

"I'm sticking to the rations," Octavian said indignantly, glaring a little at the smirk that adorned Makiut's face.

"No one would bat an eye if you took an extra," Makiut said, as he moved passed to open the refrigerator for himself.

Since the news of the potential breach of the facility, strict rations were underway, and the House Vampires had been doing a bit more hunting than they normally did, except for Dava, of course, who would never stoop so low as to feed on a common person from the street. She demanded only Martins who weren't sequestered at the facilities for her meals thus far, much to the Elders' displeasure.

"Sign it out!" Minshin hissed as Makiut closed the door, blood bag in hand. He stifled his grumble, quickly scribbling in the appropriate fields of the chart that she had posted there to track the consumption of their supply.

"What do you mean no one would bat an eye?" Octavian asked, setting the bag he had been staring at down on the counter while Makiut popped his own into the contraption Minshin had created for even heating.

That you get special treatment.

"That you're growing. You need blood differently than the rest of us," Makiut said, but Octavian had clearly heard something else at the very same time those words came from Makiut's mouth.

"A ration is a ration," Octavian said back, dropping from his perch on the counter and slipping the bag he had been staring at back where it went.

"I'm glad you think so," Makiut murmured, affection in his tone as he ruffled the top of Octavian's white head.

"Is that what the others think of me? That I get special treatment?" Octavian asked meekly, making Makiut's back go rigid where he had turned around to retrieve his now body temperature A-negative.

"I didn't say such a thing," Makiut said.

"But—"

"Does it matter what the others think, Octavian?" Minshin asked, drawing his focus from the stiff back of Makiut to her.

"It just does. I don't think I'm a monster ... but..." Makiut turned back around, taking a moment to bite roughly into the bag and take a few pulls as he considered what he wanted to say to the young Vampire.

"You know how the coven works, right, Octavian?"

"The structure is Elders, Judges, Necare, Medicus, and House Vampires. They all work together, doing their duties so the whole of the coven and the other Vampires can function and stay safe," Octavian said, as if he were reciting directly from a book.

"That's some of it, but not all. Everything is balanced. Sure, there are those who hold more power and sway, but they have earned that one way or another. Everyone in the coven has a job to do; even House Vampires are supposed to keep the house in order, in repair, as well as bring in blood when situations like this arise to help feed the others," Makiut explained. Octavian took that in for a moment, realizing that he, unlike any other being who resided there, had no job, no purpose other than to simply ... grow.

"But I am none of those ranks," he said quietly. Makiut's eyes glowed with a little pride as he realized how quickly the little Vampire had picked up the truth there.

"You are not, but someday you will be, Octavian. What the others in this mansion don't realize is how much of an asset you *will* be, how much knowledge you will have simply because you have always been here to learn it all. I don't know what is to come for you, but seeing that you came to be in such a rare way, I have no doubt eventually they will come around to see that whatever role you settle on will be well-deserved."

And needed. Another voice not Octavian's came through his mind. He looked at the two in the room with him, but none of them had spoken again.

He was going to say something about the strange voice to the others, but his words died before his mouth could even open when he saw Dava and the twins pass by the open door to the Medicus. Dava's blue eyes seemed to pierce through the room, directly at Octavian, clear maliciousness in her features as she looked upon him. She was not one he ever cared to be alone with, even if she was simply a House Vampire. She was old and set in the life she had made here at the mansion, making it quite clear in the past how she felt about him existing at all. Makiut followed Octavian's gaze, just as the blonde hair of Dava disappeared.

"Yes ... she's one you'll need to stay away from," Makiut murmured, going back to drawing deep mouthfuls of blood from his warmed bag.

The Council room was quiet as a tomb as the Elders gathered. They hadn't met for nearly a week, and so much had already happened that their previous conversation had been basically forgotten. The Council had been in talks before about their allies. The Chenjas had been silent for far too long. Though the Chenjas were weaker than them in number, they were still valuable to the Vampires, and it was a hint at what the Vampires ultimately wanted, which was to protect the other Immortals. Vampires, although thought to be the most ruthless and cruel of all the Immortals, really wanted to keep the rest of them under their wing and maintain the balance between them and the mortals that far outnumbered all of them.

The Chenjas' continued silence and the fact that they had all but completely withdrawn from the rest of the world, most of their numbers brought back to their home in Yokohama, Japan, was cause for concern.

Though there was a Vampire coven in Tokyo, there had been no contact amongst them. It was as if the Chenjas had folded within themselves, refusing to have contact with even the Vampires closest to them. Ace had once had the best relationship with the Chenjas. Her friendship with Codi had been unprecedented. Not simply just trusting one another as allies, but as friends.

But Codi was dead.

And Ace suspected that was why they no longer heard from them.

The door to the side of the room opened, and the last few Elders filtered into the room, taking their seats. Srinta came through, eyes avoiding Ace's before she took her seat, and Nero was close behind her. His body was stiff, movements showing his agitation as his blue eyes seared into the back of his sire's head. The anger and betrayal on his face toward Srinta would have been shocking to Ace, had she not heard the disgusting words from Srinta's lips herself.

"How do we start this evening's meeting?" Georgith asked, his tone clipped. They were all aware of Ace's efforts, of the way the Werewolves seemed unable to recover, but they were getting anxious now that the Necare had slowed their progress killing off their enemies in favor of gaining information. Georgith, like several of the others, was eager for the war to be over, but it seemed like it was just out of reach.

"We need to force contact with the Chenjas," Ace said, pushing her concerns about Srinta to the side in favor of the actual tasks at hand. She and Nero had discussed bringing up Srinta's actions to the Council for punishment, but Srinta had spent the better part of two days locked in Ramses' room. She had been admonished thoroughly, if not punished in a different way by her own sire. There was no need to involve the Council unless she started spouting utter nonsense once again.

"And I suppose *you* plan on being the one to do something about it?" Fredric asked, his voice not hiding the resentment in his tone. Something about Ace being so involved and active in the war, despite being on the Elder Council, needled him. It had been years since he had been actively involved in anything. Prior to being an Elder, Fredric had been a Coven Judge, and before that a Medicus. So Ace wasn't completely sure why her continuing to hunt bothered him so much, especially when he could easily help Minshin in the Medicus if he so desired to be more central to the action.

"I am the only one of us Kagami may meet in person," Ace said, narrowing her eyes at him.

"She might meet with Srinta," Georgith offered, causing Srinta to bristle beside him. Srinta had been the main Chenja contact before Ace. For centuries, even after Ace had become a Vampire, Srinta had met with their allies the most. That was only deferred to Ace once she and Codi had developed a closer relationship and made their alliance that much stronger.

"It's been many years," Srinta said quietly, still not making eye contact with Ace, despite the way she felt Ace's gaze intensify on her face.

"There's no reason to risk Srinta in such a way," Fredric spit, his head swinging around to glare at Georgith for even suggesting such a thing.

"Ace is invaluable here in London. She's got a foothold on what's happening with our enemies and commanding the Necare. We can't spare her for a trip to our allies, that, for all we know, have become our enemies as well," Georgith said coldly. Ace simply let her eyes slide from one Elder's face to the other, somewhat shocked by the interaction. The fact that Georgith was defending her was new.

"What did you discover from the Witches we captured, Ace?" Nero asked. She had already told him all of what had transpired, but it was much better for the records if things were told this way in the meetings.

"The Raven is planning on summoning something, and Alexander is not in favor of it. It was essentially confirmed that their alliance is over," Ace said, her words seeming to echo through the large open space. She didn't need to tell them that this was further corroborated by Alexander himself, but Ace hated that she couldn't tell them there was no need to question this. It was inevitable that they would be facing something far more dangerous than simply a set of Witches unprotected by their beast-like allies.

The silence hung there for a moment. Both a sense of excitement over their enemy's weakness becoming an ever-growing chasm and also the idea that The Raven was planning to summon something. It took a great deal of power, perfect timing, and sacrifice to make such a thing come to pass. If this news was coming to their attention now, that meant the Witches had been working on it for some time.

"What is she summoning?" Fredic asked, his voice having lost some of its condescension.

"The Witch who broke didn't specifically say. Her words were, 'Only Darkness can hunt Darkness. Only another monster can kill the one who stands in the way,'" Ace said, a shiver traveling up her spine as she repeated the words, remembering the way Poppy had stared into Ace's eyes, as if *she* were the one who stood in the Witches' way.

"The Books," Nero said suddenly, recalling where he and Octavian had stopped just days ago, the foreboding feeling that filled them both when they realized there were missing pages.

"What of the Books, Nero?" Srinta asked, her lip uncharacteristically curling in irritation as she turned to look at him.

"It's been rather a failure on our part that we haven't fully dissected the two books at our disposal. Ten years we've had both the Sister Books, and yet we don't know any more of what they hold than we did when Lucef brought the second book to us," Nero said. The mention of Lucef always seemed to bring a wave of fear and uncertainty in its wake. Lucef was welcomed at Kurome, only because Ace and Nero demanded it to be so. The other Elders considered him to be a liability, a target, a harbinger of destruction.

"It was never necessary before," Fredic murmured.

"Those pages hold prophecies and truths," Ace said, nodding in agreement with Nero, locking eyes with him from where they sat apart. She knew he had already begun looking through them, and perhaps Srinta had surmised this as well, but the other two didn't.

"It's too dangerous," Srinta said, her fists clenching on her lap, eyes glowing. Ace tilted her head curiously at Srinta for this reaction. Out of all the Elders, Ace was certain Srinta had read more of the Book that they held in their possession than any others, and she was the one who had pointed out they were different when Lucef brought its sister to Kurome. Why she would deny them searching the pages now, when so many unknowns hung in the balance, seemed out of character for her. But then Ace realized her reaction made more sense knowing that Octavian was also reading the Books with his father.

"It would be dangerous not to," Nero snapped, turning his glare to his sire.

"Ace, try once more to contact the Chenjas; if it fails, we'll determine which of you to send at that point," Georgith said, though his expression showed exactly how displeased he was with the idea that Ace would go to Japan instead of Srinta.

"Octavian and I will work on going through the Books more thoroughly," Nero said, standing from his throne.

"That boy should not touch those Books," Srinta hissed, standing abruptly, and turning to block Nero's exit. The way Srinta practically spit the words "that boy" made Ace tense. The hostility toward Octavian was potent still, despite whatever reprimand Ramses had given her.

"My *son* needs to learn. He's a Vampire and deserves to contribute," Nero said back, his voice barely more than a growl.

As if the other Elders knew this was no longer a Council discussion, having begun drifting into more personal territory, Fredic and Georgith seemed to shrink from the room, disappearing and leaving Ace, Nero, and Srinta to the crackling tension.

Once the room was theirs, Srinta glanced at Ace and took a deep inhale.

"What I said stands true, Nero. Even you can't deny it," Srinta said coldly.

The moment the words left her lips, Nero was in her face, towering over her as his glowing blue eyes seared into hers.

"I deny nothing because you spoke falsehoods to us that aren't even worth exploring. I have only ever thought you a goddess amongst us, and now I see that was wrong." He violently turned from her, striding not through the side door but throwing open the large doors of the main entrance and disappearing back into the mansion.

Chapter 12

Ace made her way quickly through the mansion following the Council meeting, finding herself in the Medicus mere moments later; it was much the same as when she had left not long before. Minshin and Dietris were busy working on something while Octavian sat at the counter. Though she could see from his posture he was nearing sleep with the sunrise, his hand lazily holding onto the empty blood bag before him. It was far too close to dawn, and he was fading quickly.

"Come now, Octavian," Ace whispered as she drew close to him, pulling him from the counter and into her arms. He didn't say anything, merely nuzzling his face into the crook of her neck, letting her take all his weight as the coming dawn bore down on him.

Ace headed directly for their chambers. On a normal sunrise, she would place Octavian in his own room, but for the last few nights, she didn't want him alone. She didn't trust what could happen in this mansion if she were to succumb to the sleep the sun called within her.

"What's going to happen now?" Octavian asked, as his mother set him down gently against one of the soft chairs in the room, moving toward the windows to make certain the curtains were secure. They hadn't discussed with him what occurred with Srinta, instead trying to distract him with the Books and having him stay in the Medicus, learning about the research Minshin was doing for his own growth. He hadn't spoken about what he heard and saw in the corridor a few days before, but now she could see Octavian's face was lined with concern again.

"I don't know," Ace said honestly, sighing heavily as she turned back to look at him. His face was drawn with apprehension, eyes wide with childlike worry.

"Am I a monster?" he whispered.

Ace's breath hitched as she knelt before him and looked into the silver pools of her son's eyes.

"Werewolves tear flesh; Witches need bloody sacrifices; Chenjas' main life source is draining it from anything living. There are humans that torture, kill, and even eat other humans. You, my son, have never killed someone. You may have hurt them, you may have taken their blood, but you've never taken a life by your own choice. You are less a monster than the rest of us in this house," she said, brushing her thumb over the bloody tear that ran down Octavian's cheek.

Nero had walked in but paused just outside the door as Ace spoke those words to their son. If his heart could have beat in his chest, it would have absolutely thundered. No truer words could have been spoken on the matter. It wasn't black and white; there were certainly shades of gray in all forms, mortal and immortal alike. He had suffered through many years of his own inner turmoil over what he was. Nero had not been an angel as a human, let alone when he first became a Vampire. It was Srinta, her guidance and affection without any desire for reciprocation, that changed his view on everything. Humans and the other Immortals were almost reborn into something new in his eyes, and his previous actions made doubt and guilt take hold. It took centuries until he was capable of tearing himself out of the dark chasm of remorse.

"What will happen with Srinta?" Octavian asked, taking in a shaky breath. Ace's eyes darkened at the mention of her name, her eyes snapping to Nero as he leaned against the doorframe.

"I'm sure we'll find out soon enough what Ramses decided as far as her punishment. Right now, with things so volatile, it's best not to focus on her misdeeds," Nero said.

Ramses will have to determine if she's worthy of the life he gave her.

The voice floated through Octavian's mind. Just as before, this voice wasn't his own, and those words weren't his either. He turned to look at his father who came further into the room, confused and wondering if Nero had spoken out loud, even though Octavian logically knew he hadn't heard the words—not with his ears.

"Lucef should be coming soon," Ace whispered, as she reached out to Nero once he got closer, threading her fingers through each of his.

Nero stiffened at the mention of Lucef, glancing toward the door of the chamber.

Srinta.

Again with the voices that were not Octavian's. This was odd, far too odd, and far too much happening when his life had been fairly mundane so far, for having been born as he was. Octavian stared at Nero with curiosity, as he leaned forward to kiss Ace.

"I should see about the Books," Nero said, aloud this time, gaining a nod from Ace as he went to stand, but her fingers only tightened against his, halting him from stepping away from them.

"I have to tell you a few things," Ace murmured, eyes locking with Nero, a silent communication passing between them, and though Octavian was reeling slightly from feeling like he clearly heard his parents' voices in his own mind, he wished he could, in that moment, know what his mother wanted to say to his father.

"Later," Nero murmured, eyes flicking to Octavian briefly. Their fingers slipped away from one another, Nero striding from the room and closing the door quietly behind him, plunging Ace and Octavian into darkness.

"Can I stay in here again today?" Octavian suddenly asked, his voice so small, eyes wide and glowing with his fear. Fear of Srinta, fear of what all these sudden changes meant. Fear that he was in those Books, a monster, despite his mother's soothing words.

"I wouldn't want you far from me another moment," Ace murmured, pulling him into her lap and running her finger through his hair, soothing him as she had since he was born.

Octavian fell asleep just as Ace could feel the sun peeking over the horizon. She watched him, while her ears were trained on the house around her. Unlike the solace human mothers could take from watching their children's intake of breath while they slept, all that could give her that same kind of peace was the feel of him in her arms. The magical tether between them, keeping them connected always.

There was movement outside the room. It could have been Martins or Obis wandering during daylight, or presumably it was Nero, returning from studying the Books. They needed to talk. There was too much unsaid between them, but Nero had been right to wait. Octavian was already struggling with what had happened in front of him just days ago. A fight between his parents and Srinta was not only unexpected, but highly abnormal. And they had been fighting about *him.* Octavian didn't need to hear more. Not yet.

Just as she was about to pull her gaze from Octavian and to the door where she expected Nero to enter, Octavian's body began shaking against the sheets. She stood from the desk where she had been sitting, immediately finding herself at his bedside, eyes wide as she watched his limbs vibrate and twist, his back arching off the bed dangerously. He made no sound, and his face didn't change, still relaxed in deep sleep.

The door opened and Nero stepped through, stopping abruptly when he saw what was happening across the room.

"Ace, what—?"

But she held up a hand, her eyes starting to glow as she watched Octavian's arms and legs begin to lengthen, skin becoming more taught against his muscles. His face changed, but only slightly, taking away some of the childish and rounded features in favor of more sharpened lines, looking even more like his father. The clothing on him tore, making room for the sudden growth. And then the tremors stopped.

Where their child, who looked very much like a five-year-old human once lay, now was a boy who appeared to be more on the cusp of adulthood.

Ace stayed still, watching to be certain it was over, before bringing her eyes to lock with Nero's across the room. In an instant he was beside her, looking down at their son.

"He just..."

"There was no trigger. Just as before," Ace said quietly.

"He still sleeps," Nero murmured, curiosity in his voice.

"Let him. It's done now," Ace said, turning away from the bed and going to lean over the desk.

Nero came behind her, placing a hand on her back. She didn't flinch away, but he felt her muscles tighten under his fingers.

"You didn't tell me about Srinta," Ace said after a long moment.

"I should have. I just—"

"I met with Alexander," Ace said, cutting him off before he could apologize. His hand withdrew from her back immediately. She pulled herself away from the desk, turning to look at Nero's furious face.

"What were you thinking?" he hissed.

"That he had answers we needed. The Witches are summoning something."

"That's all he said?" Nero practically growled.

"He didn't know much. He wanted to warn us ... me," she whispered.

"You risked yourself, met with the leader of our enemy for intelligence we could have garnered plenty of other ways?" Nero asked, his voice rising.

"We didn't have time, Nero! I knew something was brewing. I didn't want us scrambling when he promised answers," Ace hissed back.

Nero grabbed her hand, pulling her roughly into their bathroom and closing the door quietly. He took a harsh breath before turning around to glare at her.

"What else?" he asked.

"What do you mean?"

"What else have you kept from me, Ace? What other dangers have you put yourself in?"

Nero's anger was all based on fear. The very real fear that Ace would push herself beyond her limits simply because of the sense of duty she had toward them all. She should not have been heading this war alone, but somehow she had become the central point, having the final say and making the tough decisions on what steps they should take. Nero knew if she had to choose between her own life and the success of their kind, Ace would choose to die. And he couldn't fathom a world without her in it.

"Nothing else," she hissed, glaring back at him. "And you?" she asked coldly.

"Me?" he asked, taken aback by the accusatory tone.

"Anything else you have been keeping from me?"

For a brief moment, he was irritated, his eyes blazing. But he realized she had been reactive to his initial actions. Her meeting with Alexander, though ill advised to do alone, was what he would have done in the same situation. She was right that when she went, they needed answers that nothing thus far had proven to provide. However, her hesitance to tell him stemmed from his own admission of what occurred with Srinta.

"I have nothing else to say. I should have told you what was happening with Srinta that night," he said, stepping closer.

"She threatened our son, Nero," she whispered, bloody tears rimming her eyes as she looked into his.

"She won't again," Nero said, reaching up to press his palm to her cheek, letting her relief wash over him when she pressed back against it.

Ace couldn't hold onto her strength any longer. It was just her and Nero, the only one she could ever show her weaknesses to, and she let herself crumble. She fell into his chest, her face pressing against him, breathing in his scent deeply, before letting out a rough sob.

Octavian had been threatened, and an unknown creature was possibly going to surface, looming over them, promising destruction. Yet Nero was there, arms wrapped around her, being the strength she needed so she could unravel, if only for a moment.

Lucef was once again plunged into the depths of the Abyss. The now-familiar feel of Six settling into him as he let his eyes take in the scene before hers. Six's gaze cast over the strange corridor. The Abyss was the unkept torture level for unkept deviants in life. Mortals who let their baser natures run rampant, not only ending their lives but destroying others in the process. These weren't inherently evil people; they were just the ones who couldn't control themselves, and thus were subject to torture for years before the Underworld spit them back out to try again.

She walked past, unnoticed by demons and their screaming victims. It was as if she weren't even there, just a ghost taking in each monstrous scene after another. Severed limbs and broken bodies chained to the floor twitched and moaned as she passed them. The hall seemed to be endless, and she never passed the same thing twice. Seeing all sorts of strange horrors as she passed by.

After what seemed like ages, Six finally came to a sort of end. Two sets of stairs sat beside each other. The one on the right was glistening white, which was entirely impractical for this disgusting, filth-covered place, while the other seemed to be crumbling, stained, and covered in ash.

Without hesitation, she took the left set of stairs. Lucef assumed she sensed that she would fall into worse circumstances by taking the surreal, welcoming stairs, because the Underworld was never what it truly seemed. She started down the dirty steps, pausing briefly at each level below. Each became worse than the one previously. More bodies, more screaming, more of a thick haze of ash coming from some unknown source. Yet still she went unnoticed.

She reached the bottom of the last set of stairs and where another set should start, but instead of another level of the Abyss to pass through, she found herself at a circular room that only held three doors. The sounds that took over the levels before, desperate howls of anguish, were gone, only leaving a faint sound of wind whistling from somewhere.

Curious, Six stepped from the final step, taking in each door. One was completely plain, metal, like the door she had to remove with her blades when she was at the River. Another was made of metal as well, but it was glistening as deep crimson blood ran down its front, as if there was a never-ending stream of fresh blood to pour over it. The delicious tang of its scent filled her nostrils and reminded her of her hunger that she had so diligently been ignoring since she left Chomic's chamber. Lucef's hunger spiked at it too, a primal need to drink and devour filling him.

The door positioned between these two was a large stone, less a door and more like an oval bolder. It was clasped to the wall by hundreds of hands that seemed to have grown from the black, stone walls of the circular room. The stone was carved, but with no set pattern. She stepped closer to it, inspecting it, and found that it was a name written thousands of times in thousands of languages.

Lucifer.

At the center of the stone, with all the writing surrounding it, there was an "L" written in blood.

Lucef felt her smile, imagining it spreading over her face, feeling the sinister pleasure within her.

"The king of the Underworld, himself."

Lucef realized that this had been her intention. Of course, her plan was to escape, but to do so, she was to present herself before Lucifer, the Master of Demons himself. The darker side of the duo of gods that ruled their world.

Arrogant, perhaps, but not a plan outside of Six's abilities, clearly.

Six closed the distance between herself and the stone, licking the blood gently with her long tongue. It was a bit sticky, old and partially dried there, but tasty nonetheless. The favor burst upon her tongue, a thousand different sensations melding together there. She, and therefore Lucef, wasn't sure who the blood belonged to, or what they were—though it was obviously not human—but she was delighted by the taste. And yet, the blood was not why she was there. Her hunger had to take second place to her mission. Behind this door, and only this door, would be the path she needed to go down to get out of this place.

She stepped back to look it over in more detail. Lucef's vision darted with her eyes, taking in each of the hands clutching to the stone. Oddly, as she peered at them, she realized many of them were recognizable, though who they belonged to was lost on her. Pale, thick, manly fingers, though well-kept, stood out to her, as well as rough hands of a working human, hands that made her recoil with vague memories of being hurt by them. There were the long black claws of a Werewolf, its nails digging into the surface of the stone. She saw hands that had pleasured her, hands that had fallen limp as she killed them ... so many hands, but only one made her still heart feel tight in her chest. The long, thin fingers gracefully held their part of the stone as the silver nails dug into it. Silver nails that had extended, like the retractable blades that they were, piercing into the stone. The index finger had a spade tattooed onto it.

Lucef felt her inner turmoil, her confusion as she tried to place a name to the face she was envisioning in her head at the sight of that hand. Lucef's mind instantly flashed to images of Ace, her silver eyes, black hair, and pale skin that set her apart from so many others. Lucef realized Six knew that this hand belonged to someone she knew, someone she cared for, though everything else seemed lost in her mind. Six touched the hand lightly, hoping it might help her remember, but instead, the nails withdrew, and the hand released its hold and went limp before dissolving into black ash that fell to mingle with the other ash on the floor.

"No!" Six cried out, her voice echoing around the stone room.

Panic struck Lucef at the pain in Six's voice. Ace wasn't gone; he knew that, but Six had no way of confirming she was still exactly where Six left her, in the living plane. Seeing Ace's hand there dissolving into ash could very well mean Ace was gone. Not just from the living plane, but from the Underworld too. But before she could fall into her own despair, the other hands soon followed, releasing the stone and crumbling.

With each hand that released, the boulder seemed to become looser, shaking slightly and parting a bit from the wall. When the final few hands finally disappeared, Six stepped back, watching as the large stone fell to the ground, sending a plume of black debris into the air.

When the ash cleared, all that was left was a large, arched passageway. She stepped through and immediately was engulfed in darkness. Whatever light had been illuminating the hallway she had just been in was gone, as if it had never been there in the first place.

Lucef was startled awake from his dream. The sun was still in the sky, but it indicated late afternoon. He and Chiyo had arrived in London a few days prior, but she had been nervous about his disguise, unsure if the Vampires would catch on that Codi was the Chenja behind the different face he wore. At her insistence, he agreed to stay in a small hostel on the other side of the city from Kurome so they wouldn't chance running into any Vampires who might be out in the city, so that his fake identity was as firm as possible before they went there. Of course, Chiyo had no idea that the identity and face Lucef was wearing would be one Ace knew very well, and that he was actually deceiving Chiyo, not the Vampires.

He looked frantically around the room, trying to control his panted breath after yet another of these strange dreams of Six. Thankfully, Chiyo had fallen asleep as well, it seemed. She was still curled oddly in a chair in the corner of the room, while he had sprawled out on the bed, the sheets now damp from his sweat, and the taste of that odd blood lingering on his tongue.

Each of these dreams had been so strange, but so happily welcomed after the decade of torture, watching Six die. The change in Six, though somewhat jarring at first, he now found himself reliving to bask in the beautiful strangeness of it. Some part of him hoped that these weren't just dreams, that he was seeing some narrative play out that was truly happening. Because if she was trying to get out of the Underworld, to return to their world, she would succeed.

Chiyo stirred from where she sat curled, her form having moved between her preferred human shape to an odd, silvery shape he had never seen before during her sleep. It was also beautiful in an oddly alien way; metallic silver skin that seemed to be liquid-like, moving just slightly, and reflecting the light. But as her eyes opened, the petite human features settled back over her like a gentle ripple.

"I didn't mean to fall asleep," she said quietly, looking embarrassed as she fully sat up and looked at him from across the room.

"I fell asleep too," he admitted, glancing toward the steadily lowering sun. "We should prepare and start our journey to Kurome. It won't be long before the sun sets," he added, seeing from his peripheral the way her body stiffened.

Chiyo nodded, moving to gather the few things that had come unpacked while they stayed there, anxiety pulsing through her at the prospect of stepping into the most powerful and highly regarded coven, only to deceive and betray them. At least she wasn't alone.

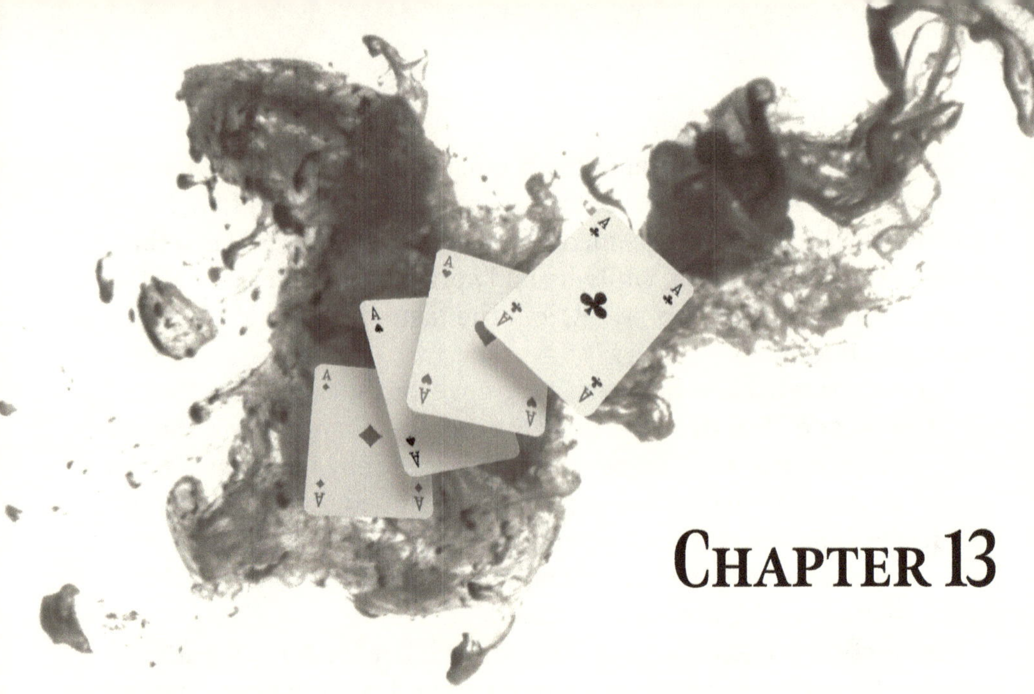

Chapter 13

The sun was nearly on the horizon as Lucef and Chiyo made their way toward the less-inhabited area of London that surrounds Kurome Mansion. They reached the gates, with Lucef's chest feeling heavy as he looked upon them. They were covered in ivy, appearing to any passersby to be long unused, but he knew better. That weight in his chest made him anxious. He wasn't sure what he was going to find when he stepped back through those doors, but the silence from Ace since he announced his return was not normal, nor was the fact he was walking an enemy into their midst.

His hand found the keypad to open the gate easily, but instead of pressing the code he had been given to gain access, he pressed the call button. The intercom played static for a moment before going silent. Standard procedure, to ensure wandering humans merely thought it was an abandoned place.

"Chiyo, daughter of Kagami, wishes an audience with our allies," Chiyo said after a beat of silence. The silence persisted for several long moments, making Chiyo visibly nervous, her hands wringing together as she glanced from the intercom to Lucef.

"We should have made contact first," Chiyo whispered, her eyes turning red of their own accord with her concern.

Lucef glanced up toward the ornate carved image of a rearing cobra that sat atop the pillar just before the keypad and intercom. He knew within its eyes held a camera that someone was watching them through. This whole plan would go poorly if the person who answered the call or the person at the door, when they were let through, called him by his name. He stared at it briefly, hoping Nyprat or Lotte were the ones watching. They would be able to see from his expression that something was happening here, that caution needed to be taken.

"We were not expecting a visit from you, Chiyo. None of our communications have been returned," came Nyprat's voice. It took so much for Lucef to hold back the relief from crossing his face.

"Kagami thought it best if I came in person," Chiyo said quietly.

Without another word, the gate started to open. Chiyo and Lucef moved up the long winding path toward the mansion. The grounds closer to the gate were kept overgrown, the trees and bushes helping to obscure the view of the mansion from those who may try their luck at jumping over their walls. Lucef knew that within the greenery sat the day guard, watching them move down the path. As they continued, the grounds became more managed. Greenery was cut back, gravel and stone cared for, and of course the mansion came into view.

Chiyo let out a little gasp as she finally looked at it. The building was rather breathtaking upon seeing it for the first time. Lucef remembered, when he came here with the Book he had stolen from his father, being slightly in awe of the magnitude of the fortress-like structure. He imagined Chiyo felt similar to how he did then, walking into enemy territory and being unsure how or if they would leave alive.

"It's beautiful," Chiyo said, astonished as her eyes wandered over the complex exterior of stone.

"It is," Lucef agreed as he walked to the steps and looked behind him, waiting for the last bit of sun to fall behind the great trees before he knocked loudly against the large wooden doors.

The great doors slowly creaked open, Lotte standing just within, eyes scrutinizing as she took in the appearance of Chiyo and Lucef standing side by side. Lucef had adjusted his appearance but made it so he was quite recognizable to the Vampires who lived here. He was hoping—desperately hoping—that Lotte would understand what was happening here, that he was in the throes of a deep deception she would need to uphold.

"Chiyo. And who is this?" Lotte asked, keeping her eyes on Lucef.

Of course she would catch on immediately. She was trained by the best, after all.

"He is my escort. Kagami didn't feel comfortable with me coming alone," Chiyo said. Perfectly reasonable explanation, especially since, as allies, they knew who Chiyo was in the hierarchy. It was rather strange that she *had* been sent all this way on her own, but she had explained to

Lucef on their train ride that Kagami had felt Chiyo would be seen as less of a threat to the Vampires if she had come unaccompanied. Interesting how easily Chiyo had gone against her mother's instruction when she happened upon him.

Lotte stepped aside, gesturing for the two of them to enter the mansion. Lucef stepped through, fighting the feeling of rightness that made him want to sigh contentedly. Being back in Kurome was like a balm, easing something within him, even though that odd ache that came from his new dreams of Six continued in his chest. But he couldn't think of that now. He needed to talk to Ace and Nero, needed to explain what he had learned from Chiyo to them as soon as he could.

"The Elders have been informed of your arrival. It is still early in the evening, so we'll show you to your rooms," Lotte said, glancing behind her at the House Vampires who were lounging on the parlor furniture, watching the interaction with fascination. Chiyo nodded. It made sense that her unexpected arrival would mean she would have to wait before she was properly greeted. "William."

William stood from where he sat, coming toward them and looking to Lotte for instruction. He had been slowly working toward becoming a Necare, a goal Lucef recalled him striving for as long as he had known the Vampire. Last he heard, William was due to complete his training soon, so he would no longer have to stay amongst the likes of House Vampires like Dava, Charles, and the twins, who sat scrutinizing everything that was occurring before them at the front door.

"Please take Chiyo to the Blue Room," Lotte murmured, eyes still assessing.

"Of course," William said, gesturing for Chiyo to follow him. She glanced at Lucef for a moment, feeling suddenly uneasy that they were to be separated.

"I'm sure I'll follow you shortly," Lucef said, nodding for her to follow William. She nodded in reluctant agreement, still looking uneasy before she followed up the stairs.

Once Chiyo and William were well away from the parlor and out of sight, Lotte turned her searing eyes to Lucef.

"I need to talk to Ace and Nero," Lucef said, easily letting his appearance slide back to what they all normally saw.

"You most certainly do. What is going on, Lucef?" Lotte hissed, turning and marching quickly toward Nero's chambers, the eyes of the House Vampires following them silently.

"It's a lot to explain," he murmured.

"There's been a lot happening here as well," Lotte admitted as they moved through the halls.

"Like what?" he asked, wondering if the weight he felt on his chest had anything to do with what had been occurring here.

"I should let Ace and Nero explain all that," she said, flashing him an uneasy look from over her shoulder as they approached the chamber doors. It was only a second after their feet stopped, before Lotte could even raise her hand to knock, that Ace whipped the door open, silver eyes immediately falling on Lucef.

"He arrived with a Chenja," Lotte said in response to Ace's questioning gaze.

"What?" Ace hissed, confusion written all over her features in a way that both Lotte and Lucef were unaccustomed to witnessing.

"She thinks I'm Codi," Lucef offered with a shrug.

Ace was astonished by Lucef's sly deception. She had never known him to do such a risky thing with his new powers. He rarely did anything at all with his vast abilities, and while she was fervently curious about everything he could possibly do, she would never push him into using or revealing that to anyone. Not even her.

Both Ace's eyebrows rose in surprise as she nodded slowly. This was going to be very interesting. Chiyo thinking this was her brother would mean everyone would have to be extremely careful until they knew her motives behind travelling all the way to Kurome.

"Thank you, Lotte," Ace said dismissively, pulling the door open further and gesturing for Lucef to step inside.

Lucef had been in Nero's chambers once, years ago, when he first came to Kurome Mansion with the Book. At the time, Nero had been in New Orleans with Six. Since then, Lucef never had a need to step in this space again. Whenever he had stayed in the mansion, he mostly kept to himself, only ever staying in common rooms or Six's room. It was what he expected from Nero's room. Rich lush furniture, deep colors, and luxurious fabrics, but it was far more lived in than it had been the previous time, with all of Nero's possessions back in place, as well as Ace's things mixed in now as well.

Nero sat at his desk, and Octavian still lay on the large bed, still as the dead and much larger than he had been the last time Lucef had seen him.

As Ace closed the door, he rushed to Octavian's side. Something about the stillness of the boy and the fact that his clothes were torn against his body made Lucef fearful.

"Is he alright?" Lucef asked, kneeling down to get a closer look at him.

"He grew as he slept. He hasn't risen yet," Nero said nervously, his eyes trained on his son from where he sat.

"You came with the Chenja?" Ace asked, pulling Lucef's attention back to her.

"I happened upon her as I was returning here," Lucef said honestly. "She thinks I'm Codi."

Ace took a sharp breath at the mentioned name. Codi.

The memory of watching her friend be reduced to a puddle of mercurial liquid against the stone slab in the basement of the abandoned hospital flashed through her mind. His death, like Six's, had torn something from her. She couldn't imagine what Kagami and the other Chenjas had been dealing with since his loss.

"How did you manage that? The Chenjas know he is dead," Nero asked, standing from his plush chair and leaning against the desk.

"She recognized some of him in me. I merely ... allowed her to believe it to be true, with a few added details. I told her you thought I had died, and I had remained under the radar ever since the ritual. She's rather naïve. She hasn't been let out of Kagami's sight for her whole life. She is next in line to take over if Kagami passes, so it was quite the risk sending Chiyo here," Lucef said, running his hands through his hair.

"Why has she come?" Ace asked as Octavian finally began to stir, his fingers twitching lightly against the satin sheets, eyes moving under the thin skin of his lids.

"Kagami has allied herself with the Witches. They're plotting something, and Chiyo is supposed to retrieve an object that resides here."

Ace and Nero exchanged a look. What could possibly reside within the mansion that the Witches needed? Nero immediately thought to ask Srinta. She was the oldest Vampire in the mansion, had been alive for longer than nearly all others. Most of the artifacts they housed in the lower level she had personally brought to their collection. Ace seemed to have similar thoughts, since her gaze found his immediately. In the past they wouldn't have hesitated to ask her, but there was no way to know what state she would be in. Given her reaction at the Council meeting, she was still struggling through her negative feelings toward Octavian and most likely was less inclined to help them.

"Where is Chiyo?" Ace asked, turning back to Lucef as he watched Octavian's continued, small waking movements intently.

"Lotte had William take her to the Blue Room," Lucef said, letting a smirk lift at the corner of his mouth.

The Blue Room was in the guest wing of the mansion. Several rooms were simply that, guest rooms with nothing special about them, but there were some rooms that held things there, things that were not quite living or dead. The Blue Room was one of those. Octavian and Lucef had discovered all sorts of interesting things about the mansion itself over his time spent there. The Blue Room held something within it that, when unleashed, could do untold damage to anyone who happened to be there with them. A very strategic move on Lotte's part.

Ace was pleased with Lotte and slightly relieved that not only was Lucef back in the mansion, but they at least had confirmation of what was happening with the Chenjas, even if it was betrayal.

Chiyo followed William hastily, her steps quick to keep up with his long strides, though she knew he was slowing down for her benefit. She hadn't noticed at first that Codi wasn't following behind them, but when they reached a fork in the long hallway they took after climbing the stairs, she realized she was very much alone. Had another Vampire taken Codi somewhere?

"Wh-where is my companion?" she asked as they paused at the fork.

"I don't know. I'm sure he's being made comfortable," William said, tone dismissive.

He took a right once they reached the fork and started into a very grim-looking end of the mansion. Chiyo assumed it was an unused wing because there were still gas lights flanking each door they passed. Most were not lit, making this area far more shadowed than the rest of the mansion she had seen. The wallpaper was not only different from the previous hallway, but it was peeling in some places.

She looked around curiously at the wooden doors. Each door or threshold had symbols carved into them: some plated in metal, some left fully unfinished, exposing the raw wood beneath the varnish. Each was different. Some looked quite beautiful, while others looked rather frightening.

"May I ask, what do these symbols mean?" Chiyo asked quietly, knowing she had let her curiosity get the best of her. She had to tread carefully, for she had a purpose to complete. Knowing all the strange things held within Kurome was not part of that mission.

William slowed his movement down the hall for a moment, glancing over his shoulder to her and taking in the curiosity that flickered over her face. He was silent, weighing how much he wanted to scare this Chenja.

Considering he was nearing completing his training, and almost a Necare, he had been told of the Chenjas' cold silence. Bearing in mind Lotte was sending her to the Blue Room, no one knew yet if she was friend or foe.

"Some are the symbols of Vampires who inhabited those rooms long ago. Most of the symbols started out as their marker. Each Vampire of rank gets a symbol of their bloodline and often uses that to make something that is completely separate and meaningful only to them," he said, nodding his head to a door that had a gold-plated symbol resting there. "They either moved on to other covens, were forced rogue or out to a nest, or died."

"And the others?" Chiyo asked, eyes landing on a particularly rough-looking set of shapes that looked more like they had been stabbed into the wood rather than carved.

"Other symbols are to ward things out of the room because they hold precious things ... some hold things in," William said in an eerily monotone voice.

As William's last words left his lips, he stopped in front of a door. The symbol on it looked menacing, with sharp points jutting from a weblike center that encircled four blue stones.

"What does that one mean?" Chiyo asked.

"It's just the Blue Room," he said, turning the knob and pressing the door open.

Chiyo didn't much like that non-answer, but she turned to look inside anyway. The Blue Room was a fitting name, covered in a metallic blue, like the stones on the door. The area rug, curtains, and bedspread all had the same regal vines in silver. Chiyo was in awe at this large room that she had all to herself. Even Kagami didn't have bedchambers this elaborate, and certainly not in this western style.

Chiyo forgot all about the meaning behind the symbol on her door once she saw how lavishly it was decorated, entering and running her fingers over beautiful cherry wood furniture and the soft down comforter of the bed. She slid her bag gently off her shoulder to the floor, as if she were afraid its presence would harm something in the beautiful room. There were claw- footed couches and tables, a hand carved armoire for clothes, and great silver framed mirrors on several of the walls. There was even another door that she assumed led to a personal bathroom.

A smile came to her face as she looked at the striking objects in this room she would call hers for a short time. She turned to thank William for the selection, but the doorway was empty, and only the dark corridor was beyond it. Chiyo was alone.

Chapter 14

"Must be silent."

Lucef couldn't see anything, but he could certainly feel and hear. The whisper of Six's thoughts echoed around them. Though she was hidden in whatever blinding darkness they were in, her thoughts were on full display to anything and anyone else here. Nothing and everything were concealed here.

He felt it as Six stepped forward, her legs moving stiffly and slowly as she ensured there was solid ground to stand on. The darkness seemed to thicken, disorienting them further. Struggling, her body wasn't sure what was up or down, whether she was swimming or walking. She wandered, hands out to find a wall that might guide her where she needed to go. She grabbed, finding one and feeling the ground at her feet, but froze immediately.

It was like fire, poison fire, had seeped into her from her fingertips and was now running through her veins. She couldn't breathe, speak, or scream: she could do nothing but feel the scorch of hellfire burning through her body from where her hands touched the rough stone walls.

Lucef felt her pain as if it were his own. He tried to scream and fight against its hold, but though her thoughts echoed in this place, his did nothing. He was simply silently there, trapped in the pain inflicted on them both, tortured further knowing she was feeling this too.

Six fought against the pain, trying with everything she had to gain control. She had dealt with pain, had suffered through so much of it for so long, and while the fire licking through her felt like it would tear her apart or burn her to ashes, she still knew her body was there. That she was still there in this place of eternity.

With great effort, she released herself, pushing off the wall and into the darkness with no anchor but what she could feel below her. It would have to be enough.

"Of course, it can't be easy," she hissed, stumbling further into the darkness. Ahead of her, the faint outlines of the tunnel she seemed to be in could be seen, the oppressive darkness and disorientation abating some. "Light," she whispered, picking up her pace.

The farther down she went, the more she could see. The shadows grew around her as she reached its source, the light making every stone wall cast harsh shadows in its wake. Lucef felt the weight of eyes on them first it seemed, immediately going on alert as she moved closer to the shadows just before the bend, where the source of the light had to be coming from. Six slowed as she too, felt it, her eyes darting toward the shadows with suspicion, gazing and trying to penetrate every crevice that held darkness she couldn't see through.

"I smell it on you," came a voice from a particularly deep shadow. The voice was odd, a cascade of whispers that culminated into one voice after a moment. Each word spoken peculiarly slowly. She kept herself in the stream of light, eyes watching for movement.

"Smell what?" Six asked.

"The blood that runs through your veins. Your line stems from the one who trapped me here," the voice said.

"You're trapped here?" she asked, curious about how a demon could be considered trapped. Demons had limitations in the other world, but to feel trapped in the only place they could be completely whole seemed odd.

"Part of me locked away on the Living Realm, the other part banished here. I am in pieces, and it's your blood that caused it to come to pass," the voice said, though it seemed to rasp more near the end, growing angrier with each passing word.

"I do not even know your name, demon, let alone who may have trapped you here in such a way," Six said, wanting desperately now to continue her pursuit. She knew that if she pushed further, going toward the light, she would somehow get to where she needed to be and, once there, she would be free.

She felt the shadow move closer, the darkness oppressive and foreboding as it drew nearer.

"I'd eat your soul if it would do me any good," the demon said, its voice nothing more than a growl that seemed to hang in the air. Six felt its power,

and though she was strong, she was not stupid enough to think she had enough strength within her to stop this creature from tearing her apart, nor could she stop it if it chose to place her back in the cell she had only just escaped. She began to back away, the darkness coming to try to consume her with each step back she took.

The light that was cast from the place up ahead seemed to grow brighter, its beams cutting through the darkness of the shadow that grew before her so she could see, if only for a fleeting moment, its true form. It hissed at the light, backing away and back to the corner where it seemed to have come from. Six's gaze remained fixed on the spot until the light grew so shockingly bright that she couldn't see anything anymore. Not the cave-like space she was in, not the corner where the demon had disappeared to, not even her own hands in front of her face.

The pure white light was shocking, all encompassing, beautiful and frightening. She both wanted to bask in it and run from it. She stumbled back, away from the source, her body hitting the walls, and, once again, searing pain swept through her limbs. A touch on her arm was suddenly there, warm strong fingers wrapping around her elbow and pulling her from the wall. She gasped at both the sudden relief from the pain and also the feel of the skin against hers.

"Lucifer?" she whispered, eyes still unseeing in the white light as she peered up at what should have been a face before her.

"No," came a crystal-clear voice that sounded more like music than words.

Octavian watched from the bed as Lucef twitched, breathing erratically in his sleep. He had awakened in his parents' chambers only to find Lucef sleeping as well, draped over one of the velvet chase lounges that sat closest to the bed. He wasn't sure what time it was or how long had passed since he went to sleep following his mother's return from the Council meeting, but the surprise of Lucef being there was enough to let him simply watch his friend for a minute or so.

"Six!" Lucef shouted abruptly, sitting up with his eyes wide and glowing red.

"Lucef?" Octavian asked quietly, edging closer to the end of the bed. Lucef's eyes snapped to Octavian, his breathing still harsh, a tremble in his limbs. It took a moment of them simply looking at one another before Lucef's eyes began dimming, the red glow no longer burning there, but now his familiar black and blue eyes.

"You're awake," Lucef said, letting out a rough breath as he raked a hand through his hair.

"You were dreaming," Octavian said, smiling weakly.

"I was... I've been having some strange dreams as of late. Stranger than normal, at least," Lucef admitted, bracing his elbows on his knees.

"You spoke. You said 'Six.' Is that who you were dreaming of?" Octavian asked. It wasn't uncommon for Octavian to ask prodding questions. He was a child, after all, but it was odd now for Lucef to experience those questions when the boy who sat before him looked closer to an adult than the five-year-old he had appeared like before. And beyond that, his dreams were rather hard to explain. He always dreamed of Six, but these were different. They were not reliving the past, but more like he was taking this journey with her.

"Always," Lucef said, letting the corner of his mouth turn up just slightly. Octavian's smile in return made Lucef feel a little lighter.

Throughout Octavian's life, Lucef had been there. Not all the time, but often enough that they had formed quite the bond. Both were very different: a Vampire born and an Ultimate Immortal. They shouldn't have had much in common, but the feeling of being an outsider, of being unusual, helped to bond them together as friends.

"You grew," Lucef said, gesturing toward Octavian's chest and causing him to look down at himself.

He hadn't really taken stock of anything but Lucef's presence since he woke. Now that he cast his eyes down at himself, he saw he had indeed grown. The clothes he had been wearing when he went to sleep were torn, having had to make room for the new width and length of his limbs. He was tall now, perhaps as tall as his father, he could tell just from how much more of his calves could be seen from the end of the pants he wore. His fingers were long, no longer the short, child-like fingers he had grown so used to seeing.

"Is that why you've come?" Octavian asked, turning back to look at Lucef.

"No. I was coming back anyway. I thought I'd stay with you if Ace had to go meet with the Chenjas, but that doesn't seem to be a necessary trip for her any longer," Lucef said, standing and heading toward the doors of the extensive closet that Nero and Ace shared. Octavian slipped from the bed and followed him in there, watching as Lucef glanced at the various clothes on his father's side.

"No longer necessary? We haven't heard from them in nearly a decade. Why wouldn't that be needed?" Octavian asked.

"Because a Chenja came to visit them, and I happened to run into her and came along. Seems like they are no longer our allies, but they don't want us to know that yet," Lucef said as he pulled a pair of trousers from a hanger, handing it to Octavian, before moving on to the shirts that hung nearby.

"How did you manage that?" Octavian asked, trying to keep the excitement from his voice as he let the fact that Lucef had said "our allies." It was the first time Octavian had ever heard him say anything about taking sides. Not that it wasn't obvious he had before. The only place Lucef stayed with any sort of regularity was Kurome. Why would this place be his home if he didn't side with them?

"I convinced her that I was Codi."

"Used your Chenja abilities, did you?" Octavian asked with a grin. Lucef turned back to him, taking in that smug look as he shoved a red dress shirt at him.

"I use them occasionally," Lucef grumbled, somewhat indignant, as he strode out of the closet and leaned on the door just outside. "I couldn't let her walk in here without knowing her motives."

"We don't know anyone's motives anymore," Octavain murmured, tearing off the remnants of his old garments and pulling on his father's clothes. They were still a bit too big for him, but clearly much better suited than anything else he would be able to find within the mansion.

"What is that supposed to mean?" Lucef asked, worried at the strange change in Octavian's tone.

"Srinta ... she tried to attack Mum. She said I'm a monster and wants me dead," Octavian murmured quietly as he stepped back into the main room. Lucef's eyes glowed once again in anger.

"She did what?" Lucef practically growled, shoving off the wall to stand.

"She's right, though. I shouldn't be. Vampires aren't supposed to procreate. It's never happened before. A myth," Octavian said, shrugging.

"She's far from right, Octavian," Lucef said, stepping closer. "Did you choose to be this way?"

"No."

"Being a monster isn't what you are fundamentally. It's only how you choose to use what you have that makes you the monster. Am I a monster because of what I am now?" Lucef asked, looking intently into Octavian's silver eyes.

"No," Octavian murmured, though his voice was a little stronger now, his eyes sparkling with understanding as Lucef's words sank in.

"Your being here is miraculous. Who you choose to be, what you choose to do, will determine if you are a monster."

Chapter 15

Chiyo stared at the darkened hallway outside her room, a foreboding feeling coming over her as she watched the flickering gas lights cast moving shadows. She wasn't unfamiliar with ghosts, souls that were trapped within places instead of making their way to the Underworld, but ever since stepping onto the grounds of Kurome, she felt that she was being watched. Eyes of hunters were everywhere and surrounding her, and now that Codi was no longer with her, she was an island unto herself.

But she had a job to do, a mission her mother set her on, and she could not fail.

Chiyo knew she would be called to meet with the Elders soon. Her arrival had not been expected, and they would want to discuss the alliance with her. She had prepared herself for the questions. They would want to know what the Chenjas had been up to in the years of silence between them, and possibly give updates they had been unable to convey.

This room she was in was beautiful, and it eased some of the fear she felt within the rest of the mansion, but nothing would be accomplished isolated in this room. Slowly, she made her way to the open door, peeking out at the dark hallway to see if there was anyone out there that might see her if she chose to leave. The corridor was desolate. Silence persisted; the only sounds seemed to be coming from so far away, she couldn't clearly distinguish it.

She stood in the beam of light that cascaded from her room, having stepped out onto the hall to see if she could get a better listen around her. Whispers seemed to cascade over the dark hall, as if the walls were talking. She had half a mind to rush back to the safety of the Blue Room, but just as she turned away from the hall, Chiyo saw a figure approaching, dark and shadowed as it walked down the dark path toward her.

"Miss Chiyo," came the deep voice of a man. The way he moved as he walked down the hall told her he was not a Vampire, his movements too erratic, lacking grace. As he got closer, she could hear his heart beating soundly in his chest. He was human. "I was sent to bring you to the Elders," he said, stopping before her.

The man was tall, blond, with the cleft chin and blue eyes that she knew were signs of his lineage. He was a Martin. She was supposed to find a Martin boy and give him the object she had been tasked to retrieve.

"Are you—?" But she stopped herself from the question that so desperately wanted to come from her mouth. If he wasn't the correct Martin, she could expose herself as a traitor, assuredly leading to her quick death at the hands of any Vampire he chose to tell.

But he suddenly went rigid, his eyes widening and his hands turning to fists at his sides.

"Yes. I am the one you seek," he said, though his voice wasn't his own any longer, having become slightly echoed as he said the words. She could vaguely feel the magic surrounding him. He wasn't betraying the alliance his family had with the Vampires by choice; he had been spelled and was struggling against it.

"Do you know where I find it?" she asked.

"It is below. In the same hall as the Council room. We must act quickly. The Vampires already know of your deceit."

Her stomach dropped. A sickening feeling slithered through her.

How could they know?

What would they do to her?

Chiyo shivered slightly, closing her eyes and trying to calm the fear racing through her. She could run now; she could run and disappear, getting away from the danger that she was most certainly in now. But where would she run? If she came back to her mother without completing this mission, it would be a great dishonor. She wouldn't even deserve to step foot into any of their buildings once more, let alone be in her mother's presence. And what of Codi?

She just got him back, and she was thinking of abandoning him?

He may not have been dead any longer, but he would be if she left him alone to take the blame of her deception.

With a shuddering breath, she looked up at the man's face once more, his eyes staring blankly down at her. She had no choice but to continue.

"Take me," she whispered, watching as he turned, body still rigid, and began making his way down the hall, back toward the main part of the mansion.

The Elders sat on their thrones, the room deadly silent, except for the shallow breathing of Chiyo as she stood before them. The walk through the mansion to get here was interesting, sometimes breathtaking in the beauty of the architecture and decor, but also frightening. Her eyes took in the sight of blood in cups, at the necks and wrists of the humans who had been brought there for the House Vampires' dinner, just like the man who was escorting her.

The whole building, she realized, smelled of old death. Stale, because nothing *lived* there. No living food was brought in. None of these creatures needed to move or breathe. It was completely devoid of the signs of true living. While Chenjas were not human, they still held signs of life that didn't exist here in this place. No wonder she felt strange and out of sorts; the Chenjas had allied with their opposite. While Chenjas also fed off the life of living things, they too were alive. Vampires were not.

The man, who she had learned during their slow journey through the mansion was named James, had guided her down to the lowest level. The temperature dropped significantly as soon as they stepped foot in the long stone corridor. There were some modern lights placed here and there, but they did little to help with the darkness that persisted. Dread filled her as Chiyo stepped further from the stairs and deeper into the depths of the mansion. They passed many doors, but James came to a stop before one door, tilting his head as if to indicate she should look inside.

What she had been tasked to find was the vessel that held the final piece needed. The object which held the part of the demon The Raven planned to summon, who had been trapped here to keep him weak, broken, and unable to move through the planes as he once had. The Raven hadn't told them the whole story of the demon, or why this particular demon was significant, only that it was imperative to their plans. And, as usual for Witches, the timing had to be just right.

The Raven had been preparing this for some time.

Chiyo took a deep breath, closing her eyes and remembering the way her body had felt when she had sat in on the meeting with The Raven and Kagami, as they put this plan in place. The Raven's voice echoed in her mind, telling her she would know it by the darkness it exudes. The light would almost seem to be swallowed by it; shadows pervasive around the object that held *him* within.

Her eyes snapped open from where she stood just outside the threshold of the room. Her irises were no longer the changed brown they had been for her travels, nor were they the red she liked to put on when she was in her human shape. These were the black of her true form, her face becoming strangely alien as it stretched around the enlarged orbs. Her gaze took in the room and its contents. Everything within this room was old. She could see and feel the power that radiated from each one, the darkness and light. Finally, after several long moments, where she felt James tensing and shifting his weight beside her nervously, she zeroed in on the black obsidian box that sat on a shelf across the room.

"The black box," she whispered to James, his body going rigid for a moment, as if his real self, the one hidden under enchantment, was fighting for control.

"I'll take it," he said quietly, turning away from the room to gesture toward another set of doors a bit away from them and further down. "That is where you'll meet with the Elders," he said, not making a move to join her.

"But—"

"Just go, Chiyo," James said, his voice flat, eyes glossed over as he stepped into the room full of strangely beautiful yet dangerous objects. Had things been different, Chiyo thought she'd love to see what all was in this room, but she couldn't risk being seen there, especially with what was to come next.

She headed down to the double doors, and now, here she was before the Vampire Elders, each of them with their eyes trained on her.

"Miss Chiyo, it's been a very long time since we've heard from your kind," an Elder at the end said. She hadn't seen him or one of the other Elders before, having only ever met Ace, Nero, and Srinta, so she assumed the one who spoke was either Fredric or Georgith.

"It has, and we are so sorry it has taken us this long to reach out. It has been very difficult since Codi's passing," she said quietly, trying to keep out the sharpness from her voice at the mention of her brother. He was here somewhere in the mansion, hopefully keeping up his façade as the companion she had brought along with her.

"Many things have changed. Has Kagami been receiving our intelligence?" Ace asked, keeping her tone unconcerned. If the situation had been different, if Ace hadn't known that Chiyo was here to betray them, she may have tried to convey more warmth, but that knowledge kept her from showing any sympathy for the fate the Chenja was undoubtedly going to have befall her.

"She has, and that's part of the reason she sent me here. A show of good faith. We have appreciated the updates, keeping us knowledgeable, but it's time now to put aside our grief and continue to work together."

The silence took back over the space. There was a heaviness in the air that made Chiyo uneasy. She could feel it now, the weight of the knowledge that she was lying to them and essentially completely alone within their domain, alone and defenseless against them.

"We have only ever looked out for the Chenjas, have we not, Miss Chiyo?" Srinta asked, her tone not giving away anything about her thoughts.

"We have been fortunate in our allies."

"You know it is for the betterment of all the Immortals that we fight and win this war. You should feel that especially, as a Chenja, you are very likely to be taken advantage of by the others," Nero said. His words made Chiyo shiver. Taken advantage of, indeed. That was certainly how she was feeling at this moment. The Witches were using them, using their proximity to the Vampires to gain the last piece they needed to summon their demon ... and Kagami had fallen right for it.

"I do," she whispered, her hands shaking as she clasped them in front of her. She was regretting everything very suddenly, and she fought herself to remain calm in the presence of these old and powerful Vampires.

"I'll have some things written up for you to take back to your mistress, but until then, enjoy your time here," Ace said, watching the way the Chenja before them began to shake, the enormity of the situation finally hitting her.

Chiyo bowed to them all, her eyes not rising again to meet any of theirs before she swiftly left the room. Her gaze landed on the room she had been in only a few minutes prior, taking in the lack of James. He was gone. Her breath quickened as she stepped closer to the open doorway, eyes landing on the now very empty place where that black box had been. He had already taken it, the box most likely very close to being in the hands of The Raven.

Chiyo dashed from the door, quickly and quietly making her way down the corridor along the path she had followed James down. It was like the stone walls were closing in on her, the very house itself was trying to bury her with the guilt she felt at what she had just done.

Halfway up the stairs to the main floor, she suddenly found herself face to face with a boy. He looked to be a teenager, dressed in clothes a bit too big for him. His face was mildly familiar, silver eyes set just above a sharp Roman nose, taking her in with curiosity.

"You must be the Chenja," he said quietly, his voice deeper than she had anticipated. "Where are you going in such a hurry?" he asked, crossing his arms and leaning against the wall of the stairway, clearly not intending to let her pass.

"To my room. I was dismissed," she said, tearing her eyes from his. Vampires were not supposed to be able to affect the minds of Chenjas, but she felt a presence pushing on her slightly, like his eyes were boring within her mind.

"I'm not sure you'll know the way. It can be rather confusing for those that don't stay here," he said, smiling lightly as he pushed from the wall and gestured for her to follow him.

Octavian wasn't certain if the Chenjas had been made aware of his birth, but based on the confusion and mild fear he could sense from her, she was not aware. She followed behind him, slowly walking through the much busier halls of Kurome as the Vampires went about their nightly activities. It was interesting to see the House Vampires all chatting and lounging, almost behaving like normal humans, but Chiyo could still feel the eyes on her, watching her every move through their space. They passed open doorways, one leading into a large room where a few Vampires stood over a computer, talking quietly, so quiet that Chiyo couldn't hear them, even if she shifted her ears to be a bit more sensitive.

"This is the Medicus," Octavian said, pausing there when he noticed her slow even further at the entrance.

"Your doctors?" she asked, watching as he nodded.

"And more, but that's probably the best understanding," he said quietly. Minshin and Dietris looked up from what they had been pouring over, taking in Chiyo first, since having a Chenja in their midst hadn't happened in so long now that Codi was dead, then Octavian's changed appearance.

"You grew?" Minshin asked, coming before them an instant later and observing Octavian more closely.

"While I slept," he confirmed.

"I must measure you. To record this," she said, her voice full of excitement as she grabbed his arm, beginning to pull him further into the room.

"I have to take our guest back to her room first," Octavian disputed, making Minshin stop and return her gaze to the small Chenja beside him.

"I'll take her," came Lucef's voice. Octavian turned, his excitement over Lucef's return evident on his face. They had only talked briefly when they both woke, but Lucef had made it quite clear that he wasn't to mention or even hint that he knew Lucef at all in front of Chiyo. A task that was much more difficult for him than he originally thought it would be now that he was in this situation.

"Come, Octavian," Minshin said, her voice seeming to pull Octavian from saying something to Lucef that he shouldn't have before she yanked him through the room to begin the exam.

Lucef turned, quickly striding down the hall, Chiyo following behind him with quick steps to match his long strides.

"What are you doing?" Chiyo asked him in a whisper.

"I needed to check on you," he lied, having really gone to the Medicus to wait for Ace and Nero to return from the meeting. He was eager to know what had gone on there with Chiyo. He didn't want ill will to befall the Chenja, necessarily, but he realized that since that encounter with her on the train, and the fact that the Chenjas were betraying their centuries-long allies, he couldn't stand by and let anything happen to the few people left in the world he cared for.

"Where have you been?" she asked, as they finally made their way up to the second floor, passing through the maze of hallways until they got to the long hallway where her room sat.

"I was sequestered in a room. They only just let me out. What have you been doing?" he questioned, even though he knew very well that she had been in the Council meeting.

"I had a meeting with the Elders, but..." She wrung her hands together, eyes flashing between red and black as she nervously thought about what had just happened.

"What is it?"

"There was a human. He was entranced, I think. I found the piece The Raven needs, and he took it while I was in the meeting. But, Codi—" She grasped at his arm, clutching it as she looked at him, worry and devastation written all over her changing features. "I think we made a mistake. We shouldn't have done this."

Lucef's heart seemed to squeeze painfully at those words. Chiyo was fairly innocent. His memories from Codi showed she was kept safe and by Kagami's side throughout her whole existence. She, of course, came here blindly following her mother's orders. What else could she have done? That was all she knew.

But something had transpired in the meeting with the Elders that allowed her to see past that. And now there was no going back. It was already done, which meant it was only a matter of time before the demon would be summoned. Depending on how closely the Witches had planned this, it could be the summoning was already taking place.

Lucef's features changed, returning to his normal state, and very much not like Codi. Chiyo's breath seemed to stop, realization dawning on her as he looked down at her with a mixture of hatred and sadness.

"You're not Codi," she murmured, stepping back and closer to the Blue Room.

"No. Codi did die that day. He was sacrificed, just as the Vampires told Kagami. What is left of your brother lives in me now, and while both of us understand your deception, your devotion to Kagami, you still chose to betray the Vampires, under their roof, and may bring death upon us all," he said through gritted teeth, his eyes glowing ominously.

"I-I..."

"Stay in there until they decide what to do with you," he hissed, pushing her further into the room before slamming the door shut.

Chapter 16

Lucef's unbeating heart seemed to squeeze within his chest. The Witches had it, whatever the item was. It could be days, hours, or minutes before calamity broke, and they had no way to prevent it from happening now. He immediately returned to the Medicus. As suspected, Ace was there with Nero right beside her, as Minshin discussed Octavian's rapid growth.

"He hasn't changed in years, but his excessive blood consumption over the past few weeks makes sense now that we see how much he's changed. He grew nearly to full adulthood in one day," Minshin said, pointing at the charts on her computer for them to all look over. The sharp upward line where it had once been stagnant looked so dramatic on the screen.

"Ace," Lucef said, his voice barely more than a growl, making all eyes turn to him.

"What is it?" Ace asked, immediately on alert at the way he looked when she let her eyes take him in. Vibrant eyes, hair shockingly red, his fangs were extended, and his chest heaved with the breath he took to hold back his anger, and power.

"It's already happened. The Chenjas sent one of the humans in the mansion off to The Raven with whatever it was we held here. It was the last piece they needed."

"No!" Came a scream from behind them. Srinta fell to the floor in the hall outside the Medicus, her nails dragging through the thick carpet there as shivers wracked through her body. "He will come and kill us all."

The shock of Srinta's outburst caused the room to still for a moment. There was admission in those words, knowledge Srinta had of what was to come that she hadn't disclosed. If there was time, Ace would have her pinned to the wall, extracting every ounce of information she had, but as it was, they were on borrowed time. Humans couldn't move very quickly, but who knew how long he had been gone?

"Which human?" Nero asked, his eyes snapping back to Lucef.

"Chiyo didn't say," Lucef murmured.

"No human should have been escorting a guest like that. Wasn't William told to fetch her?" Ace asked, glancing at Nero who nodded.

"Dava told him not to. She said, 'One of the minions can do it,' and sent a Martin," Octavian said, sliding off the table.

"How do you know that?" Ace asked.

"I went in there to see if William or Charles had clothes that might fit me better," Octavian said with a shrug, gesturing to his father's clothes that were a bit too big on him.

"Dava," Ace practically spat, immediately storming through the room, barely sparing a glance at Srinta, who was still curled into a ball on the floor of the hall.

Ace tore through the mansion, travelling faster than she ever had until she could hear the commotion coming from the hall, just outside the cluster of rooms the House Vampires called theirs. Without even a knock, Ace kicked the door open, the wood splintering as it rained over the room, causing shrieks to fill the air as humans and Vampires alike were pelted with the shards.

"Which Martin did you send to take the Chenja?" Ace asked, after she spotted Dava lounging on a bed, two humans on either side of her in various states of undress.

"What do you mean?" she asked dreamily, licking her bloodstained lips.

"Which one? I need a name or a picture. You sent a human to do a Vampire's job, and now something was stolen from us and given to The Raven. Your stupidity and laziness have most likely gotten us all killed. So, tell me, Dava, who did you send?" Ace asked. Her voice had gone from frightfully level and low to a feral scream.

Dava sat up, eyes wide and filled with horror as she registered what Ace said. William similarly seemed shocked from where he sat against a chair, pushing the Martin girl who had been on his lap to the floor as he stood up.

"It was the male. He volunteered," William said when Dava remained silent, mouth open in shock. Ace would have found amusement in the devastation on Dava's face, if it weren't for the fact that what she had done may have destroyed everything. Perhaps now she would rethink her flippant ways, but Ace doubted it.

"James," said the woman William had shoved to the floor.

"James?" Ace asked for confirmation, mentally going over the Martins she knew by name. She had seen him when Dava returned with them the night before.

"I-I don't remember which one that was," Dava murmured.

"I know which one," Ace snapped, turning to leave the room, but pausing and looking back at Dava with glowing white irises. "This was unforgivable. We will have to decide on your punishment if any of us live."

Without another word, Ace left the room, the hall outside filled with bodies, since apparently everyone from the Medicus had followed her.

"I'm going to track him, see if I can catch him before he hands it over," Ace said, not breaking her stride as she moved through the mansion to the front doors, having caught his scent at the stairs.

"You aren't going alone," Nero protested.

"We don't have time to gather a party. We must track his scent now," Ace practically growled, still barreling toward the front doors, where he most likely left through.

"I'll go," Lucef said, as Nero was going to continue his protest.

Ace paused at the door, looking at everyone who continued to follow behind her. Octavian's face showed both excitement and fear, Nero deep concern, Srinta looked as if she were about to fall to pieces, and Lucef stood confidently at the front of them all.

"Fine," she said to Lucef, nodding at him as she pulled the doors open.

"Be careful," Nero said solemnly. But there was nothing for Ace to say in return. She would do exactly what she had to do, careful or not, to avoid bringing death down upon them.

Lucef followed hastily behind, watching as Ace moved swiftly, only stopping once or twice to take in a large inhale through her nose before she caught James's scent again. It was strange watching Ace work. It had been many years since Lucef had followed along with her while she hunted, though at that time, the only creatures that Ace hunted were Werewolves.

He never joined her on the hunts as anything other than a witness, but this time he was prepared to shed blood if necessary. Whatever this demon was that the Witches were summoning into their midst was frightful enough to have Srinta on her knees. It couldn't be let loose in the world.

And what would they do if they did get to James before he handed this object off to the Witches?

Would Ace eat him? Spare him?

Would they make it there in time?

The path wove through the streets, meandering as if he was trying to outmaneuver anyone who was to pick up his trail, but clearly not enough. The scent was getting stronger, though they had to slow to a more human pace as they came into the busier areas of London, where humans were plentiful.

Ace slowed to a stop, reaching out her arm to halt Lucef as she finally spotted James. He was stepping closer to the mouth of a narrow alley between old buildings, the two of them just on the other side of the road, still hidden in shadows from him. In James's hands, he held the obsidian box that had sat in the antiquities room for as long as Ace could remember. She had never thought to inquire about it, though it had always seemed to give her a foreboding sensation when her eyes landed on it throughout the years.

James's body movements were strange and unnatural, his eyes seemed muddled and unfocused. His hands shook, fingers gripping the box so tightly that his skin was white with the strain.

"Entranced," Ace murmured to Lucef. He nodded, glancing down the street as two women walked by chatting happily as they passed. They would have to be very careful in this part of the city. There were human eyes everywhere here, and Ace knew if they moved too quickly or unnaturally to a human, they would be spotted. Her eyes scanned the exterior walls of the buildings around them for CCTV cameras, and just as she suspected, there were plenty.

Yes, this would have to be done rather precisely if they were to avoid having a lot of evidence to clean up.

Another small group of humans began to pass them, and Ace knew this would be their last opportunity, since James was slowly inching closer to the shadowed darkness on the other side of the road, as if he were fighting his own body not to enter there.

"Just in time," came a voice from within the shadows. Two green eyes were the only things that could be seen in the darkness for a moment before a woman stepped from the obscurity. Red hair flowed out from beneath her hood, a thin-lipped smile playing on her face as she took in the image of James holding the box. "Just as she told you, Martin-boy.

Want to or not, you've done exactly as we asked." She held her hands out, and James shivered uncontrollably as his arms forcefully pushed the box into her waiting fingers.

Ace saw a break in the human traffic and quickly stepped from where she and Lucef were hidden on the other side, causing the Witch's eyes to snap to her.

"Too late, Vampire," the Witch said with a smirk, before she seemed to melt back into the darkness she had come from.

As soon as Ace was at the mouth of the alley, passing James without a second glance, she let herself move at her full speed, her eyes quickly adjusting to the strange pit of blackness in the narrow space before she saw the Witch once more, toward the end of the passage, stepping through what looked like a portal in the air. Ace was there in an instant, but it was too late. The portal closed with a harsh crackling sound that split through the air and echoed off the brick walls. The Witch was gone.

When Ace turned again, her fingers curled into her palms, cutting through her skin with the sharp edges. Lucef had pulled James further into the alley so the cameras couldn't see any more, his large hand pressed against James's throat, pinning him to the wall as he snarled.

"How dare you? Do you know what you've just done?" Lucef asked harshly, his voice rumbling with the growl in his chest.

"P-please! Spare my family!" James cried, tears and snot running down his face as he struggled against Lucef's iron grip.

"Why would anyone want to spare you anything after what just happened, human? You've killed us all!" Lucef practically screamed. Ace came close now, eyeing the humans that were passing just feet away from them.

"Lucef," she murmured, placing a hand on his arm. He took a deep breath, trying to calm himself. He may have been tortured these last ten years since the ritual, but it didn't mean his desire to live was any less. "James Martin, you were spelled, were you not?" Ace asked, looking at the sobbing man now and seeing him nod.

"Please!" he begged again, sagging against the brick wall when Lucef's grip finally released. Ace crouched before him, watching as he continued to shake and cough.

"James," Ace said, moving her head until she finally caught his eyes. They were blue, but rimmed in so much red from crying it was off-putting. "How soon until the ritual begins?"

"S-soon. They had it all set up for a very long time. They needed the final piece either tonight or tomorrow, or the time frame would have to reset."

Tonight or tomorrow.

That wasn't much time at all, given they had no leads on where it would be taking place. The Witches had been moving locations frequently enough to evade the Necare for quite some time. The last lead they had was a townhouse, but that had long since been abandoned.

"James, look at me," Ace said softly, reaching out to touch his chin gently and turn his face back to hers. Pink-tinged tears were freely flowing from his eyes, his shivers and shakes becoming more pronounced. "Did they tell you what they're summoning?" He shook his head. "Did you *hear* what they are summoning?" His body became wracked with convulsions for a moment, his sobs turning into desperate painful gasps of air.

"Sh-shadow demon," he managed to choke out.

"What's happening to him?" Lucef whispered. It had been a matter of seconds, and his lips were turning blue, the veins in his face and neck becoming more prominent against his skin, which was mottled and looking more like a corpse than a living man.

"Took poison ... their magic ... it wouldn't l-let me die unt—"

"Until your task was complete," Lucef murmured, watching in sadness as James nodded, his limbs going rigid, foam spewing from his lips with every harsh exhale.

"Do you know where the Witches are? Did they take you somewhere?" Ace asked, feeling his fluttering pulse as his body tried desperately to fight the effects of the poison coursing through him.

"Tomb," he said, sputtering blood on Ace's face as he coughed the word out.

"A tomb," Ace whispered, her mind immediately trying to think of all the places they could be. There were so many places in London that held tombs. A city as ancient as London housed more dead than living.

"P-please!" he managed to choke out one last time, his fists tightening as he grasped the front of Ace's shirt, forcing her eyes back on his face. She looked down at him, pity playing over her features as she watched his mouth fill with foam and blood. All that could come from his lips was the horrific sound of choked gurgles.

"Your family will come to no harm, James. The Martins are safe," Ace assured him quietly, pressing her cold hand upon his burning forehead. Relief and comfort flashed in his eyes as he stared up into Ace's face before his body gave one last, great shudder, going still a moment later.

CHAPTER 17

The moment Ace had left the mansion with Lucef behind her, Nero turned to where Srinta had been a moment earlier, but she wasn't there.

"Octavian, go to the Necare. Have Makiut get a team ready and scour any intel we have on where the Witches may be located currently," Nero said, jumping down the remaining stairs and moving swiftly toward the only place he thought Srinta would go to hide. He didn't hear a protest from Octavian or any further questions, so he felt assured his son was doing what he was told.

Nero may no longer have used the pull between him and Srinta, their bond as sire and progeny having long been outweighed by the one he had with Ace, but he could still feel her as he stepped into the lower level, as if his feet were attuned to follow where hers had touched. It was no surprise when he rounded a corner and saw her exactly where he thought she'd be; however, her state *was* quite a sight.

Hair a mess, still thin from her lack of taking in any blood, and eyes wild as she tried desperately to pull open the doors to Ramses' chambers, which were staying firmly closed.

"Srinta," Nero said loudly, his voice echoing off the stone walls, making her flinch.

"I need to speak to him," she hissed, glaring over her shoulder at him.

"You need to explain yourself. You know something."

Those shoulders tensed further, her fingers tightening on the handles of the door.

"I-I don't know what to do, Nero," she finally whispered after several long moments of silence.

"I have read every page in both Books. There is no prophecy that speaks of summoning something, which could only be a demon. You spoke earlier as if you already knew *who* was coming."

"No!" she protested, though the words came out weak.

"'He will come and kill us all.' That's what you said, isn't it?" he demanded, having moved closer as he spoke.

"You're an old Vampire, Nero, but you haven't seen what I have seen. You don't have the memories of so many years bearing down. Things get lost until it is too late." Her shoulders sagged, fingers slipping off the handles to hang at her sides. "I should have seen the signs earlier. I should have known what was coming for years, and yet I didn't see it until Ramses' silence made my mind wander," she whispered, looking up but past him, as if she was no longer standing in the corridor with him but in the past, seeing things she once did.

"What signs? If there were signs of what was to come, shouldn't they have been recorded?" Nero asked, temper flaring once again.

"It was recorded, just not in either of the Books we possess. That prophecy is held in The Witches' Book."

Ace and Lucef raced back through the city after stopping at a Vampire nest nearby to safely tuck James' body away. They didn't need human authorities discovering him and trying to determine what had happened to him. James was wealthy, a Martin, and, therefore, it could raise too much attention their way if other humans began asking questions. Don, the leader of the nest, had been gracious enough to agree to stow him there until they could retrieve him. Don didn't like to get involved with the war, preferring to have the run of his nest and his club, The Gast, where the war was put on pause within its four walls. But he was still a Vampire and seeing Ace at his back door, holding the horrendous corpse of a young man that was unmistakably a Martin, left him with little choice but to help her.

"I'll be in touch when things have ... calmed," Ace told him, turning without any additional platitudes to join Lucef near the street.

"What's going on?" Don asked, his voice quiet as not to alert the neighbors.

"You don't want to know. If I haven't reached out to you in a week, take his body to the Facility, to his family." Then she and Lucef seemingly disappeared in the night.

Now they were heading back to Kurome. There were very few things they could do at that moment. The box was gone, in the Witches' hands; they had only the word "tomb" to indicate where their enemies were located; and a timeframe of "tonight or tomorrow" gave them very little time to discover what they needed to prevent from happening. She hoped Nero had started getting the Necare ready. They would spend the remainder of the night searching the city until they found where the Witches were residing. They had no other choice.

And what was so significant about this night or the next?

Ace looked up toward the sky. There was cloud cover, as there usually was, but even with that, Ace could tell exactly what moon phase was approaching in the inky sky beyond the clouds.

A new moon.

"I'll go with the Necare," Lucef said, as they climbed effortlessly over the vined walls surrounding Kurome.

"No. You'll stay with Octavian. You aren't a Vampire, and you don't want to be part of this. I understand it. The only thing I ask of you is to keep him safe," Ace said, just as she opened the main doors, finding the parlor completely empty.

Ace went to charge through the mansion, but Lucef's hand wrapped around her arm halting her.

"I was made this way for a reason, Ace. There was a prophecy about me becoming ... *this*," he said, gesturing at himself, as if his outward appearance held insight into what he had become during the Ritual. "I shouldn't have stayed out of this as long as I have."

The fire in his eyes as he spoke was something Ace hadn't seen there since before the ritual took place. He was going to step into this war, and not only that, but he was also doing so on the Vampires' side. On Ace's side.

She thought about thanking him, praising him, telling him he had become family, despite their differences, but before she could, she felt Nero's anger surging, flashes of Srinta's face and the antiquities room swimming through her mind.

"Come," was all Ace said, before moving through the mansion and down to where she knew both of them would be.

As she and Lucef approached the antiquities room, she was greeted with a strange sight. The ancient Books lay on the floor, Srinta pressed against the wall with Ramses' staff digging into her back, and Nero's hand around her throat.

"What is this?" Ace asked, standing just inside the room, her bladed nails already extending as if there was an impending battle.

"Tell her what you told me!" Nero screamed, squeezing at Srinta's neck before releasing her and letting her slump to the floor.

"Thousands of years of memories, Nero. It took me time to remember," Srinta protested, not looking up at him.

"I don't want to hear the excuses! Just tell her!" he hissed.

"Tell me what?" Ace asked, her eyes snapping between them, finally settling on Srinta as she moved to stand.

"Before the war, when Immortals were less foes, a demon was made. I do not know why Lucifer made this creature, nor why he was unleashed upon the world, but he brought unprejudiced death everywhere he went with no regard for maintaining the balance we had in place."

"Narthadis," Nero said, snatching one of the Books off the floor and flipping through the pages until it fell on the page Octavian had come across previously. The Shadow Demon. The description had been vague, the story of his banishment even more so, almost flippant like it didn't matter. The other Book held no information about it.

"We came together, the leaders of the sects. All of us having lost many of our ranks and all of us facing not only extinction of ours, but of the mortals as well. The Sparrow was leading the Witches at the time. She came up with a plan, one in which we all had to work together, but if we succeeded, we would trap Narthadis in a broken state. Two parts of him separated between planes, unable to move at will as he once did, unable to tear the world to pieces," Srinta said, a shake in her voice as she reached out to the shelf the black box once resided on, touching it softly.

"And you succeeded?" Ace asked.

"We did, but almost immediately after, The Sparrow had a vision."

A chill came over them all, the room suddenly feeling darker and more sinister.

"Out with it," Nero snapped.

"Three things would come to pass. Three things that would signal his return to this domain. A creature that possessed all the abilities of the Immortals would be created. A child born of two Vampires would come to be. And the silence of an Ancient one for a decennial era would be broken."

"And what happens once these things occur?" Ace asked, since Nero was silently vibrating with rage.

"The creature would be made whole once more. A Witch gone mad would bring him forth, and he would once again be free to move through the shadows, feasting on the death and fear of his victims without ceremony as he once did," Srinta said, turning finally to look at the three of them who stood there, taking in her words.

"You thought killing our son would fix this? Would make this demon's summoning somehow not come to pass, Srinta?" Nero asked, after several long moments of silence. His anger was now far more justified to Ace once those words echoed through the room.

"I-I wasn't sure ... I didn't even recall the prophecy until Ramses' silence became too much for me to take any longer."

"What was it that made you recall the prophecy?" Ace asked, moving so she was between Nero and Srinta, having seen the tension in his body ramp up with her non-response.

"It was Ramses," Srinta whispered, looking down as if ashamed. Nero's chest swelled as he took in a menacing breath, but Ace placed her hand there, shaking her head and looking into his glowing eyes.

"We don't have time for this," Ace said, glancing back at Lucef who stood in the doorway, hands clenched to fists. "The Necare need to be out searching for the tomb."

When Ace, Nero, and Lucef reemerged into the main hall, the Necare were already moving toward the parlor, gathering to start their search. It was the early hours of the evening now, so there would be less human traffic. Therefore, this would be better for them to go out on foot in search of the Witches than taking vehicles that would attract more attention. Makiut stood at the front doors, looking out at the crowd of Necare who was gathering there, when he spotted Ace at the back of the room. Octavian stood just beside him, still looking slightly strange in his father's clothes, but his face was full of determination as he looked out at all their warriors.

"Ace," Makiut said, bringing attention to her as she moved through them.

"I'll tell you what we know now, which is still not enough," Ace said, letting those words quiet the Vampires from their side conversations so the room fell deathly silent. "The Witches have gained the final piece they need to summon a demon. The timeframe we were given was tonight or tomorrow. The only clue we have to where they are staying is that it is a tomb. Until dawn breaks over the sky, we will be hunting through every cemetery and graveyard. Find them." Her final words came out as a growl, and the Necare broke into their duos, moving seamlessly out the doors and into the night.

Makiut stayed behind for a moment beside Ace, waiting until the lingering Necare was gone.

"You need to stay here," he said as she moved to follow behind them.

"I am going out with them. I'll not abandon my Necare right now," she protested.

"You are needed here, to monitor our progress, to prepare for whatever is coming next," he said, the look on his face daring her to argue with him.

"My place is by their side," she hissed.

"Your place is leading us to victory, Ace. It always has been," Makiut said, pulling a facemask out of his jacket.

"Why are you bringing that?" Ace asked, furrowing her brow at her old partner as he placed it over his face.

"I won't stop even once the sun rises," he said, slipping his gloves over his hands as well, before disappearing out the door and into the darkness.

Chapter 18

Octavian stood in the guest wing of the mansion, though calling it that was rather laughable, considering there was little that was friendly or welcoming about these rooms. But then again, the visitors that Kurome often housed were other Vampires from visiting covens, not Chenjas.

Nero had gone with Lucef and several House Vampires to keep watch over the comms and the CCTV footage for Ace, so she could clean the remnants of James Martin from her skin, leaving Octavian to his own devices. In normal circumstances this may have been fine, but Octavian, though quiet throughout the events that had unfolded, was internally raging. The Necare were out searching desperately for the Witches, since the Chenja in their midst betrayed them all, Srinta had kept secrets from them, and there was an impending attack they were unprepared for.

What had really struck Octavian was Srinta's reaction. When a Vampire who had lived longer than recorded human history was saying things like, "He'll kill us all," it was clear that whatever this Chenja set in motion was not something to underestimate.

Octavian was also under no illusion that suddenly he would be allowed to be part of any fight now that he had grown. No, he would be kept separate from any fight that would happen. His parents would never allow him to be part of this, not at least until he was properly trained. But this ... this he could do.

He approached the only door in the hall that had light pouring out from beneath it. The Blue Room. Though it was beautifully decorated, the magic stones fastened into the door really were a ward, holding the ghost of a very powerful Oracle, a woman born between a Witch and a human. Oracles had limited powers, if any at all, and most were prone to madness, but none were like Helem.

In life, Helem had been feared by the people in her village, not only being thought mad, but making anyone who dared cross her mad as well. The Witches wanted nothing to do with her, despising their own half-breeds if they were anything other than perfect. The story Octavian had been told about Helem was that it was Dava, oddly enough, who had taken the Oracle in. Her blood had been delicious and her unusual skills helpful to the House Vampires in the days when they were tasked with luring prey to the mansion.

As Helem aged and ailed, it was she who created the ward, trapping her own soul within the room that they had fittingly called the Blue Room. She knew better than to use her gifts on anyone the Vampires didn't expressly tell her was an enemy. Placing Chiyo in this room had been strategic on William's part, and Octavian was ever so grateful for that now as he silently stepped closer to the door.

Raising his hand, he gently touched the stones in the pattern Makiut had once shown him, thankful for his perfect recall. There was no outward indication that anything had changed until the blue stones shimmered lightly, as if the light had changed within the hallway.

"Little Vampire, what is it I shall do to the girl in my room?" came a whispered voice, the cadence of the words slightly strange, but Octavian supposed it could have been a product of the time she lived, or perhaps the fact that she wasn't completely sane when she was alive. He could almost feel cool breath against his face, as if she were standing right before him.

"Do your worst, Helem," he whispered back, just before a low chuckle sounded, and the soft sound of Chiyo's pacing steps within the room stopped.

Meanwhile, Chiyo stood in the center of the beautiful Blue Room, her fingers wringing nervously. She had been left there for hours after her encounter with Lucef, her mind reeling from the revelation and revival of her devastation that her brother, Codi, was once again dead and had been dead the whole time. The minutes ticked on, quite literally ticking in the ornate silver clock that sat beside the fourposter bed.

What would happen to her now?

She was far from the protection of her mother, unsure of how true this new alliance with the Witches was, and trapped in Kurome Mansion, surrounded by Vampires who now knew she had betrayed them.

She shouldn't have done this.

Shouldn't have come here in the first place.

How had The Raven managed to convince Kagami to send her here alone so far away to betray their longest-held allies?

Perhaps it was sorcery of some kind. Magic from the Witches tricking Kagami into doing their will, but Chiyo knew this was impossible. No matter how much she wished it were the case, no creature, Vampire or otherwise, could influence a Chenja's mind that way.

Chiyo paced the room, her footsteps making a specific creak each time she passed a certain part of the floor. That and the continuous tick of the clock started to make her feel almost meditative. It was only when these quiet sounds were accompanied by a whisper that she paused her pacing. The whisper sounded like it came from within the room, even close enough to have been beside her.

She hadn't been anticipating another voice or sound, so she didn't quite catch what it said, but she remained still, eyes searching the room for the cause. Perhaps it was a radio? The cellphone in her bag? She went to retrieve the phone, but as she stepped toward her discarded bag, she felt a chill run through her.

Frozen in place, she looked around. She couldn't see anything with human eyes, so she immediately shifted, changing her eyes to that of a dog. The strange eyes jutted slightly from her still human-shaped sockets but allowed her to see with different vision. The muted colors gave her the ability to see beyond the surface. Vibrations, magic, and currents in the air were observable now, and with that, she could see a hazy figure standing in the spot on the floor that had creaked when she walked past it. It was standing exactly where she had stopped a moment prior.

"What is this?" Chiyo asked aloud, her eyes never straying from the figure, though it was hard to keep focus on it. But all she could hear was harsh, whispered voices, too low for her to make out. The figure disappeared from where they stood just a few steps from her, but in the corner, she saw another hunched figure. It was shaking, huddled there as if it were scared, though for what reason, she didn't know. Its appearance frightened her of course, but its features were too ambiguous, almost like it was smudged, and no solid features could be made out.

"Who are you?" Chiyo asked, her voice hushed with fear, as she gripped the phone in her hands. The figure stopped its shaking, limbs going still for a long, drawn moment before it slowly moved to stand. The motion was beautifully and frighteningly fluid.

"Chiyo," the whispers in the room suddenly said, sending a renewed jolt of terror through her body. The figure stepped closer, her name being whispered over and over the closer it came. It was with the smooth movements, the line of the figure's body, that Chiyo realized who it was she was supposed to be looking at.

"You're dead," she whispered harshly, the features of her brother's face coming more into focus with each step.

She continued backing away, eyes trained on the face that was becoming Codi's with each passing moment. Did Lucef come back here to torture her? How was he able to do this? How was he creating the taunting whispers that were now becoming clearer, spewing horrible things into her ears as she watched her dead brother materialize before her very eyes.

"It's all your fault, Chiyo. If you had been better."

"If you had been braver."

"If you hadn't listened."

"If you went with him."

"You let me die."

"You're a monster."

"You're nothing."

"He's dead because of you."

Images began flashing through her mind. Visions of her letting Codi leave. Visions from when they were young. Visions of their mother, Kagami, forcing him out into the world and holding her close. Visions of his death, the ritual that pulled his very soul and essence from him, leaving nothing but the very base of his mercurial form, like a puddle against the stone slab he had lain upon.

"No!" she screamed, grabbing either side of her head as if that would somehow relieve the pressure of the heartache she was feeling.

It didn't matter though; the images came with more frequency, countless deaths, blood, gore, and everyone and everything she had ever cared for dying and flashing through her mind as she stumbled back further, finding herself pressed into the wall of the bathroom with the eerie, unreal image of her brother pursuing her each step of the way.

CHAPTER 19

Ace reluctantly left everyone where they were, going instead to clean herself of James's blood that had splattered across her face and chest. She wasn't sure what to do following that. Part of her planned to go listen in on the comms with Nero, but she knew it would only tempt her to leave the mansion and join the search. Instead, she moved down to the depths of the mansion, planning to look at the few pieces of information that were listed about this Shadow Demon in the Books.

She slowed as she moved down the corridor, her eyes inadvertently traveling to the ornate door of Ramses' chamber. The doors were firmly closed. The last time she had been in that room alone had been when she sought his counsel on her pregnancy. And then the disastrous encounter with Srinta. Part of her wanted to enter the room, to talk to Ramses now that he was once again awake, to seek his guidance. They knew so little about the threat they were about to face, had no true way of preventing it, and she wasn't sure how she was going to protect those who were hers.

But what could Ramses tell her? He wasn't a god. He was a Vampire, just as she was. The first, the most powerful, yes, but still merely a Vampire. With a shake of her head, she turned to go to the antiquities room, but before she could get too far down the hall, a whisper echoed off the stone walls.

"Ace."

She stopped, turning around to look around the corridor. It was empty.

There were ghosts in this mansion, she knew that. Many things had died within these walls over the years, some souls trapped here, but this was not one of the places they frequented. Nor was this a voice of any of the ghosts who knew Ace's name.

"Ace." Neither was it the voice of any of the Vampires who should have still been in the mansion, and at a time like this, no one would dare play games like this with her, not with a threat so imminent.

"Come here," the voice said this time, and with the command she recognized it, her eyes widening in surprise.

The doors to Ramses' room opened, just as they had days before when Nero had been pinning Srinta against them. Ace stayed where she stood for a moment, staring at the open doorway and feeling uncertain. This had been quite a strange night; the dawn would be coming soon, if the quiet of the mansion was any indication. She didn't want to be away from Octavian and Nero any longer than she needed to be. Ace didn't want to miss the moment Makiut and the other Necare located where the Witches were.

"Come now, Ace," Ramses' whisper persisted.

She moved slowly, at a human's pace, to the doors, pausing for a brief moment at the entrance before stepping past the threshold. The doors closed sharply behind her, the darkness of the room enveloping her. This room was always dark; only one flame ever illuminated the space, just enough to enhance the movement of the wall that Ramses inhabited. Ace watched the ripples in the wall for a moment, waiting.

"Ace, I know you have questions. There's a lot of unknowns," Ramses' voice said, seeming to come from every direction within the room.

"Which is why I'd like to get back to work," she said, trying to keep the mild annoyance from her voice. She felt like the clock was ticking. Ten years had passed, with little to do but decimate their enemies, and now they had a countdown to their own doom, a battle that they had no way to prepare for because so much was still left in the shadows.

"Always so focused. It is part of what makes you so formidable," Ramses said, a hint of humor coming through. "You are special, Ace. Different. You know that, do you not?" he asked.

On some level, Ace had known she was not like others. She had abilities no other Vampire had ever possessed until she changed her progeny, Six. The fire she could wield seemed to warm under her skin at the very thought of it. Had she known she was truly different, though? She had worked hard, just like every Necare before and after her. She had fought, been injured, suffered, just as the rest of them. She hadn't wanted special treatment, despite who her sire was, and she worked to prove her place for centuries until she was leading them all.

"I am no different than any other," she said, even though she knew that wasn't fully true.

"Oh, no, Ace, you are different. You have fire at your fingertips; you can move things without touching them; and you have a strength within you that is unprecedented. Do you know why?" Ramses asked. Ace shook her head. She had no idea why she, and no other than Six, had these abilities.

"Come closer," Ramses said, the wall shifting so a face started to appear, instead of the intense swirling and pulsing it had been doing previously. Ace did as she was told, stepping closer so she and Ramses were face to face, only a small distance between them, so small she could nearly reach out and touch him. His features were sharp, a long narrow face, prominent nose, and square jaw. She had seen this face many times in portraits and sculptures, and here again it was before her. "Your human parents ... what do you remember about them?"

Memories flooded her mind. Her parents doing their chores, working on their farm. She and Alexander, sitting by the fire after supper while the younger ones played and their mother sang quietly. Her father's face as he smiled at her, as if she were the most precious thing in the world to him.

"They were just people. Regular humans," Ace said, confused by his line of questioning.

"Your father was, but your mother was a little more," Ramses said, the face he had generated in the wall smirking ever so slightly.

"More?"

"She had descended from a line of women who were the mistake of the Sparrow. Do you know who that was?"

"The Witch Queen before The Raven," Ace whispered, letting her brows pull together.

"Yes. Sparrow had taken many human lovers. She wanted her magic blood to be prominent, and the male Witches at the time were all impotent. Her daughter, Graciella, though a powerful Oracle, ran away. She was never found and presumed to be dead, but in reality, she had simply moved on, made her way in the world as a human, and avoided detection from the others until she ultimately died from a fever she refused to treat with magic.

"But her children lived on. Each generation holding less and less power, but that magic remained there, in the blood. Dormant ... until you."

"How do you know this?"

"Do you remember coming to me the first time?"

Of course, she remembered. How could she possibly forget? She went to him, offering her blood for guidance. She wanted to be a Necare. She wanted to avenge her family's death, and though Ramses hadn't provided words, necessarily, she came away from that with a renewed sense of purpose and determination.

"Yes."

"And do you remember offering your blood?"

She had. With a blade, she had slashed her palm, laying it against the wall and watching as it absorbed the crimson fluid, leaving nothing behind before her wound closed up.

"Blood holds memories. Not just your memories, Ace, but memories of all who came before. I knew Graciella. I had met her long ago, and *that* blood in your veins stems from her line."

Ace wanted no more revelations. Too much was already happening, and she had no idea what her next move should be. Now, Ramses was putting even more on her mind to consider, and she simply had nothing left to give to this.

"Why are you telling me this?" she asked, her voice coming out as weary as she felt.

"Because what is coming will require my help, but I am bound to this form for now, unable to join in any battles unless it were to happen in this room."

"What does that have to do with me?" she asked, toeing the line between suspicion and curiosity.

Suddenly, a pair of golden bangles seemed to melt from the wall. They hovered beside Ramses' head, just barely touching the wall to keep them from falling to the ground.

"Only someone with Witch blood can wield these. They are needed for what is to come."

Ace reached out, plucking the bangles from the wall and held them in her hand. They would be fairly plain, if it weren't for the intricate pieces on each end. The pieces looked delicate, with elaborate edges, but she realized the two bangles could fit together, like a puzzle, interlocking.

"And what is to come?"

"I do not fully know, but I *feel* that I might be needed, and only you can make that happen," Ramses said. Ace wasn't sure what these things were or what she was supposed to do with them, but anything to help them with the impending doom she felt hovering over their heads, she would gladly take.

She slipped the bangles on her wrists, marveling at the way they seemed to re-size to rest snugly against her skin, before looking up into Ramses' face once more.

"You will know what to do when the time is right. Your instincts have yet to steer you wrong," Ramses said, another small smile gracing the lips of the face on the wall, before it dissolved back to the swirling stormy surface it had been.

Alexander paced in his room, bourbon untouched, as his mind raced. It had been days since he had met with Ace, but there was something off within the den. Werewolves had been coming and going in ways that were not dictated by his orders. Kyle had been strangely absent from this part of the den, and even Melissa was no longer pestering him, not since their encounter when he returned from the church.

All this and the fact that he had no additional information about what was going on between the Witches and the Vampires made him uneasy. Something within him knew that summoning was going to be coming to fruition soon, and he wasn't sure that anything he had offered Ace had been enough to keep that plan from moving forth.

He slowed his steps, moving toward the decanter of bourbon, thinking perhaps a drink may settle him enough, when he spotted an envelope sitting near the hearth. It was partially charred, but not burned completely, the black paper and blood wax seal still displayed there. The Raven sent a letter, but that was clearly not one she had sent him. No, all those letters he had watched burn himself, making sure they were reduced to ashes before he turned his back on it.

So, who, then, had this been sent to?

He stooped, pulling the envelope from the ashes, feeling the slight burn of the residual magic there, telling him that he was correct, and this letter had not been intended for him at all.

"I thought I'd find you here, drinking instead of leading. Very typical of you, Alexander," came Melissa's voice from behind him. He had heard her approaching but was unconcerned. He had planned to seek her or her brother out, especially now that he had discovered this interesting letter.

"Typical, yes. I see now why Lukis struggled so long with his mental health. It takes quite a toll on someone to lead our kind," Alexander said, standing and turning the envelope over, letting his eyes rest on the name at the top. Kyle.

"Weak, both of you; that's why neither of you should have been leading us at all. Lukis went mad, but he was always going to. You are just incapable of being a true leader. Simpering off alone for most of your years while Kyle did all the hard work. Why, Deca thought you—"

"It matters so little now why Deca would have chosen me, Melissa, wouldn't you say? Especially now that I see I've been betrayed," Alexander said, turning to face her, holding out the remnants of the letter for her to take in. Her smug smile slipped from her lips, eyes widening as she saw the page there between his fingers.

"Alexan—"

"It really doesn't matter. I have no interest in this any longer."

"No interest?" came Kyle's voice, him having rushed down the hall just a moment before, his large frame taking up the doorway behind his sister. "You have no *interest* in your own kind? No *interest* in leading us when that has been your duty for these last ten years?" Kyle was practically vibrating with rage as the words spit from his lips.

"I have been loyal to the Werewolves for centuries, Kyle. Centuries of working for Lukis, being his blade in the shadows, his unseen force that did all the dirty but necessary things to keep us from losing this war. I did it because despite the fact that Werewolves were the very reason I lost everything and everyone I held dear, I was convinced that I had to. I had become the very monster I hated. I thought I had to protect my new family."

"Of course you should be protecting us!" Melissa hissed, stepping forward, eyes shining with anger.

"Of course?"

"Yes! Humans are weak, Alexander. Your family died, but you became powerful. Immortal. Why would you ever blame us when we set you free?" Her words were like a shot of electricity going through his body. The callousness of throwing away the love of his human family, so shocking to him, filled him with rage. At least they had each other; they were not torn from their whole family when they were changed. He had spent hundreds of years thinking his entire family had died in that brutal attack.

"You know nothing of them. I should have never allowed this to go on as long as I did," Alexander practically growled, crumbling the letter in his fist as he glared across the room at the siblings.

"No, I should never have allowed it," Kyle said, stepping further into the room. "I've taken steps, Alexander. You are no longer going to lead us. It has been pathetic, and I won't watch it continue."

"I suppose that's why The Raven wrote you, to tell you of the summoning happening tonight? She wishes you to do something for her, Kyle?" Alexander asked, throwing the now crumbled letter toward his former second in command, watching as it hit his chest.

Silence stretched for a beat or two, the two men staring at each other as Melissa fumed between them.

"I have only one task to do tonight. The summoning must happen on the new moon and is to have no interruptions. And after this, we are back to our alliance with the Witches. We are too weak right now to turn down answers to our problems. She is offering to kill the Elders for us, why would you have refused that?" Kyle asked.

Alexander didn't need to respond to that question, because neither of them truly wanted the answer. Kyle's task was quickly revealed when Melissa seemed to burst from where she stood between the two men, lunging with extended claws toward Alexander, her face contorting with the promise of a change before she tackled him to the floor.

Her claws were everywhere, tearing and piercing through his skin repeatedly before he could grab her wrists, breaking them quickly and tossing her across the room as she screamed from the pain. Kyle lunged a moment later, but Alexander was too quick, moving before Kyle got to him and easily rolling to his feet. He took less than a moment to look over at the two of them: Melissa still recovering, her wrists healing slowly as the rest of her began to change into her wolf form; Kyle turning once again to face Alexander, who was now at the door.

Alexander opened his mouth, thinking to continue arguing, but he knew it was useless. No one within this den was truly a friend or his family. He owed them all nothing, not even another word. Without pause, he turned to the door, easily moving through the tunnels and out through the little side entrance that was no longer secret, making his escape from the underground tunnels that had once been a safe haven, but now felt more like a prison.

That was not, nor was it ever, his home. He would not return. He would not lead. He was finished. He may have been one of them, technically, but he didn't want to be. Kyle and Melissa had just made it so simple for him to make the choice with finality. He would protect Ace at all costs.

Chapter 20

Ace came to the parlor, phone in her hand. She had no idea how long she had been in the room with Ramses, but she knew she was far behind getting an update on the Necare. Some teams had come back, several of them awake despite the sun having risen hours prior. Makiut was still gone with Lotte and their team, doing just as they said they would, searching despite the sun having risen. The idea that the day had already nearly turned to night surprised Ace. How long had she been in the depths of the mansion with Ramses?

Nero left the control room to William when he rose just as the afternoon turned to evening, who was doing well and proving himself to be taking his Necare training seriously. The whole mansion seemed to be vibrating with tension; even Fredric and Georgith had come from their chambers to the parlor, Ace noticed, the two Elders looking almost out of place as they stood near the stairs' banister, whispering to themselves about their own speculations.

Ace could feel the telltale final burst of the sun's rays as it dipped below the horizon. If they were to look out the drawn curtains at that moment, she was certain she would see a blood-red sky. The energy in the room shifted as each Vampire felt the same, eyes glowing briefly as they felt the night, their time, descend upon them.

Ace's phone rang from her hand, and everyone within the room seemed to pause, looking at her as she answered it.

"Makiut. Tell me," Ace said, not bothering with a greeting.

"We waited when we saw the signs of life at this mausoleum. Smelled of magic too. But now it's confirmed. I saw Witches heading inside just a few minutes ago, and the air already is permeating with whatever spell they're casting," he said quietly, his voice so low and hushed that only those very close to Ace could hear his words.

"Which mausoleum?" Ace asked, glancing at the Necare that were eagerly awaiting instruction near the door. Nyprat's fingers flexed over the gun at her hip repeatedly. She hadn't liked being separated from Lotte during this excursion and was eager to get to killing Witches with her partner.

"The one on—"

Makiut's sentence was cut off by a loud screeching sound. It was a cross between a high-pitched bird squawk and a horrendous spine-tingling scream.

"Makiut?" Ace hissed, her grip tightening on the phone in her grasp.

"Ace, i-it's—" The screeching rang out again, then the distinct sound of a blade being drawn rang out. "Lotte!" Makiut screamed just as the mangled cry of Lotte came through the phone, followed by gunfire and an eerie humming chant. The line went dead in Ace's hand, and Ace looked up at the Necare who were gathered by the door, all of them tensed and ready to run out and into the night to help their fellow soldiers, Nyprat's eyes glowing with fear and rage at the sound she heard ripped from Lotte's mouth.

"What do we do?" Nyprat asked, her voice slightly choked as she tried to remain in control after what they heard.

Ace looked around at all the faces surrounding her. Everyone was there, every Vampire, no matter their rank, age, or status who lived within Kurome was in the room, save for William, and all their eyes were on her. Nero and Octavian stood close by her, having moved to her once the phone call cut off. Srinta stood against a wall not far, but her eyes were also on Ace.

Ace was their leader. Their general. She was the one they all looked to for guidance. She had been running this war, leading them all to where they were now. Whatever victories they had won had been because of the decisions she had made, both as Head Necare and now as that of an Elder. Even the other Elders were deferring to her, and she wasn't sure what to do.

They didn't have the location, and though Makiut's phone could possibly be tracked, they didn't have time for that, not before whatever battle those Necare were fighting was already complete. The only thing the Vampires in that room could do was wait. Wait and hope that Makiut and his team would win.

"We—"

But before Ace could get out another word, an odd humming seemed to slowly build. The few lights that illuminated the parlor dimmed and flickered as the scent of ozone and magic breached their noses.

Ace's eyes started to glow, her head whipping to look down at Octavian, who had just reached over to grasp her hand. He may have grown to be taller than her nearly overnight, but that didn't mean he wasn't still a child nor that he wasn't her son. The comfort of his hand in hers could only last a moment, though. He couldn't be there for whatever was about to occur.

She scanned the room, her gaze finally landing on Minshin, who stood near the doors to the hall. She was ready to do what she needed to do, Ace could tell by her stance, but the brilliant Medicus was no warrior. They would need her if any of them were to survive this.

"Minshin, take Octavian," Ace said suddenly, reaching out their clasped hands to transfer him to her. Minshin immediately came to their side with a nod, reaching out for him.

"No! Let me stay and help!" Octavian demanded, tearing his arm out of Minshin's grasp as she took hold. He already knew it was futile. His parents would never let him if they could help it, but the idea of leaving them in this room, perhaps to die, was unbearable. They were everything to him. Nothing else in this world made any sense if Ace and Nero weren't in it.

"If we survive this battle, Octavian, I will personally train you to fight in all other battles to come, but this one you will hide with Minshin," Ace said, her voice firm and so strangely even that the whole room took it in, as if her calmness was catching.

You cannot die. I love you too much.

The words echoed in his mind. His mother's voice there, but no spoken words aloud. Whatever was to come, it was going to be catastrophic. He could see the fear she only ever showed to his father in her eyes.

"I don't want to leave you," Octavian murmured as he continued to stare at his mother, their silver eyes mirroring each other.

"And I can't live in a world where you don't exist. It's our job to protect you," Ace said as Nero's hand wrapped around her waist, his eyes glowing blue with anticipated battle as he watched Minshin dragging Octavian back through the doors.

"Stay hidden. Stay safe," Nero said, just before they disappeared down the hall, the humming growing more intense with each passing second.

The magic started to increase, the lights flickering, and a murmur began joining the vibrations in the air.

"Anyone unprepared to die for our kind, leave now," Ace said, as darkness seemed to be taking over the room. A few House Vampires seemed to shiver, moving closer toward the stairs, as if they were ready to dash to their chambers at a moment's notice. All lights slowly went darker until there was nothing left to illuminate the space but the small sliver of light from the stars cascading through the singular curtain, which had been drawn by Melody. She was peering out as if Makiut's team would be strolling from the shadows any moment.

"Dava, get the curtains," Nero said, just as the room plunged into total chaos.

The darkest corner of the room, where the shadows were deepest, even to a Vampire's eyes, seemed to expand, then a chorus of low melodic chanting filled the room. The Witches' voices resonated throughout the room, and yet the shadow in that corner persisted, as if nothing was there but a black void of space. All the Necare stood still, eyes glowing and bodies on alert, as they waited to see what was going to happen.

Lucef stepped forward, having been hanging back toward the hall, watching and waiting. Now, he stood at Ace's right, while Nero stood firmly on her left, the three of them the nearest to the growing shadows.

"A portal," Lucef growled quietly, his own magic seeming to be pulsing along his skin with anticipation.

As soon as he said it, Ace could suddenly see everything. There in the dark corner sat a strange circle shimmering ever so slightly in the air. Beyond that was somewhere completely different. Rough stone walls circled a candlelit room, a summoning circle with the obsidian box and a book at the center. Witches were there, bare feet exposed and covered in what Ace could only imagine was sacrificial blood that was also covering the ground, splattered, and used to draw ancient symbols. The Raven stood over the box, her body shaking as her arms moved in frighteningly beautiful patterns that matched the rhythm of the chants. Her body was naked, painted in the blood that Ace assumed was used on the floor, her hair down and wild, like a dark flame surrounding her head.

Everyone was still for a moment, taking in the scene on the other side, before Ace made a move to head into the portal, but there was no need. Witches, dozens of them, were flooding into Kurome from the opening in space, stepping through, their bloodied feet sullying the floors of the mansion. The magic sizzled in the air along with their chants.

It didn't take a moment for the Necare to move in for an attack, Vampires descending on the Witches like a wave, but they were prepared. Defensive spells were being kept up by Witches toward the back of the emerging group. Attacking Necare were immediately repelled, flying back when they hit the strong protection, doing nothing to the Witches at the front. Georgith hissed loudly as he was thrown so far, his body shattered part of the stone banister on the stairs. The scent of his blood hit the air. The spell had been strong enough to not only throw him back, but the force of the blow against the banister had broken his skin.

As the Vampires continued trying to get past the shield, bursts of sun-like power began being hurtled into the chests of some of the repelled and slightly stunned first attackers. The effect was instantaneous. Those on the front lines burned. The burst would hit them in the chest, tearing through the flesh there and spreading through their bodies. There was no way for them to fight it, no way for them to be saved once it hit them. The scent of scorched Vampire filled the room as their screams broke through the now overwhelming sound of the Witches' spells.

Ace grabbed for the gun at her hip, aiming toward the Witch who was sending fiery blasts toward not just the Necare but the huddled House Vampires as well. When it became obvious even the Necare were not making headway on the invading Witches, they pulled back even further, untrained and unsure what to do. They had no way to fight against this sort of attack, and yet they stayed, Melony and Melody holding firmly to Dava, who was the only one to try and turn and flee toward the stairs.

Ace's bullet was also repelled by the protective magic, ricocheting off and into the knee of Nyprat. Her knee exploded, with blood, tissue, and bone raining out as she went to the ground. But Nyprat barely made a sound, her eyes filled with determination as she continued to try to shoot toward the ceiling over the Witches' heads.

Chunks of the beautifully molded plaster began raining from above and smashing down on their attackers, but none of the falling pieces seemed to hit the Witches, who were keeping their protective spell in place, though it did seem to slow the fiery attacks. Ace moved swiftly, pulling Nyprat behind a piece of furniture and barely dodging a flame that was hurtling their way. It hit a tapestry, which immediately burst into flames, spreading up the intricate wallpaper just behind it and filling the room with black smoke.

"Don't stop," Ace said, nodding toward the ceiling, gaining a grin from Nyprat, as Fredric and Georgith moved to put out the flames that were threatening to burn the entire mansion to the ground.

Ace moved swiftly back to where she had been, touching both Lucef and Nero's shoulders, before glancing toward the grand fireplace that sat not far from where the portal was. It was taller than any of the Witches in their huddle. She didn't need to say a word as both took no time to move there with her. Ace climbed up first, pushing her body from the mantle and gracefully landing amongst the Witches gathered. Though she could see the terror on their faces at her breach, their chant never wavered. Ace wasted no time, immediately going after the protectors, her blades lengthening from her fingers and taking purchase on one of the Witches' throats, her chanting being replaced by the sickening gurgling of her choking on her own blood.

Ace felt the shield weaken immediately with one down, her eyes shining with burning, silver satisfaction as Lucef and Nero joined her amidst their enemies. Lucef seemed to unleash himself, letting his beastly nature toward the surface. Blood lust shown in his eyes as he began tearing the women apart, his eyes a vibrant, glowing red so reminiscent of the way Six's eyes had looked when she hunted years ago that Ace nearly stopped to watch him.

His face had not changed other than his eye color, hands little more than long claws at the ends of his arms that were now caked crimson in Witch blood. Limbs were torn off and tossed aside, as well as large chunks of flesh.

Nero had procured an axe that had been mounted over the fireplace. With his strength and the dull ancient blade, he easily hacked away at the Witches. But no matter how many of them the trio took down, it seemed like more continued to flood out from the portal, crowding the small space they were in. They must have brought Witches from other covens to London; there was no other way the Necare would have missed how large this coven had gotten. They couldn't reproduce Witches as easily as Vampires and Werewolves. Witches had to be born.

The Raven was still in the center of the circle on the other side of the portal, concentration unbroken as she continued to move through the spell.

Fire and electricity sparked from the offensive Witches, cracking like lightning through the air as the shattered arch reached through the room, striking at the House Vampires behind the Necare who were still desperately trying to break through. Screams and yells of frustration were becoming almost as loud as the chanting, but despite how many of the Witches Ace, Nero, and Lucef took down, more were there to take their place, the protection going mostly unbroken.

The door to the mansion burst open suddenly as Ace tore out two more Witch throats. She spared a glance toward the now open doors to see not Makiut and the other Necare, but Alexander. His chest heaved, long hair mussed from running, and his silver eyes glowing on the precipice of his change. Ace couldn't fathom how or why he was there. Their greatest enemy and somehow still her brother had not only risked everything to warn her, but now he was here.

His presence seemed to startle some of the Witches at the front lines, their voices faltering, attacks dropping off as they watched his body begin to change. Skin tore, bones breaking and reshaping as fur seemed to grow through and over his flesh. A savage growl ripped from his throat before he moved quickly, still not completely through his transformation before he lunged toward the Witches at the front. He managed to grasp the foot of one who was now trying to aim her fiery spell toward Nyprat. Still hunched behind a smoldering lounge chair, Nyprat's gunfire didn't waiver, still raining pieces of ceiling from above the Witches.

But Alexander's presence made no difference. Ace, though making her best effort to push through and get to the portal, trying to get to The Raven before she could summon the creature they all feared, saw it as it began to happen. The candles in the room beyond the portal were snuffed out, leaving eerie whisps of smoke trailing upward. Everything was quiet and loud at the same time. A throbbing, almost like that of a heart, seemed to thrum in the air, and suddenly the lid of the obsidian box shattered, the sound less like stone breaking and more like the screams of a hundred voices.

Somehow between the Witches Ace still fought, the darkness, and the portal, her eyes locked with The Raven, who was now still, her strange but beautiful dance having stopped. A smile spread over her face before truer darkness like pitch seemed to pass over them all, accompanied by a gust of wind that held the sharp scent of brimstone and death.

Chapter 21

Silence overtook everything; even the Witches stopped chanting, the scent and feel of their magic dissipating with their voices quieting. Everyone seemed to pause, waiting as pure darkness seemed to pour forth from the box at The Raven's feet. Ace stood at the center of the now motionless, silent Witches, Nero and Lucef at her sides. Her fingers and blades dripped with magical blood; her body splattered with it like some gruesome piece of art.

"I am whole," came a voice that seemed to echo from every shadow.

"Summoned and free," The Raven said, her voice smug as she continued to look across the space between her and Ace.

"And why, Witch, have you done this? Do you not know it was your kind who tore me apart and trapped me before?" the voice said again, ending in a sinister growl as a large black claw grasped at her pale throat.

"I have summoned you to destroy the rest. Those who cast you out before, if you would spare me and mine," she said, trying to keep her voice firm, but failing as the clawed fingers squeezed against her throat.

The Raven meant to have them all wiped out. She wanted the only Immortals roaming this plane to be her own. If only Kagami could bear witness to this. Would she see the error she made in aligning herself with such a woman?

Ace seemed to snap out of whatever shocked stillness she was in, taking the opportunity to slide her blades quickly into all Witches easily in her grasp. The chanting had stopped, and therefore so did the shield that was being created. As if Ace moving prompted the rest of them,

Necare, Elders, and House Vampires alike charged forward at full speed, taking Witches out. The spray of their blood and screams filled the room.

Nero savagely tore at their throats with his teeth, having abandoned his axe, while Lucef and Alexander ripped them apart like the beasts that they were. Gunfire was renewed by the Necare that surged forward, and the sounds of blades through flesh and bone began drowning out some of the sounds of pain and terror.

Without their spells up, the Witches were no match for the true might of the Vampires.

"Now!" The Raven cried toward the darkness, watching in horror as the Vampires decimated her forces.

The claw disappeared from her throat, the darkness growing like slithering snakes through the portal and spreading out against the walls of the parlor. Ace didn't stop, even as the Witches tried to fight back with quick bursts of magic. She felt when the magic grazed her, saw when Alexander was not only thrown across the room, but a tear ripping into his side and exposing a white flash of bone surrounded by blood and tissue. Ace watched as Srinta's beautiful hair was set ablaze, which she easily snuffed out and was seemingly unfazed as her eyes scanned the shadows that were spreading over the room.

This creature that The Raven had summoned was not solid, or perhaps not *always* solid. A screech from the other side of the room rang out, causing Ace to look in that direction. As if suspended in the air by nothing but shadow, Melony, one of the twin House Vampires, was dangling upside down, her face locked in horror as she wailed. What looked like black snakes made of smoke held her by the leg, the rest of her thrashing uselessly. The sound of her cries was quickly cut off as a black hole formed on her chest.

The blackness spread like a poison, eating the fabric and flesh equally as tentacle-like inky black spread from the spot on her chest and enveloped her. It was as if everything was being sucked from her: the glow left her eyes, her skin pulling toward her bones, before she crumbled to nothing. Dust on the floor.

A strange sound of satisfaction seemed to radiate out from the shadows surrounding them. The guttural sound came from everywhere the deepest darkness was within that room, even Ace's own shadow beneath her feet.

Melony's agonizing scream could be heard but was blotted out by others. The remaining Witches seemed to know it was time to leave. Their duty was done, the demon was released, and their lives would be forfeit if they stayed within the walls of Kurome. Because despite the fact that the demon was ripping through the room, draining the life from Vampires one by one, just like Melony, the Vampires were showing no mercy as they angrily tore down the Witches who remained.

Alexander seemed to see their attempt at fleeing, him and Lucef both moving before the portal, tearing Witches apart as they tried desperately to push through back to their mistress.

Nero looked at Ace, their eyes locking with a strange sense of longing. They had no way of knowing if either of them would make it out of there. For one moment, they basked in their connection, letting it consume them, before turning their attention back to the death that was being rained down all around them.

Ace jumped back up onto the mantle, her eyes scanning the dark room as more horrifying screams rang out. Narthadis was picking through her ranks, sucking each Vampire he touched until they were nothing but dust on the floor. She knew she needed to get to him somehow, that these bangles Ramses gave her would help her trap him in some way. But he did not remain solid, instead moving through the shadows, both the ones he created and the true shadows in the darkened room. His power seemed limitless, only being solid when it suited his needs, but even then, the darkness seemed to ripple from him, as if he was made of black mist.

"You all thought you'd lock me away," the echoing voice of the demon said as Fredric let out a sharp cry, his entire body seemed to be engulfed in shadow, disappearing without another sound.

"You're a danger to the world!" Ace hissed from where she was. If she could focus his attention on her, perhaps fewer would die. She was fast and smart. She'd be able to evade him long enough to perhaps decide what she could do to use these bangles on him.

"I am inevitable. I am how this realm is meant to end."

Ace glanced down at her hands, coated in blood, but the bangles still stood out against her pale skin. Ramses had given these to her for a reason. Somehow these thin bands of metal would help her. She had to get closer to Narthadis; he had to come to her.

Ace watched as the shadow moved through the darkened space. If she wasn't paying attention, she might not have seen how the shadow seemed to have an even deeper level of darkness when Narthadis inhabited it. Lucef seemed to notice it too, abandoning Alexander to deal with the fleeing Witches, to follow where the demon was going.

With a roar ripping from his throat, Lucef's hands, which had formed into monstrous claws, glowed as balls of fire burst forth from them. The light from the fire seemed to cause Narthadis to shrink back, dropping Nyprat who had begun firing the remaining bullets from her gun at the claw that grasped her injured leg. The bullets flew through the shadow into her own flesh, and she let out a cry as she collapsed on the floor, her knee and foot now horrifyingly damaged.

Makiut, Lotte, and what remained of the other Necare who had gone with them appeared in the doorway of the mansion. Mud and blood spattered, they too joined the efforts of the other Necare who were left, shooting at the shadow as it passed, having been repelled by Lucef's flames. Ace could see it now, the potential, the possibility. She wasn't sure what it would do, or how the bangles would work, but she knew now that the flames within her would only aid her.

With one powerful jump, she soared through the air, her body aimed toward the shadow just as it grasped toward Srinta, who up until his summoning had been trying to protect the House Vampires from the blasts of the Witches. Ace felt the warmth of the fire within her fingers, letting them burst forth until her arms were aflame. She circled her flaming arms around the shadow, her wrists coming together, the bangles locking as they trapped Narthadis in her grasp.

The scream that came from the demon was nothing short of ear-splitting. Between the fire that was illuminating and consuming both of them, and the magic that seemed to pulse and surround them both, keeping them locked together, Narthadis grew frantic in his need to escape her clutches, but the bangles held him firmly in place.

Now what was she to do?

Ace had trapped him, yes, but she could feel her fire starting to wane, never having tried to keep it blazing more than a moment or two before. Usually rage sparked this in her, and while she was angry, her mind was far more calculating, wanting to know how she could successfully keep this creature trapped beyond her arms wrapped around him.

The portal that the Witches had opened was starting to close. Apparently, The Raven had decided whatever Witches were still trapped within Kurome deserved their fate, since it closed with a sharp crack. The small sliver of magic that separated Kurome's parlor from wherever The Raven had been was gone, as if it had never been there in the first place. The handful of Witches who remained fought as hard as they could, their faces full of both determination and dread as they tried to repel the Necare and Alexander from getting any closer, but it was no use. They were torn apart, either from the mighty claws of the leader of all Werewolves or by the blades and hands of Ace's Necare.

"Ace." The voice echoed in her mind as she fought against the strength of the demon thrashing before her. She knew this voice of course. Ramses called to her. But she was far from his room, from his wall. A level away, amidst the aftermath of the fight that was finally complete. The final cries of the last few Witches dying out as their lives were taken were heard, leaving the room quiet, save for the strange, alien sounds of the demon struggling in her arms.

"Come," he said, his voice such an odd whisper in her ear, she was certain she was the only one to hear it.

Everyone in the room had halted, their eyes trained on Ace as she continued to fight for control over the creature.

"You cannot trap me forever!" Narthadis roared, claws scraping against her face and throat, like a cat cornered and trying every violent means to escape.

"Ace. Do not hold back. Feel my call. Come to me," Ramses said, this time his voice was louder, more forceful. She felt it within herself, a pull she had never experienced before. There had been times in the past that Ace had thought Nero had used his influence as her sire to force her to do things. She knew now that he had never and would never do such a thing. If there had been any lingering doubt in her mind, it was now truly banished. She felt Ramses' influence, his demand was far too strong for her to resist now that she realized what it was.

Her eyes glanced out at all those who had stopped their fighting now that it was done, catching onto the white glowing orbs of Nero. She didn't know what succumbing to the call of the First Vampire would mean for her. Ace wasn't sure how she would continue to contain the demon trapped in her clutches. Neither mattered, so long as their kind could continue, so long as their son could live. She tried to convey all this to him through simply the connection between their gazes, giving it only a moment before she let Ramses' call take her.

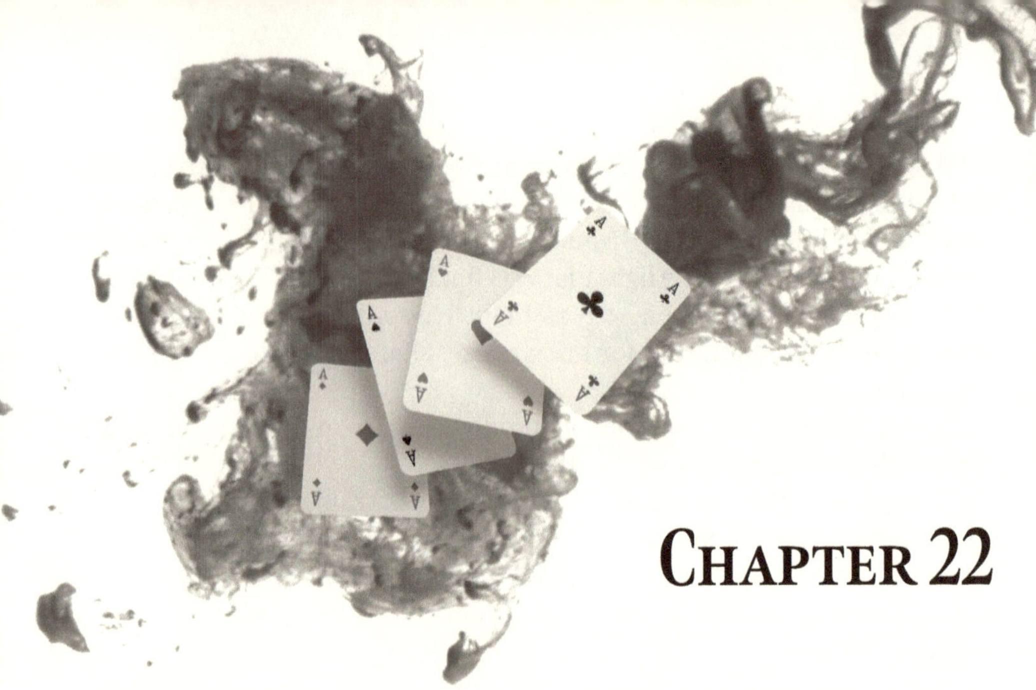

Chapter 22

One moment Ace was in the battle-ridden parlor: the furniture broken and scorched; a massive hole in the ceiling where Nyprat had been firing; blood, ash, and the bodies of both the enemies and fellow Vampires scattered across the ground. The next moment she was encased in darkness. Though this wasn't the same darkness that Narthadis had brought with him, nor was it simply darkness that came with being in an unlit room. This darkness was deep, like a void in and of itself. She could feel her body and knew she was still herself, still whole, but she had no idea where they were.

Narthadis was still firmly attached to her, the metal bangles nearly cutting into her flesh as she continued to fight to hold him against her. She recalled the summons that Ramses had given her as he whispered to her, but nothing more when she released herself to it. It was as if his call had been fulfilled, but she had no idea how that could be. She didn't travel through the mansion to the lower level and had no recollection of pushing through the doors of his chamber.

She wasn't in his chamber.

Was she?

"What is this?" growled the demon in her clutches still, though she wasn't sure how she still had the strength to hold him to her, but she was managing somehow.

"I-I don't..." Ace muttered, just as confused as her prisoner.

"I brought you." Ramses' voice broke through the still silence in the darkness. Suddenly the presence, the voice, the *feel* of this place made it all click in her mind. They were not simply in Ramses' room. She had not travelled to this place by foot; she was *called* here. Ramses moved her here. And where had she been summoned?

Within the wall.

Within Ramses himself.

"Traitorous beast!" Narthadis wailed, thrashing even more violently against Ace's hold than he had been a moment prior.

"This is the only way to make sure this demon cannot roam the earth as he once did millennia ago," Ramses said, his voice more solid than anything else surrounding Ace.

"How do you plan on doing that?" the demon rasped, sharp tendrils like tentacles jutting out from his body, as he tried and failed repeatedly to shift out of the solid form he was forced into now.

Ramses didn't answer; instead, the place they were in seemed to change, the darkness shifting to a warmer light in a way that allowed Ace to see herself and Narthadis, as well as take in the room they were in. Ramses' wall had always appeared to be made of dust or sand, the surface of it rippling and changing, creating shapes, and even, as she had witnessed just hours prior when he summoned her to give her the bangles, his own face. Now it created a space that was familiar, if not bland. A floor, walls, and a ceiling appeared, though they, too, seemed to be made of dust or sand, their surfaces irregular and moving.

Ace felt Ramses everywhere here, for despite how strange the concept was in her mind, she knew that they were ultimately inside of Ramses. But the sands shifted, on the floor, and from one moment to the next, Ramses himself was standing before her. He looked mostly as he had been depicted. The shape of his face was long, his lips full, though he looked just as strong as one would expect a Vampire to be, his muscles defined behind taught, tan skin. Ace had only seen the impression of his face through the wall, but she had never been privy to the real form of the father of them all.

"You may release him now, Ace," Ramses said, opening his eyes, his gaze searing into her.

She twisted her wrists, the mechanism unlocking itself, and Narthadis ripped free of her hold. He was still solid, and there were no shadows for him to hide within in this place, even if he had been able to use his abilities fully. Ace fell to her knees, the soft sands of the floor seeming to cushion her as she fell there. She was bleeding, her face, neck, and chest torn apart with gaping wounds from Narthadis's struggles.

Narthadis merely stood between her and Ramses, heaving a breath as his many eyes, like that of a spider, looked around searching for a way out of this place. But being within Ramses meant there was no escape, not unless he wanted to let you free. Ramses walked confidently past the creature, kneeling before Ace and gently touching her chin to tilt her mangled face toward him.

"You did well," he said, his eyes sparkling with pride as he took in her damaged form.

"Free me!" Narthadis screamed, though he did not approach. Ace's eyes slid from Ramses' face to look at the demon.

She hadn't really gotten to look at him fully during the battle. He moved too quickly, his shadows hiding his appearance, but now that she saw him, he was almost beautiful in a frightening way. His skin was the color of pitch, deep black, so dark you could get lost looking just at the flesh upon his body as you would the night sky. His many eyes were also black, though they shined minimally in the soft light of the room. Two sharp slits sat between his eyes and mouth, which were flaring with fury as he heaved in panicked breaths. His mouth was large, lips nonexistent, simply a wide slash in the flesh, making way for rows of razor-sharp teeth. He was a terrifying creature, something only made to fuel nightmares, but there was something undeniably stunning about something as fearsome as that.

"You will be freed," Ramses said, giving one final pet to Ace's head before standing once more and moving toward Narthadis.

"Now!" snapped the demon, though he stepped back a bit as Ramses advanced on him.

"You will be freed from all planes of existence. Never to walk as you are now once more."

"You cannot kill me. I would only return to the Underworld, but renewed as I am, I would return. There is no escaping me, Ramses," Narthadis said, chuckling sinisterly as all eight eyes fixed on the Vampire before him.

"I am not merely a Vampire. The first is always more," Ramses said, just as Narthadis moved to take yet another step away, but Ramses merely continued his pursuit, striding ever closer with calm steps against the soft ground.

"I am the first of my kind!" Narthadis protested, his form only becoming that much firmer with each passing moment in this place. There was nowhere for him to hide. No shadows to play in. The movements of his claws and tentacles only became more frantic as he realized this.

"You are the only one of your kind, Narthadis. Yes, other shadow demons exist, but only you were made to create your own shadows, and only you create shadows from your prey. You are a plague on any realm you step foot in," Ramses said, his eyes beginning to glow, like twin amber flames.

"And what are you, if not Vampire?" Narthadis bit out.

"I am a little more. To create me, I was fed the blood of our creator himself. Made from human to this and given the ability to pass it on in much the same way. But his blood straight from the source," Ramses paused, closing his eyes and savoring the memory. "I can still feel the power of it running through my veins. Can you?"

Narthadis opened his mouth as if he were going to answer, but suddenly found himself pressed against the rippling wall. In an instant, Ramses was there, his hand crushing the thick throat of the creature before him.

"You hold no more power than I," Narthadis hissed roughly, his tentacles and clawed arms trying to fight against Ramses and his hold but failing. Each swipe at Ramses' flesh was like pressing into a figure made of sand. All Narthadis's attempts yielded were a moment where Ramses seemed to be missing a piece of flesh, only for his image to be renewed a moment later, as if nothing had happened at all.

"My power is different. Your power is to move through and create shadows, to take the life from your victims, leaving only darkness in its place. My power is to take that life and make it *mine*," Ramses said, just before he yanked the demon forward, fangs extended as he let out a strange predatory sound, just before sinking them into the rich black skin.

The scent of demon blood hit the air, and Ace was suddenly starving for it. Her broken body was the only thing that seemed to be keeping her back from lunging toward them and taking her own sampling of his blood. She tilted her head down, her head slumping as if sheer will had been holding her head up to watch before, not muscle. Blood was everywhere. Her body was coated in her own dark blood, as well as the Witches' blood from the earlier battle. Her chest no longer held flesh but was a gaping hole, stark white bone peeking through the sea of ravaged flesh and blood.

Ace knew that she would die. Had she enough blood within her to survive this, she would be healing by now, at least minimally, but there was no hint, no tingle of her tissues moving back together, only pain. She had been ignoring the pain well, as she had to complete the mission, be certain Narthadis was secured. The bangles that sat on her limp and broken wrists did their jobs. She succeeded. Octavian was safe. Nero was safe. Lucef and Alexander were safe. The surviving Vampries in Kurome were safe.

Somewhere within her she felt the pull between her and Nero. His agony over the sensation of her dying was almost more terrible than the physical pain she felt, but she couldn't do anything to save herself. They would have to carry on without her, but knowing they were alive, that she had kept this monster from killing everything she held dear, meant she could find a sense of peace in the magic that made her living slowly slip from her body with each passing moment. She could close her eyes. She could let herself go now that Ramses was taking care of the creature.

Ramses seemed to sense the tone of her thoughts, eyes moving to look upon the slumped figure of Ace on the ground. Her eyes were dulling, the glow fading within them. Blood was still oozing from her wounds, indicating she was not healing. He detached from the creature's flesh, turning to look at her more fully with the white eyes of a hunter that he was.

"Come," Ramses said, his voice a command for the second time that night. Ace didn't have the power to do so on her own accord; she had nothing left within her to move from where she sat, but with the force in his voice, she stood. Her body and its movements were unsteady as she slowly made her way over to where he and Narthadis stood. "Drink," Ramses commanded, cupping the back of her head and pulling her closer to the wound he had created with his own fangs.

She didn't hesitate, pressing forward and taking the black, bleeding wound into her mouth. The taste of the demon was like nothing she had ever experienced. It almost sizzled against her tongue, rich and warm as it slid down her throat. For a moment, it was as if she was simply drinking the strange blood, sating the hunger that came from her injuries, but after a few moments, it was almost as if the very blood in her veins was on fire. The flames within her seemed to rear back up, alive and far more vibrant than they had ever been before.

A switch seemed to flip within her, no longer simply pulling on the wound but now she wanted to drink. She wanted to sink her own fangs within this flesh, to tear it open and gulp the blood down. She wanted it to fill her, to crackle within her.

"Yes, drink. Take in the demon blood, let it become part of you," Ramses whispered, his fingers trailing through her short black hair, encouraging and comforting her before he took to the other side of Narthadis's neck, savagely breaking through the flesh there with his fangs.

They drank in tandem, pulling the essence of the demon from his body and into theirs. Fangs and tight-gripping hands tearing open his flesh even more to let it rain down upon them.

Ace felt Narthadis thrashing against the hold she and Ramses had on him, but it was as if there was no resistance at all. She had no trouble pushing back, taking his blood as he screamed, the many voices within him crying out as the final drops of him were stolen into herself and Ramses.

Ramses pulled back, taking Ace with him by the back of her neck. She heaved in long breaths, gazing at what remained of the creature she had brought here. Narthadis's limbs shivered strangely, the final pulses of life releasing from the body as the now dull and lifeless black eyes looked out at nothing in the strange room of sand. And then she realized she had power within her body once more. She felt it surging through her, not completely different, perhaps merging with her own, the two melding together and making her feel charged instead of the near dead she felt only minutes previous.

Ace turned her gaze to Ramses now, who looked at her and smiled broadly. It was as if he hadn't at all been drinking from the demon just moments before. Not a bit of him was out of place, the black blood that had once been dribbling down his chin and coating his chest was nowhere to be seen.

"What just happened?" Ace asked. Though there was some part of her that knew, she wanted to confirm.

"You are changed now, Ace. No longer just a Vampire. Like I was never just a Vampire," Ramses said.

"Is it...?"

"Over?" He chuckled darkly. "With Narthadis, yes. He will never again walk amongst any plane of existence. What is left of him now lives here, in me and in you."

Within her.

Did she feel different than she did before?

She wasn't sure.

But she didn't have time to process that fully, because suddenly she found herself not within the warm glow of the sandy room of Ramses but instead in the cold, shadowed room of his chambers in Kurome.

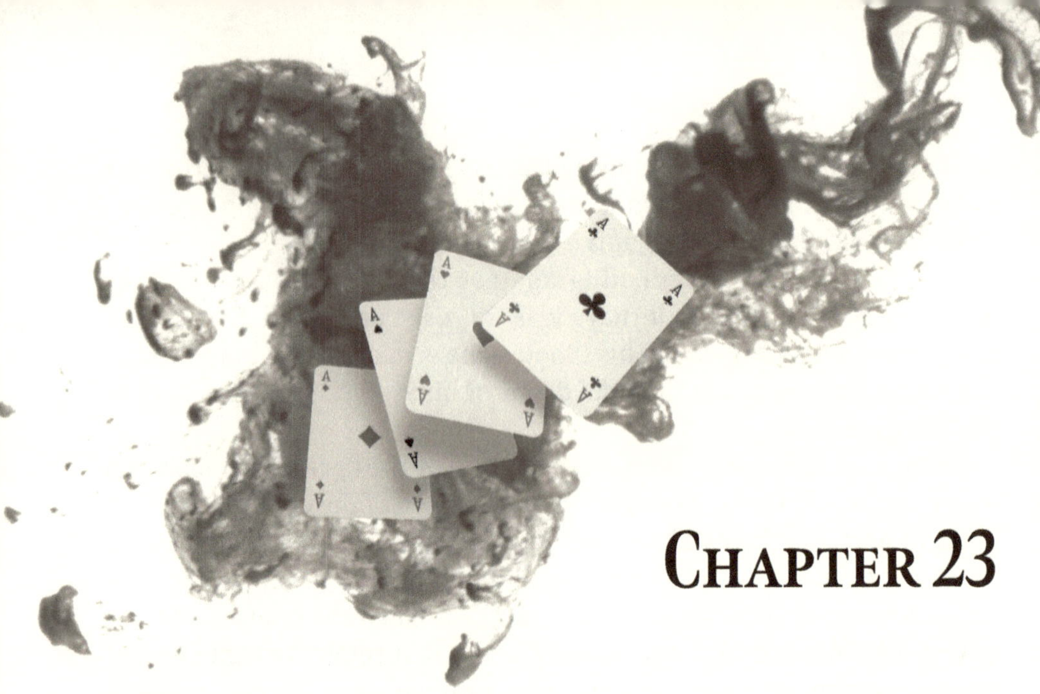

Chapter 23

The doors burst open not but a moment later, Nero at the front, the brighter light from the corridor outside the chamber casting him in silhouette, but Ace would know him anywhere. His eyes glowed vibrant blue as he looked across the distance to her. She had no idea what she looked like to him, so she wasn't sure if it was agony or relief that caused the desperate sound to rip from his throat before he took nothing but seconds to stand before her. His arms reached out, fingers slowly and gently moving to cup her face between his hands. Ace was vaguely aware of others there as well, but she couldn't care less as she looked at Nero once more.

When she had been leaving the parlor, Narthadis was trapped against her, and she knew she had to relinquish herself to whatever was going to happen next. They had said all they needed to say in the look that passed between them. But there was nothing better than to think your death certain, and have that not come to pass, especially when your soulmate was there to hold you once again.

"I thought I'd lost you," Nero whispered, fingers trailing over her lips and chin, down her neck and to her chest, before pulling her close and crushing her to his own. She wrapped her arms around him, holding him equally as tight, taking in deep breaths of his scent.

Behind Nero came Lucef and Srinta. Srinta's gasp was the only thing that could have possibly broken Ace from Nero's embrace, and so it did. She tore away, looking toward the door where Srinta stood. She was also covered in blood and ash; her usually long, beautiful hair had been set ablaze and looked frazzled and lopsided. But that didn't seem to matter, since her eyes were unwavering as they looked beyond Ace and Nero to where the wall should have stood before.

Ace turned to face it, expecting to see the wall there, but perhaps with Ramses' face showing on its surface. Instead, there was no longer a rippling wall; there was a man.

Ramses was once more in the flesh. His body was whole after so many years of having gone to living dust, and everyone in the room seemed to shake from the enormity of what it meant that he was standing there.

He was tall, his body roped with muscles and skin bronze and shining like he was dusted with gold. His face was unmistakable, and the power radiating from him was worthy of awe as he stared back out at all of them with eyes glowing golden.

"Ramses!" Srinta gasped, letting out a choked sob as she moved through the room toward him.

"Black Dove, stop," Ramses said, and immediately Srinta halted where she was, flinching as if he had threatened to hit her, though his words had been nothing but soft. His eyes slid from her to take in Nero and Ace, still holding one another, and Lucef behind them. His eyes glowed a little brighter seeing Lucef there before turning them back to his progeny.

"How?" Srinta asked in a whisper, shaking with the need to go to him.

"Ace," was all he said, turning his attention to her, and thus everyone else's.

Lucef stepped closer to her, his eyes shining in the dim light. They were all still bloodstained, but none as much as Lucef, who looked like he practically bathed in the blood of the Witches. Srinta turned to look at Ace too, and as if she had never seen her before, her face took on the uncharacteristic look of surprise. It was hard to surprise someone who had lived for so many thousands of years. The shock on both Lucef and Srinta's faces was odd, considering what the rest of them looked like. They all looked battle-ridden, so what was so strange about her?

"Your face," Nero said, as explanation to the questioning expression that bloomed on Ace's features, touching her cheeks once more, fingers brushing over skin. Not blood. Not exposed bone and muscle. "Your chest," he said again, hands drifting down to where Narthadis had torn at her there, trying desperately to free himself from her grasp. She looked down, thinking she'd see the flesh there healing, being that it was the last place she had looked on her body before Ramses commanded her to drink.

There was no gaping hole, no splatters of blood or ragged chunks missing, no bone showing through. There was only her pale, luminescent skin.

She was whole.

She was clean.

She was wearing nothing, just as was Ramses.

"Reborn," Ramses said, as if it was all that needed to be said, a small smile adorning his lips.

"I am not reborn," Ace said, casting an odd look over her shoulder at him. Ramses' lips quirked up in a smirk. So few would challenge his words. Even Ace had now borne witness to his power, being cared for by him and taken under his wing, and yet she pushed back on some of the absolutes he said. She was a pleasure, indeed.

"I am reborn. Made whole again, and you have been changed." He turned to Srinta, who still seemed to be struggling to stay the distance from him that she was. "That was what the Witches' prophecy foretold, Srinta, not the end of everything because a demon was made whole once more. That I would be brought back." Srinta whimpered, glancing at Ace and Nero, eyes filled with regret at her previous actions before her gaze inevitably turned back to Ramses. She could no longer hold herself back, leaping at him and throwing herself in his arms, which he wrapped securely around her.

This moment was no longer for witnesses. Srinta deserved her time with Ramses now that she had him back again, and there was plenty to do now that this battle was over.

Ace had no idea how long she had been within Ramses. She wasn't sure what had come of those who remained in the mansion, but she knew by closing her eyes that her son was still within these walls. She needed to see him to know that it was real.

"Octavian," Ace whispered as Nero pulled his shirt from his body, placing it over Ace's naked form, before taking her hand. The shirt was dirty, but it didn't matter. Ace was far beyond modesty at this point, as was everyone else it seemed. Nero, Ace, and Lucef passed through the lower corridors, seeing Georgith holding the shoes of Fredric in his arms as he descended the stairs. He didn't even seem to see them as he passed, his eyes shimmering between dull and glowing.

"Everyone moved to the Medicus," Lucef said from behind them as they turned away from the Elder. He was whole, though not mentally, perhaps, but nothing they could do would help him when there were others upstairs needing care.

The three of them moved swiftly through the mansion, the usually pristine and ancient halls marred with blood and ash. The whole mansion seemed to echo with the sounds of pain. The Medicus was already full of injured Vampires when they got to the doors. Octavian was helping Deitris and Minshin with them, getting instruments they asked for or pulling blood from their refrigerators.

"Nyprat. It will grow back," Minshin said, as Nyprat thrashed on the table she was lying upon. Lotte, who had a burn covering half her face and down her neck, was holding her still. The bullets to her knee and foot were such that there was no tissue left, merely wide holes, dripping viscous blood.

"I don't want to wait for it to grow back!" Nyprat screamed, as Minshin tore the remainder of her pant leg from the injured limb. Makiut glanced over, clearly feeling sympathetic about growing back a missing limb. He had done that before, but he was too busy helping William hold Melody down as Dartri began sedating her. It took a lot of sedative to put a Vampire to sleep, but she just hadn't been able to stop screaming since she watched her twin die.

Ace moved closer to Nyprat, placing her hands firmly on her upper arms and pressing down as she leaned over to be face to face with her Necare.

"Minshin is going to cut off your leg from just above your knee—"

"NO!"

"If you don't let her, you will be crippled. A Vampire with a limp."

"I can't be down that long. Months!" Nyprat sobbed, bloody tears running down her dirty face.

"My Necare must be in top physical form. I won't let you go with Lotte if you refuse this," Ace said, as she tightened her hold on Nyprat's shoulders. That seemed to get her attention, since she abruptly stopped thrashing, her body going still as she finally let her eyes drift above her, focusing on Ace.

"What?" Nyprat whispered, seeming in awe of who she saw hovering above her.

"The only way for it to grow back correctly will be to regrow the whole limb," Ace continued, though Nyprat wasn't calming simply because of the explanation; no, she was getting lost in the way the shadows danced against Ace's skin from where she hunched and how her silver eyes, which they all knew well, somehow seemed *more*. She was lost in the fact that they had watched Ace take hold of the demon who killed their kind as if it was nothing, her body being torn apart as she fought to keep her hold on him, and yet there she was. Ace was alive and whole, staring down at Nyprat and demanding she get the treatment she needed.

"We lost too many of us this night. I need you, Nyprat," Ace said, her voice a little softer.

"Okay," Nyprat whispered, her voice quivering.

"Okay?" Ace questioned, raising an eyebrow at the quick change in Nyprat's demeanor. If Nyprat had been human, Ace would have thought she was in shock, but as it was...

"Three," Minshin said suddenly, her hand holding the bone saw moving faster than Ace had ever seen the Medicus move. The limb gave way, blood spraying out as Minshin quickly moved to stanch the wound. "Blood!" Minshin yelled without stopping her process.

Ace pushed off Nyprat's shoulders, her eyes immediately being pulled to the white-haired boy who was coming toward them with a new bag of blood.

"It's not warm," Octavian said, setting the blood beside the newly removed appendage, before looking up to see Ace standing on just the other side of the table.

"Who isn't injured?" Ace asked, realizing everyone was in this room. The whole coven was here except for those they had lost. Shockingly, even Alexander was standing off in a far corner, a cloth pressed to his shoulder that was soaked with blood. While they needed to recoup, she didn't want to let any Witches get away if she could help it. They were weakened from the amount of magic they had just used, and it was the perfect opportunity to take down The Raven, making the whole of the Witches fall apart without a leader.

Makiut raised a hand, but remained where he was holding down Dava, who was having glass pulled from her face.

"We need to get back to the mausoleum," Ace said.

"I'll come," Octavian said, gaining a sharp look from Ace and Nero in quick succession.

"I'm going to put clothes on. Anyone able to needs to come with us," Ace said, leaving the room without another word and heading straight to her wardrobe in her chambers to throw on pants. She didn't have time to care that she was still in Nero's shirt.

When she returned to the decimated parlor, Makiut, William, Lucef, and Alexander were standing at the ready.

"Lotte wanted to come, but we need someone keeping watch on the others. We're vulnerable now too," Nero said, to which Ace nodded. There wasn't any more time to waste.

"Alexander, this isn't your fight," Ace said, glancing at her brother who had been given some pants, since his clothes were destroyed during his transformation into his wolf. His shoulder still held a nasty gash in it, but it was no longer bleeding. He had tied his long black hair up in a knot at the back of his head.

"There's no other fight for me now," Alexander said. The weight of his words clung to Ace as she realized what that meant.

"But—"

"There are far more important things than being with other Werewolves, Ace. Being able to be your brother again, or if nothing else, making sure I am not the cause of your death."

Ace held his gaze for a moment, nodding finally and putting back on her mask of the bloodthirsty Necare she was, before nodding for everyone to head out the doors into the night.

It hadn't been long since the sun had set, but somehow it felt like it had been night for ages. That battle had taken so much out of all of them. It had taken so many away from them. They couldn't lose more, but they couldn't let the Witches get away, even if their forces had been depleted as well.

Makiut led them to the mausoleum where they had encountered the Witches. The scent of magic still permeated the air, but it was quiet there. They moved swiftly between gravestones, entering the building silently. Makiut showed them a false wall that revealed a set of stairs down. It was dark; the stone walls of the stairwell lent nothing to improve sight, but it didn't matter. Soon they were in the depths of the structure in a long hallway that had several doors. Ace could smell the blood of humans down here, James Martin's blood predominately.

Ace signaled for the others to stay back as she stepped into a set of doors that were slightly ajar where vague light was flickering. The room was in chaos. The circle of blood where The Raven had stood was still there, bloody symbols now smeared. Tables and shelves littered the place covered in all sorts of things Ace imagined they used for rituals of various kinds. A few candles were still lit, but as she suspected, there wasn't one soul left in this place. Not one Witch was here, or at least not alive.

Ace looked down at a few of the bodies of Witches. Ones that made it through the portal they had created to come back here but had clearly gotten the end of Lucef and Alexander's fangs and claws, meeting their demise just as they reached safety.

"Gone," Ace said quietly when Nero stepped into the room beside her.

"The other rooms looked to be where they slept and a holding cell," Nero said.

"Smelled like the Martin boy," Lucef said, looking around at the mess the Witches left in disgust.

"They're weakened, Ace; it will take them time to recover from what they lost with this, both magic and numbers," Alexander said as he picked up a black feather from the table, absently moving it through his fingers.

"I need a moment," Ace whispered, still only looking at the corpses of Witches and not turning around to the others.

She clenched her fists, anger rolling through her. This war was a never-ending task. For so many years, centuries, she had dedicated herself to it, and yet they were still just as far away from it being over as it was when she was made Vampire. Fire licked within her veins with the fury she felt. She wouldn't tire of fighting, of bloodshed, but she would tire of seeing those around her die and suffer at the hands of her enemies.

"Ace," came Alexander's voice from behind her. The others had left her to her peace, but he had stayed behind, still holding the feather in his fingers. As children, they loved to collect feathers as they walked from their farm to the town. She had fashioned a fan from some, others they had just played with until they were lost or broken.

"I said I needed a moment," she said quietly, her voice pinched with her frustration. Even Nero had given her space, leaving her to her thoughts when he would have much rather stayed by her side, but not Alexander.

"There's nothing else we can do right now. You need to be with your coven," Alexander said.

She whirled around, the fire burning within her coming forth to encase her in flames. Her eyes glowed like molten silver as she pinned him with her glare. She was frightening and beautiful as she seemed to glow with the fire that crackled as it surrounded her.

"What do you care about my coven, Alexander? Why are you here?" Ace yelled.

"I left them!" he yelled back, stepping closer despite the fire that seemed to whip toward him with malice.

"What?" she hissed, eyes narrowing as she glared into his.

"I left the den. I left the Werewolves."

"Why would you do such a thing? You are a Werewolf, Alexander!"

"I was your brother first!" he screamed.

Silence overtook the space once more; the only sound was Alexander's harsh breathing that echoed slightly off the stone walls surrounding them. Ace looked at him, seeing now the pain in his eyes, the truth behind his words.

"Ace, for years I thought you were dead. I thought I had lost you in the attack, suffered wanting to avenge our family, just as you. But when I realized what you had become, when I saw you fighting, my purpose changed."

Ace simply looked at him, the fire having died down around her, but her eyes continued glowing.

"Watching you as I just did, what you did for them…" Alexander shook his head, his face transforming into awe. "The attack on our family may have been because of Werewolves, but you were always meant to be this. You were supposed to be a Vampire."

The enormity of everything that happened seemed to crash down on her. What Alexander was saying, what occurred with Ramses earlier, all the revelations that had come forward in such short succession hit her. Her fire died down, bringing them back into the dim light of the filthy room once more as she took in a gasping breath.

Ace had dealt with prophecies several times over, had seen the effects that fate had, but she had not considered that she may have had a path she was taking, one she was meant to go down. But just as Ace was about to say to him that perhaps he was meant to be a Werewolf then too, she realized she didn't have to. He already knew. They were meant to become what they had, but the reason for it was still very much unknown.

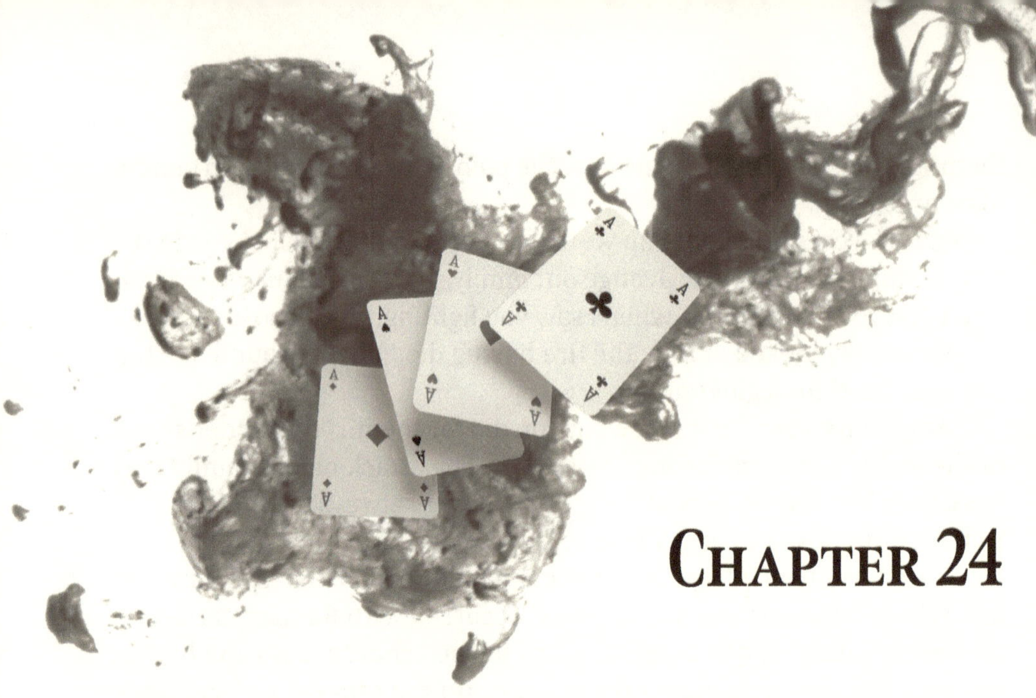

Chapter 24

The foursome made their way out of the mausoleum's depths, out into the night sky. Rain had started to spit from the dark clouds above as they raced back to the mansion. As they approached the gates, Alexander stopped short, making the rest of them pause.

"Are you coming?" Ace asked him. Though it would have been uncomfortable for him initially, as it had been for Lucef to stay there, Ace knew no one would question it if he stayed in the mansion, especially after the battle he had just helped them win. But Alexander smiled sadly at her, his grey eyes that looked like hers once did when she was human, taking her in for a moment as the rain began coming down harder on all of them.

"I don't belong there, Ace. Go to your coven. I'll see you again someday," Alexander said, turning his gaze to Nero and Lucef, nodding with respect before turning and walking down the dark road that led to the center of London.

Alexander not being the leader of the Werewolves anymore caused two things to click in Ace's head. Whatever hesitation to fully destroy the Werewolves she had been harboring since he had taken over that position a decade prior was now gone and that the Werewolves as a whole were, at least temporarily, weak again, as they would be trying to rearrange their ranks. Any new forces Alexander had managed to procure may once again scatter. They would have a good opportunity to take them out or at least down a rung lower than they already were.

Though Ace's heart ached to follow him and bring him back, she knew there was far too much to concern herself with now. She couldn't be wasting her time on something that she hoped would be an inevitability. She and Alexander were born together in this world and had somehow found their way back to one another after centuries. She would be surprised if they didn't find each other once again.

Ace turned back toward the gates, climbing over with ease and dropping onto the gravel drive. Nero and Lucef followed suit, and they moved quickly toward the front doors of the mansion. There was still chaos within, the sounds of cries could be heard like a symphony of pain.

"I'm going to see if we can track any of their movements away from the mausoleum. Maybe I can follow them during the day," Lucef said, turning to head back to the communications room.

He was uncomfortable. He hadn't slept in days, not since he had arrived at Kurome with Chiyo, but a strange feeling had begun creeping within him, filling his chest. The sensation reminded him of how he felt when he had been having the strange dreams of Six. It was like a tug from within him, like Six had reached through death itself to touch his now still heart within his chest. He had smelled her too, her scent flooding his nostrils as if she were there with them, but she wasn't.

She was dead, just as she had been for the last ten years. Only his recent dreams had been taunting him about her, and there was nothing he could do but try to make himself useful. He was in this with Ace and Nero now. He had chosen a side, the side Six had been on.

"You wouldn't go alone, Lucef," Ace said, grabbing his arm to stop him before he took a step.

"Ace—"

"Don't argue with me, Lucef. You're one of mine. I'm not losing any more than I already have. We'll go with you if you find something. Don't leave before seeing us," Ace said firmly, her eyes locking with his, which were still the red of Six's eyes.

"I'll get you if I find something," he said with a nod after a moment, and Ace released his arm from her grasp.

Nero and Ace moved back to the Medicus, Makiut right behind them. There was still plenty of movement, Minshin seeming to flit from one patient to the next trying to use what she could to help them. Most seemed to have been already on the path to healing, simply needing projectiles removed from where they had been embedded in their flesh and blood to promote healing; others, like Nyprat, would take much longer to heal.

Octavian was still active too, getting more blood bags and giving them to the seriously injured. He had smears of red across his cheeks and the shirt of his father's he still wore. Ace went to him when he brought yet another bag to Nyprat, whose glowing eyes turned brighter as she bit savagely into the fresh one he offered her.

"What's the status?" Ace asked him, as she reached out and brushed his blood-smeared cheek with her thumb. He looked at her with an odd expression for a moment before glancing around him and the now quieting room.

"We lost Charles, but that, I think, is the last one who we should be concerned with. The others are going to heal," Octavian said, looking back toward his mother.

She looked different, he realized, not fully but there was a change about her. He wasn't sure what happened in that battle, but based on the looks that she was getting from quite a few of the Vampires throughout the room, he imagined she did something monumental to secure the victory for them. And though he would have preferred to be in the thick of the battle with everyone else, his mother's words before it began rang true. Based on what he saw of the aftermath, he wasn't prepared to be of any help in that situation.

"Minshin," Ace said, making the Medicus pause as she was heading over to her tablet, which had been left by her desk in the far corner. "What can we do?"

"We're going to need more blood," Minshin said mournfully, glancing around the room at all the injured who had been downing blood. Their stores had already been low because of the Witches stalking their facilities, and now ... there wouldn't be enough blood there to last them the week. Perhaps not even a week, given what Ace saw behind the glass door of the cooler.

"I'll reach out to the Martins. I still want the facilities guarded, but we can't risk this many injured Vampires going hungry," Nero said, a little nervousness passing over his face.

"Other than the blood, they're all as good as I can get them for the time being. Most of them need to stay in here so Dietris and I can monitor them, but the others can return to their rooms," Minshin said, nodding as several Necare finished the blood they had been drinking to heal a few small wounds and moved to leave.

"You two, start cleaning up the parlor. Lotte, you keep an eye on the perimeter," Makiut said, casting his eyes around at the other Vampires. "And anyone else who is able, start on the clean up too. Any salvageable blood from the Witches should be drained until we get our supply back up."

"Come, Octavian," Nero said, putting an arm over Octavian's shoulders and steering him out of the room.

"I can keep helping. Or go clean," Octavian murmured as he went out to the hall with his parents on either side.

"Dawn is approaching. You don't last long once the sun breaks through," Ace reminded him.

"And tomorrow night, we put the studies on hold and teach you something different," Nero added, as they got to the door of Octavian's chambers beside theirs.

Lucef saw the shock of brilliant white light, felt the curiosity and wonder that wasn't his own—he was feeling dread—and heard those words once more from a voice he knew so very well.

"Lucifer?" Six asked, her vision, and therefore Lucef's, straining to see past the all-encompassing light that was surrounding her.

"No," again came the voice that sounded like a song, not human ... more ethereal, perhaps. "We are Acim and Acimony. You are Six. Once called Sinthia. Blood child of Ace."

As the voice said her name, the light dimmed, and she could then see them fully. These were not demons, not creatures created by Lucifer's hand, but angels. They were in the form of two men, completely identical, tall, and broad-shouldered, with white hair that fell to their shoulders in thick curls. They wore white suits and held silver canes, but their eyes were hidden behind black cloth.

"Fallen angels," Six whispered, eyes taking in the sight of them with strange fascination.

There had been stories of angels, of course. Every Vampire who was made at Kurome was taught the histories. It was imperative for them to know how Vampires came to existence, how their enemies came to be there too.

The brother gods, Viginiti and Lucifer, created the world and its Underworld, but they differed in opinion over what creatures should be in domination. While Viginti created angels, powerful, beautiful, and supposedly perfect, Lucifer created demons, equally powerful, perhaps not beautiful, and certainly not what Viginti considered perfection. They, together, created humans, but it was the demons and the angels who made some of those humans more. Six, for the life of her, couldn't remember exactly what occurred to create the first Vampire, but at the moment, staring at the twin angels before her, she couldn't be bothered to care.

She wasn't sure what was going to happen to her here. They were powerful, far more so than she, and they could easily do exactly as she suspected the Shadow Demon would have done.

Lucef shivered at Six's thought of the Shadow Demon. They had just barely defeated him. Ace very nearly sacrificed herself to keep him contained. Yes, these angels were not to be taken lightly, not when a creature of similar strength and magic just came and helped the Witches attempt to destroy everything and everyone within the walls of the only place any of them seemed to be able to call a sanctuary.

"Why have you come here, Six?"

What a question. She wasn't sure what to say. Should she be honest? Should she try to get away from them? Could she get away from them?

"I—"

"Do not think for a moment that any lie you might say will not be cause for us to erase your soul," the one on the left said. She decided he was Acim and seemed to be the only one that spoke.

"I wish to leave this place," she said, raising her chin defiantly. The one on the right let a small smile peek at the side of his mouth.

"How do you plan to do that, little one? You have died in that world," Acim said, eyebrows rising over the top of the black cloth.

"I don't exactly know. I thought I'd plead my case to Lucifer; he is the man in charge, isn't he?"

A deep chuckle that seemed to carry like a low tinkle of bells cascaded around the stone room.

"You thought you'd just wander through the levels of the Underworld and happen to come upon him? That he would set your soul free unto the world, did you?" Acim asked, a smile that she would have liked to smack off his face sitting there and mocking her.

"I wasn't sure what else to do," she grumbled, crossing her arms and glaring back at them.

Silence settled there, Six glaring at the angels before her, while they seemed intrigued and studied her.

"She's what we've been waiting for," Acim said after a moment of watching her anger-filled eyes glare at them. Somehow, Six knew they could see her, despite the coverings over their eyes.

Lucef felt like however it was they could see, he was somehow being viewed through Six as well, especially when at that thought, the mute angel, Acimony, let a strange smile play at the corner of his mouth.

"Waiting for?" she asked suspiciously.

"Yes. We have been awaiting your arrival for some time," Acim said, shifting his cane from one hand to the other so he could grasp his twin's arm. The two of them seemed to glide across the floor, coming closer to Six once more. Before Six had a moment to comprehend what was happening, Acimony's free hand reached forward, the same strong, warm hands covering her bare shoulder.

Acim and Acimony's faces were trained on hers; now the three of them linked by touch. And without another moment, there was a flash of red light, and everything around her changed.

It was as if the volume had been turned up to its maximum capacity. The stark quietness of the caves they had just been in was so different from the now deafening sound of where they were now. There were no dark tunnels surrounding them; now there was one open area that seemed to go on forever. The room was filled with bodies, demons, humans, and even some dead Immortals. Screams and chatter from all of them seemed to surround her, filling her ears with their horrific symphony of sound.

"Where are we?" she asked, feeling somehow reassured with the pressure of Acimony's hand still on her shoulder as he gently pushed her, guiding her forward through the masses of bodies that filled this place.

"The Portal. The only way to leave this place if you have not been summoned," Acim said from behind her.

"And I am leaving?"

"We are leaving," Acim said.

Six contemplated that for a long moment. These angels couldn't leave this place; they had been waiting for her, or someone like her, to help them out of the Underworld, just as she was hoping to get help in her own escape from this place.

"Why couldn't you leave?" she asked as they pushed through a particularly thick group of screaming bodies that all seemed to be clustered around a particular spot.

"For now, you focus on this. Leave the rest for later. We will have time," Acim said.

"Focus on what?" Six hissed, shoving a woman out of her way who tried to grasp at her.

"You must go to Orion," Acim said to her, his voice now quiet and right in her ear.

Orion?

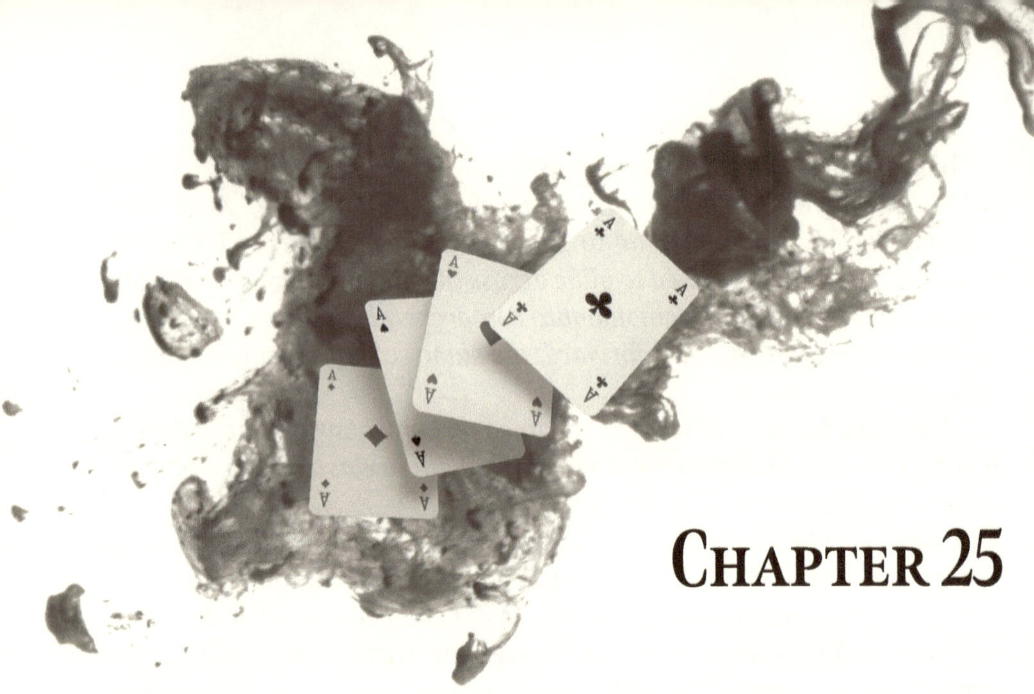

Chapter 25

Kagami's black eyes took in the appearance of the Witch The Raven had sent in her stead to update their new allies about what had occurred with the summoning. Kagami's face gave nothing away of what she felt, the stoic mask of a queen firmly in place as she looked over the woman. The Witch before her may not have been The Raven herself, but she represented her, and it baffled Kagami to realize The Raven had somehow convinced her to turn her back on a centuries-long alliance with Vampires.

"Kagami—"

"Where is Chiyo?" Kagami interrupted, no longer interested in the excuses the Witch gave for the complete failure her plan had turned out to be. She was now only interested in where her daughter was. She had taken a big risk, sending the next in line for the throne out to be part of this mission. The risk had thus far turned out to not have been worth it.

"I-I don't know," the Witch said, fidgeting. It wasn't the awkward moments before this that made her nervous, but the flash of Kagami's eyes, the way her skin rippled like a tide of fury moving over her form and under her skin.

"The Raven failed. The Vampires are still the most powerful, and my successor is missing?" Kagami asked, turning away from the Witch to look back out the window.

"We will find Chiyo, but we had to secure and protect ourselves first. We lost so many in the battle—"

"I don't care how many you lost. Chiyo is worth more than a legion of you," Kagami said, her voice cold. "Our alliance only continues out of complete necessity. The moment I don't feel your kind is of use to mine, it will cease to be. I expect word on Chiyo soon."

But just as the Witch was turning to leave the room, relief evident on her face as she turned around, the doors opened, and two Chenjas came in, holding a box between them. The box was made of silver, blue crystals inset into the metal with intricate filigree engraved within it. Beautiful.

"What is this?" Kagami asked, turning to look at it. It smelled of Vampire and death.

"It just arrived from Kurome Mansion with this note," one of the Chenjas said, speaking in English for the benefit of the Witch present. Kagami glided forward slowly, her eyes never straying from the box as it was placed delicately on the floor. The sound of liquid sloshing within made it even more strange.

Surely the Vampires knew of Kagami's betrayal, and if that was so, why would they be gifting her with something in the first place?

Kagami,

> *It pained us to learn our alliance was over. We had tried to reach out to you many times in these long years since the ritual, to no avail. Then we learned that you had aligned yourself with The Raven, sent your successor as a show of good faith, only to have her steal from us and ultimately cause the death of some of ours, while destroying our central and sacred home.*
>
> *This is the last contact we expect to make to you before the war is complete. The final step to be certain both of us know where we stand with one another.*
>
> *You are no longer under our protection or in alliance with us.*
>
> *Your kind will be hunted and destroyed if you interfere with what we have planned for the others.*
>
> *Whatever you know of how we operate, and our methods should be forgotten, or else you risk those methods being used on you.*

Let this gift we've brought you be the last warning you shall ever need. For we know how difficult it is for your kind to procreate.

The Elder Council

Below it was signed only four names, though Kagami was certain there had been five, since Ace had become an Elder herself.

Kagami glanced at the Witch who was still as a stone where she had turned around. Her eyes glued to the silver box with a look of horror. She knew what kind of box that was, perhaps she knew what was held within it too.

"Shall they open it?" Kagami asked her, curious about her reaction.

"I should get back to The Raven," the Witch said, trying to move a bit closer to the door, but being unsuccessful with the strong arms of one of the Chenjas who brought the box into the room wrapped around her from behind.

"Open it," Kagami said to the other once the Witch was secured.

With slow, but methodical movements, the Chenja pulled at the closures on the box until a strange hiss of air came out, indicating the pressure within had released. As the lid was removed, a horrible sound came from the Chenja's throat. Anguish was the only way it could be described.

"Open it!" Kagami screamed this time, her body looking more like ripples on the surface of water, giving off simmering slivers of her silver form.

The Chenja pushed the lid of the box the rest of the way off, the metal clanging loudly to the floor. Within the box was, indeed, water, but not only that. A silver liquid was floating within it, like oil would when set in water. Immediately Kagami knew what it was—or rather who it had been, and her body seemed to stiffen, the rippling ceasing as her human form melted away, revealing the alien mercurial form that was natural for her.

Black eyes snapped from the remains of Chiyo to the Witch who still stood there, seemingly stuck to the ground with her own fear.

"You knew!" Kagami accused, and only then did the Witch manage to shake her head stiffly, eyes wide as she heard the words from the queen but didn't see any movement from her mouth.

"We suspected, but—"

"And yet you come here with false promises. What kind of ally is The Raven if I cannot even trust what she sends her messengers to say? I always was able to trust the Vampires. Truth, the good and the bad, were never withheld from me. Like everything else you creatures touch, you've sullied it!"

The Witch opened her mouth to try and defend her kind, but she didn't have a moment to. Kagami's arms reached out, stretching an impossible distance between them, her hands turning into inorganic-looking claws, clamping around the Witch's neck.

"The Raven will not appreciate me not coming back," the Witch said quietly, unable to speak louder with the tightening of Kagami's grip.

"The Raven will understand why you had to die after arriving here at the same time as the remains of my murdered daughter, or she will be adrift in this world. Alone and weak to face the Vampires and Werewolves."

"So will you."

"We have survived worse," Kagami said, before closing the claw around the Witch's neck with such force, her neck collapsed. The skin began tearing with the sharp ends of the claws, and with a rough tug, her head fell free of the body, blood spraying everywhere.

Silence fell over the room once more. Kagami turned her cold black eyes away from the Witch's corpse, looking again at the remnants of her daughter within the poisonous water in the box.

"Remove her from there and bring her to me. Send the head of the messenger to the last address we had for the Witch. The Raven will get it eventually," Kagami said, before turning back toward the windows, not bothering to change back into her human form.

Ace watched closely, leaning against the wall that seemed to vibrate with the thumping rhythm of the base in the club. Lucef watched from the other side of the room as Octavian worked to lure a girl who had begun dancing with him. Ace hadn't been completely sure that Octavian would have passed as old enough by human standards to have not only been in this club, but also to be intriguing enough for him to catch someone's eye. Lucef disagreed, and thus, much to Octavian's excitement, they brought him out of the mansion to help him with more of his training.

Hunting humans wasn't exactly training to fight, but it was a different sort of gaining control over his abilities that he hadn't yet been exposed to, or at least not outside of the watchful eyes and comfort of Kurome. Here, he was not at home; he was in a neutral zone. No Immortal was protected over another within these walls. It took everything in Ace not to go to him, to help guide him, but she managed it. This was for his own good. He would not always be by her side. She knew he would inevitably want to try to be on his own for periods of time, and she had to be sure he was prepared for that in whatever way she could.

Octavian's eyes flashed a little brighter as the girl slipped her hand in his, seemingly unable to look away.

"Do you want to come with me?" Octavian asked, gaining a nod from her as she stepped even closer to him. He gently guided her through the crowd, never letting his eyes stray from hers as he did so, finally making it to a wall, not too far from where Lucef stood, and pressing her against it.

His nostrils widened, eyes glowing white as he took in her aroma. He could smell the warm blood flowing through her veins, making his fangs extend involuntarily.

"I'm going to kiss you," he whispered, bringing his lips closer to the pulsing of her skin at her neck. He heard the little whimper come from her throat. Was it fear or desire that she was feeling from this encounter? He wasn't sure, but he wasn't wasting another moment.

His hands grasped her tightly, fangs descending and piercing through the flesh of her neck, letting that warm blood fill his mouth.

And oh, was it magnificent. The taste, the scent, the feel of her heartbeat against his chest as it sped up before gradually slowing with each pull he took of the wound.

It was then, as the thumping of her heart grew dangerously slow, that he felt a hand on his shoulder.

"That's enough," his mother said behind him.

"Is she...?"

"Dead? No. Just unconscious. We'll leave her here. Either she will have friends that take her home, or Don will be sure that she is safe before he goes to bed for the day," Ace said, glancing around the club to be certain there weren't any Werewolves in their midst. It was rather fortunate that they had not encountered any Werewolves on this particular outing, but Ace didn't want to chance it much longer, not with Octavian out with them.

"Must we go home now?" Octavian whined, as she pulled him behind her back through the doors and out into the night.

"Yes," Ace said, deciding against giving him any additional details of why, because that would lead to more questions she just didn't have it in her to answer.

"Did you see it, Lucef? Do you think I did all right?" Octavian asked, as they moved through the streets of London, barely being noticed by anyone.

"You did great, Octavian," Lucef said, smiling down at the boy who continued to seem to grow in bursts over the last several weeks. His need for more blood during these growing times was another reason Ace had thought of bringing him there. They simply didn't have enough blood from the families to support all the injured Vampires as well as his growth-induced appetite.

Nero had stayed back at the mansion. While he had been assisting in Octavian's training, he was just as uncomfortable with his son being out and hunting humans as Ace was, and he wasn't prepared to witness it until he heard how it went from Ace. Instead, he was working diligently on documenting what had occurred, a task that was once Fredic's responsibility.

Octavian moved a little further ahead of them once they got past the busier part of the city and were now on the winding roads that lead to the mansion. They could have, since there were no longer as many human eyes and cameras to spot them, raced through the streets and made it back to the mansion in moments, but the night was perhaps the least chaotic one they had experienced since the Witches' attack, and Ace was enjoying it. She even enjoyed the feel of the rain that started, peppering her face with water as she turned it up toward the moon.

"Have you had any more dreams?" Ace asked Lucef suddenly. He glanced at her, anticipating seeing her stern and stoic face, but instead got to see her walking beside him, eyes closed and turned up toward the sky. She looked oddly relaxed, even though he knew it was only temporary.

Ace was referring to his dreams of Six. He had finally told her about how strange they had been since he decided to come back to London, but since the attack, they had stopped. In fact, he had only one dream since then. The feeling was a bit like waiting. He was in a holding pattern, but for what?

Thunder rumbled in the clouds above and a moment later, the streak of bright white lightning lit them up.

"No more dreams yet," Lucef said, though as he said that a strange feeling tugged at his still and silent heart.

Ace opened her eyes and looked over at Lucef, her expression surprised and confused. She could feel an odd sensation, one she hadn't felt since her progeny had been turned to dust before her eyes during the ritual ten years prior. She could feel Six. But that wasn't possible.

"Mum?" Octavian asked, having paused before the gates of the mansion. Each step closer to their home seemed to make the feeling grow. That invisible tether that held sire to progeny was being strengthened the closer she got to Kurome.

Ace and Lucef looked at one another once more, an understanding passing silently between them, as Ace scooped Octavian's larger form from the ground, jumping over the tall gate with him in her arms, before racing down the gravel path to the mansion with Lucef right beside her.

There was electricity in the air as the rain began pouring down on them like a sheet. The sky rumbled, and they paused with mere meters between them and the front door of the mansion as lightning crackled and hit the stone steps in front of the mansion with a deafening roar.

What was left in its wake was not what Ace or Lucef were expecting.

Standing there on the now charred steps of Kurome Mansion were three figures.

Though the appearance was slightly different, Ace would know the one who stood at the center anywhere.

Six, naked, dirty, and steaming as the rainwater hit her sizzling skin, stood before them.

Her eyes were different, snake-like as they looked out across the short distance, taking in the three of them.

The two other figures Ace had never seen before. She had never seen anything like them at all. They were men, completely identical, with skin, hair, and clothes perfectly and impossibly white. The contrast was such that they almost seemed to glow and emit their own light as they stood on either side of Six.

"Six," Ace said, her voice carrying over the roar of the storm that began raging around them. Six's eyes snapped to Ace's from where they lingered on Octavian. An expression of… knowing seemed to pass over Six's face.

"Ace," Six whispered so quietly, it seemed to disappear under the sound of the storm, though Ace could hear it. "I'm back."

Book Club Questions

1. With so many of the other Immortal Sects being weakened, why do you think the Vampires don't simply take them out and dominate as the only Immortals left in this plane?
2. How do you think the characters mentally deal with living so long and dealing with the changes they have to see, as well as watch those around them die?
3. It seems so many things are fated to be, and the answers are never clearly laid out for the characters. What do you think the implications of a third Book are? What additional secrets do you think are held there?
4. It seems the alliances are all in shambles. The Werewolves may be trying to realign with the Witches, but the Chenjas are also begrudgingly remaining on the Witches' side as well. With all three other Immortals going against the Vampires, do you think Ace and the others stand a chance?
5. Six has returned from hell. What do you think her presence within Kurome Mansion will do to the dynamics of the coven?
6. Lucef is now no longer the only Immortal with mixed abilities. What do you think it means that there are more and more who are being changed?

7. Ramses, the first Vampire, has returned to the flesh. What do you think his presence will do to change the war?

Author Bio

Chelsea Burton Dunn is a Kansas City native—the Missouri side, not the Kansas side. That matters to locals. Where is that, you might ask? Right smack-dab in the middle of the country. She has two beautiful children and is married to a superb partner, but let's not forget their two snuggly cats and eager-eater of a dog.

Having always been a little strange herself, Chelsea instantly fell in love with paranormal, supernatural, and fantasy books, movies, and TV shows as a child. Did everyone think it was a phase? Absolutely. Was it? Absolutely not. Being weird is a blessing, not a curse. She's always embraced that part of herself and those around her.

She started writing from a very early age, initially starting and completing one of the *Deadman's Handbooks* in high school. She is a lover of music, having her other love and talent for singing. She performed on main stage operas in the children's chorus from grade school to high school.

Chelsea loves to delve into the difficulties of life, love, and loss, while spicing it up with a little magic and monsters. As she liked to say when she was younger, "The monsters in my head need to come out to play every once in a while," so giving them life on the page seemed appropriate.

You can see more about Chelsea, her projects, and find her social medias by going to www.chelseaburtondunn.com.

www.ingramcontent.com/pod-product-compliance
Lightning Source LLC
Chambersburg PA
CBHW020503310726
48979CB00016B/2770/J

* 9 7 9 8 8 2 3 2 0 6 0 4 4 *